**Praise for Terry Lynn Thomas**

'I was gripped from page one… An atmospheric read which I really enjoyed'

'Wow!… You won't be disappointed'

'Gripping and enthralling… Wonderful'

'Fantastic!… Such an amazing read!'

'An entertaining and engrossing read, highly recommended'

'A suspenseful, compelling plot that kept me up late reading'

'Brilliant book… Brilliant author'

'Fast-paced and gripping'

**TERRY LYNN THOMAS** is the USA *today* bestselling author of six historical mysteries. *The Drowned Woman* (previously published as *Neptune's Daughter*) won an IndieBRAG Medallion, *The Silent Woman* and *House of Lies* were released to critical acclaim and became *USA Today* bestsellers. *The Betrayal* is Terry's first foray into the world of domestic suspense.

When she's not writing, Terry likes to spend time outdoors with her husband and her dogs.

Keep up with Terry on Facebook (www.facebook.com/terry lynnthomasbooks) Twitter (@TLThomasbooks), Instagram (@terrylynnthomasbooks) or via her website at www.terry lynnthomas.com.

## Also by Terry Lynn Thomas

### The Cat Carlisle Series
*The Silent Woman*
*The Family Secret*
*House of Lies*

### The Sarah Bennett series
*The Spirit of Grace*
*The House of Secrets*
*The Drowned Woman*

# The Betrayal

## TERRY LYNN THOMAS

ONE PLACE. MANY STORIES

HQ
An imprint of HarperCollins*Publishers* Ltd
1 London Bridge Street
London SE1 9GF

First published by HQ Digital 2021

1

First published in Great Britain by
HQ, an imprint of HarperCollinsPublishers Ltd 2021

ISBN: 9780008364809

Printed and bound in Great Britain by
CPI Group (UK) Ltd, Melksham, SN12 6TR

# Prologue

*Sunday, October 5*

When the alarm blared the Sunday financial recap, the woman woke with a start. She didn't care about the Dow Jones Industrial Average, nor did she care about market volatility. Fumbling, she unplugged the old-fashioned clock radio and tossed it under the bed. Her thoughts, as they often did, went to her lover. She rolled over and pressed her face into his pillow, taking in the scent of him, that strange concoction of vanilla and citrus that made her senses reel.

Rolling over on her back, she took a deep breath, and cradled her belly, thinking of the baby that grew inside her. The positive pregnancy test lay on the table next to her, its vertical pink line a source of unimaginable joy. She snuggled under the duvet as the automatic coffeemaker kicked into gear, filling her apartment with the aroma of the dark roast coffee her lover preferred.

She saw the card on the doormat just as she poured her first cup of coffee.

*I've rented a beach house for us tonight. I'll send a key and the address by messenger. Meet you there around ten?*

Leaning back against the counter, the woman closed her eyes, anticipating their rendezvous. Dear God, she craved him.

She did not know she had less than fifteen hours to live.

# Chapter 1

*Friday, October 10*

Olivia Sinclair's life fell apart on the day of her sixty-second birthday. The morning started with promise. She and Richard lay entangled in the sheets, their limbs intertwined and glistening with sweat. Olivia marveled – as she often did – at the way their passion had withstood decades of marriage. Somehow, she and Richard had managed to keep passion alive.

"Happy birthday, beautiful." Richard ran his fingers along her side, taking his time at the curve of her hip. "I've got something for you."

Olivia watched her husband, his body still athletic and strong as he moved to the dresser and opened the top drawer. When he turned to face her, he held a familiar blue Tiffany box.

"This is for you, for your birthday and your retirement, a celebration of your accomplishments, if you will. I don't tell you this enough, but I'm proud of you, Liv." Richard always gave Olivia jewelry from Tiffany's at birthdays and Christmas. This year's gift was a platinum necklace, the pendant an antique skeleton key studded with diamonds.

"It's beautiful," Olivia said. She held up the platinum key to the morning light, the sunbeams making the diamonds dazzle.

Richard took it from her. "Let me help you put that on." He hooked the clasp and kissed the back of her neck. "When do you and Claire sign your paperwork?"

"She's coming in today. I'm going to ask for all the changes you suggested. Assuming she agrees, we'll wrap things up.

"She's got the capital?"

"She does. I think she's probably borrowing the money, but she'll be fine."

Richard ran his fingers through Olivia's thick hair. "I hear she's a go-getter. Are you okay with walking away from all that success, the notoriety?"

"Notoriety? That's your department. You're the television legal guru. I just help beleaguered women get their fair share."

Richard laughed.

"At least we can travel now, or at least I can come with you when you go away for weeks on end for depositions and trials," Olivia said.

"That's great, honey."

"We need to talk about your plans, Richard. Do you have any idea when you might walk away from Rincon Sinclair?"

Richard turned to Olivia. "I'm not ready, Liv. Not now. Maybe a year or two?"

"That long?"

"We'll talk about it later, okay?"

Olivia recognized this ploy. *We'll talk about it later* meant they wouldn't talk about it again until Richard was good and ready. She was about to push him, wrangle a commitment to retire out of him, when the alarm by his side of the bed started blaring the morning news.

"You shower first. I'll make the coffee." Richard tied his bathrobe around his waist and turned off the radio. "Are you sure you don't mind cooking tonight? It's your birthday."

"I'm sure," Olivia said. "I want to cook dinner for my family."

"Maybe you can strike a truce with our son-in-law," Richard said.

4

Olivia held her hand over her heart. "I swear, I'll try."

As she headed into the shower, she thought of the promise of freedom, and the time she would have to garden, travel with Richard, and tackle her toppling To-Be-Read pile of books.

After Richard left, she took her time over the morning paper and was going over her calendar when the front door opened and Denny called out, "Hello? Anyone here?"

"In the kitchen," Olivia said.

Her daughter stepped into the kitchen, a sweet smile on her face, her golden hair cascading around her shoulders, a huge bouquet of flowers in her hand.

"Happy birthday, Mom." Denny kissed Olivia's cheek before pouring herself a cup of coffee.

"Thanks, honey." Olivia watched her daughter over the rim of her cup, trying to ignore the dark circles under Denny's eyes and the tight lines around her mouth.

"How's David?"

Denny smiled to take the edge off her words. "Come on, Mom. We both know you don't care a bit about my husband. But he's fine, thank you very much."

She set her coffee cup on the table and pulled her hair back into a ponytail, a gesture that reminded Olivia of Denny when she was an outspoken, opinionated little girl. Richard and Denny would debate at the dinner table, Richard subtly teaching his daughter to argue like a pro. Olivia suspected that those arguments were Richard's attempt to get Denny interested in the law.

Olivia loved that irreverent spark in her daughter and had been dismayed to see it diminish when David Grayson came into her life. Now Denny watched what she said, and if David was around, she would cast anxious glances his way, worried – to Olivia's mind – that what she was doing would make David angry. Denny never argued, never expressed an opinion these days. That impulsive, no-filter child had married a man hell-bent on putting out her fire.

5

"Honestly, Mom, I don't mean to sound harsh, but I wish you two could spend some time together. If you got to know David, you'd come to realize what a good man he is. You're just not used to his traditional values. You're a modern woman, Mom. I'm not."

Olivia longed to ask her daughter about her marriage, to make sure she was okay, but she was afraid that her inquiry would be seen as an intrusion, which would push Denny even further away, so she let it go. For now. "Honey, I'm never going to believe that women need to be told what to do by their husbands or boyfriends. Marriage should—"

"—be a partnership." Denny laughed as she finished the sentence. "You look nice. Court today?"

"Very tactfully done, Den. I see how you changed the subject. No court today. I'm meeting with Claire Montreaux about selling my practice."

"Somehow I can't see you retiring, Mom. Are you sure you're ready?"

*Was she ready?* Her small practice was nothing compared to Richard's illustrious career, but Olivia and Richard had planned it that way. Olivia's office was close to home, so she had been able to care for Denny, freeing up Richard whose relentless litigation schedule kept him away from home. While Denny was young, Olivia had attended her plays, piano recitals, and pageants. As Denny got older and became more independent, Olivia turned her attention to the vast sloping hillside behind her house, turning the wild grassy area into a terraced garden. She did all the backbreaking work herself and soon had fruit trees, a large plot dedicated to vegetables, and a vast picking garden, which kept Olivia and her friends in fresh flowers all summer long.

Olivia had spent a lot of time alone in her marriage. Even though she kept herself busy, she missed her husband and looked forward to spending more time with him, even if that time was spent traveling for his work.

"So to answer your question, yes, I'm ready. I can travel with your father now."

"I don't see Dad retiring anytime soon. He likes the limelight. I honestly don't think Dad would know what to do with himself if he retired."

*And therein lies the problem.*

Richard worked long hours and each week spent a night or two in their condo in the city, with its galley kitchen and an even smaller bathroom. Nestled on the top of California Street, the condo had a beautiful view of San Francisco, and since it was the first place they had purchased – mortgaging their souls after Richard passed the bar – they kept it out of sentimentality. That was thirty-two years ago. Olivia consoled herself with the knowledge that after all these years, despite him sometimes seeming married to his career, she and Richard still loved each other. *Thank goodness for that*, Olivia thought.

"I'm hoping I can get him to slow down a little bit. As for me, I'm happy in the garden. Maybe I'll take up painting or something." Olivia sipped her coffee. "Den, tell me the truth. Did your father plan a surprise party for me?"

"Of course not," Denny said. "You made it perfectly clear you absolutely didn't want one."

Olivia sighed with relief. She was looking forward to an intimate family gathering. Maybe tonight she would come to see her son-in-law in a new light. For Denny's sake she would try.

"Are you having your birthday lunch with Lauren today?"

"I am," Olivia said.

"Tell her I said hello. Maybe the three of us could meet for lunch sometime?"

"That would be great," Olivia said. "I know Lauren would love to see you." This wasn't the first time Denny had mentioned lunch with Olivia and Lauren, but despite half a dozen invitations, Denny always had some excuse.

"Are you sure you don't want me to bring anything besides the cake? It doesn't seem like much of a birthday with you slaving away in the kitchen."

"It's not slaving when you enjoy the labor. Anyway, I've got it all under control. Shopping's complete, most of the prep is already finished. I'll come home early and get the lasagna in the oven. Want to come and keep me company while I throw things together?"

"Can't. We're going to struggle to get here by 7:30 as it is. David's busy at work right now." Denny hoisted her purse onto her shoulder and kissed Olivia's cheek. "Love you."

Her conversation with Denny left her troubled. Olivia had meddled in Denny's life behind the scenes, hiring an investigator to follow Denny's husband. The investigator had reported back, worried that David had spotted him. Of course, Olivia had terminated the relationship, but it left her unsettled. If Denny knew what she had done, she'd feel so betrayed, and David wouldn't miss an opportunity to exploit Denny's anger. After all, Olivia had no concrete evidence that David was having an affair, but her years as a family law attorney had honed her intuition to a sharp edge. She knew a cheater when she saw one. David Grayson was a cheater.

"Love you, honey," Olivia said. She walked Denny to the door and stood for a moment in the cold October sun, watching the daughter she loved with her heart and soul drive away.

\*

Fifteen minutes later, Olivia pulled into her reserved spot in the downtown Larkspur municipal parking lot and headed on foot down Magnolia towards her office. It wouldn't do to be late for her meeting with Claire Montreaux, the young lawyer who was going to buy Olivia's practice. After her meeting, she had a lunch date with her best friend, Lauren Ridley. Although the two women had lunch once a week, birthday lunches were always special and often involved champagne.

Situated in a store front and snuggled next to the historic Lark Theatre, the Law Office of Olivia Sinclair had no sign in the window. Given the incendiary nature of the divorces she litigated, the front door was kept locked at all times, and clients were seen by appointment only. Digging the key out of her coat pocket, Olivia let herself into the office, taking in the thick carpets and the comfortable sofa with fresh eyes. She had done her best to make this part of the office welcoming. A huge bouquet of flowers rested on the waiting room coffee table.

"There you are." Mary Chadwick, Olivia's assistant since she started her practice, hurried to her desk, a stack of files in her arms. "Happy birthday, Olivia."

"Thanks. Who sent the flowers?"

"Blythe Harden dropped those off. She said to tell you they were a small testament to her gratitude. I'm also to tell you that if you ever need any favor from her, not to hesitate." A small slip of pink paper was tucked into the corner of Mary's blotter. She set the files on her desk, pulled it out, and waved it in the air, a sly smile on her face.

"There's a west wind today, a portent of big change."

After twenty-seven years of working with Mary, Olivia knew that in good time Mary would tell her what the west wind had brought them today. Her assistant – a trusted, intelligent woman who masterfully found needles in haystacks – was driven by age-old superstitions handed down from her equally superstitious grandmother.

"I've found Roland Rainwater."

"What?" Olivia didn't bother to hide her surprise. Certain that Roland Rainwater had vanished into thin air, Olivia had planned to hand the whole Rainwater file, along with its hefty retainer, over to Claire once she came on board. Claire could hire a private investigator to track down the deadbeat husband and get him served with a summons.

"How did you find him?"

Mary giggled. "On an Internet dating site."

"Do I want to know about this?"

"It's legit, don't worry. I put up a fake profile of a woman who is very similar to Hetty. You know, bohemian, artsy. I made sure to hint at wealth untold. Sure enough, Roland was looking for a new meal ticket."

"Well, where is he?"

Mary looked at her watch. "Probably on his way to Peet's. I'm meeting him for coffee in twenty minutes." The Rainwater file sat on the corner of her desk. She pulled the summons out with a flourish and grabbed her purse. "Back soon."

Olivia laughed. "Just make sure he doesn't follow you to your car."

"Don't worry. I've got my pepper spray. Oh, Claire Montreaux will be here in ten minutes or so. Want me to get some sandwiches for your birthday lunch with Lauren while I'm out?"

"Thanks, Mary. Use the company card. Get something for yourself, too."

"Will do. Back soon." Mary waved and headed down the street, walking as purposefully as a bloodhound who had picked up a scent.

Olivia surveyed the small office, the home base of her work life for the past twenty-seven years. Her eyes roamed over the various diplomas and certificates that hung on the wall, the bank of filing cabinets, the stacks of files and papers. She had worked hard for all of this, but the time had come to pass the baton. There was a gentle knock on the door.

Claire Montreaux waited while Olivia unlocked the door.

"Good morning," Claire said.

"I always keep the door locked," Olivia said. "I had an angry husband come after me with a baseball bat once."

"Really?"

"Yes. I was lucky there happened to be a policeman down the block. But I wound up with a smashed-in window, so lesson learned."

Claire was young and fresh and very much like Olivia had been when she started practicing law so very long ago. A tiny thing with black hair that hung down to her waist, Claire looked like a fifteen-year-old cheerleader. Although Olivia had never been opposite Claire in court, word on the street was that the young lawyer was whip-smart, had a photographic memory, and could out-argue the best and most seasoned litigator. Today Claire wore a very short skirt along with stiletto heels so high Olivia's lower back threatened to spasm at the very sight of them. She felt old all of a sudden. Out of touch with this new generation of lawyers.

Claire stood in the reception area, surveying her surroundings. She turned a slow circle. "This office has a really nice feel to it. Uncluttered with lots of light."

"Thanks. Of course, you can change things as you see fit," Olivia said.

The women didn't waste time with small talk. Once they were situated in Olivia's office, Claire reached into her spanking new Mark Cross briefcase and pulled out the partnership proposal that the two women had hammered out a month ago, when Claire first approached Olivia with the idea of coming on board as a partner. Several pages had been tagged with Post-its. Claire opened to the first one and said, "I need your assurance that Stephen Vine will still be sending referrals from his criminal practice this way." She leaned back, confident and in charge, and continued. "My position is that Mr. Vine's influence will be needed, especially since I'm new to the area—"

*You're new to the profession, darling.* Olivia didn't say the words out loud. Everyone had to start somewhere, and she couldn't find fault with Claire's attention to detail. Granted, Claire was taking a risk, sinking her time and capital into her own firm so early in her career. Stephen Vine, Olivia's long-time friend and well-respected criminal defense attorney, didn't take family law cases and had been referring clients to Olivia for years. Claire would need those referrals, especially in the beginning.

"—so will that be a problem?" Claire said.

"Not at all," Olivia said. "I've already spoken to Mr. Vine. He's agreed to meet with you alone or with me, whichever you prefer."

Claire exhaled. "That's great. Is he easy to get along with? I've heard rumors that he can be prickly."

Olivia settled back into her chair. "Stephen doesn't like liars. Be honest and genuine and you'll get along fine. Pardon my French, but he can spot bullshit a mile away." She thumbed through her copy of their agreement. "And I have an issue I would like to change. I'm looking to be out of the practice in six months instead of a year. I'm willing to adjust the financial aspects accordingly . . ."

And so the meeting went on. For an hour Claire and Olivia negotiated, easily agreeing on changes and amendments. By 11:35 Claire was gone, off to type up the agreed changes. Next week Olivia would sign it. After Claire left, Olivia turned her attention to her computer, methodically sorting through the thirty-plus emails she had received overnight, making note of things that needed her attention and forwarding the rest on to Mary.

"I'm back," Mary said. Olivia heard her putting food in the fridge. She came into Olivia's office and sat on the couch. "Dear Roland wasn't very happy. Silly ass. I got you sandwiches and a bottle of champagne. Will you be back after lunch?"

"Nope. I'm going to check my email and head out."

"Good. How did it go with Claire?"

"Well. She's agreed to everything."

Mary kicked off her shoes. "Today I feel like a tired old woman. I have really enjoyed working with you, Liv, but won't deny that I'm looking forward to retiring."

"Hard to believe, isn't it? We've had quite a run, haven't we?"

"That we have," Mary said. "And I don't mind admitting that I'm a wee bit exhausted."

Olivia had just deleted the last email, when a new message

12

from an unknown sender popped into her inbox, with a subject line that read: *Check out your husband!*

"I've got an anonymous email. It mentions Richard and looks like it's coming from someone's phone," Olivia said.

Mary put her glasses on and leaned close to the computer as Olivia opened the email. The body said, "You think you know everything, don't you? You stupid bitch."

Olivia didn't think twice before double clicking the attachment. Grainy footage slowly came into focus. Thinking there was an error with the download, she started to close the file just as it popped into focus, revealing a nubile blond, younger than Denny, astride her lover.

The couple went at it like rabbits, and Olivia was just about to exit the video, when the man – hidden by the camera – flipped the girl, so she was underneath him. From this new angle, Olivia recognized the man's face. Richard. Her husband. Screwing someone young enough to be his daughter.

"Oh, God," Mary gasped, stepping away from Olivia, her hand over her mouth.

Olivia closed the laptop and pushed it away from her. The sound of crashing waves filled Olivia's ears. She pushed her chair away from the desk, as if distance would make the wretched thing go away. It didn't. Her stomach clenched into a painful cramp. She picked up the glass of water that rested on her desk, but it slipped from her shaking hands, drenching her lap in water.

Ignoring the mess she'd made, Olivia said, "Mary, would you excuse me. In fact, why don't you take the rest of the day off."

Mary waited, her embarrassment balanced by a look of worry and concern. "Are you sure?"

Olivia nodded. She waited until Mary had left and locked the door. Taking deep, steadying breaths, she pulled the laptop towards her, and ignoring the cold water that puddled in her lap, she forced herself to watch the video, this time with the sound on. When it finished, with Richard and his lover satisfied, Olivia

13

sat at her desk, numb and unable to move, her stomach feeling as though she had eaten a bag of rocks. Olivia couldn't quite catch her breath.

When the office walls started to close in, she snapped the laptop shut and tried to stand, and despite her weak knees, somehow managed to find her way to her car.

# Chapter 2

*Friday, October 10*

After pulling to a stop at the bottom of Lauren's driveway, Olivia took a moment to collect herself. What a hideous rollercoaster her day had become. First the productive meeting with Claire and the promise of freedom from her law practice, only to be turned completely upside down by the horrendous video of Richard screwing some young anonymous girl. Hours ago Olivia had felt secure in her marriage, confident in the love she and Richard had shared for more than three decades. All that was gone, obliterated.

Olivia took a deep breath in an attempt to quell the nausea that once again threatened. Clutching the bag that held the sandwiches in one hand and a bottle of cold champagne in the other, she headed up the steep cobbled walkway to Lauren's house, unable to shut off the images of Richard naked and entwined with another woman. *No, not a woman. A girl. A very young girl.*

Lauren opened the door before Olivia had a chance to knock. At first glance, Lauren Ridley looked like any other aging hippie, a common sight in Marin County. Today she wore a tie-dyed maxi dress in bright turquoise and yellow, which fell to the floor and brushed against her bare feet. Her thick long hair, white as

15

Sunday linen, fell into corkscrew curls to her shoulders. A chunky Indian turquoise necklace hung around her neck, the blue stones bringing out the brightness in her eyes.

Humble to the core, Lauren never spoke of the six gold records that hung on the wall in her tiny office at the back of the house. Lauren Ridley was a bona fide rock and roll legend. Despite the passing years – Lauren's star went supernova in the late 1960s – people still smiled when they recognized her. She always had a moment to chat, sign autographs, and reflect on the good old days of rock and roll. Tough, cynical, kind, generous, Lauren Ridley was Olivia's closest confidante. Now she eyed the bag of food.

"You didn't have to bring food. I told you I was cooking . . . What's the matter?" She took the food from Olivia and held the door for her.

"The last time you cooked, the kitchen caught fire," Olivia said, trying for humor but failing miserably.

Lauren took the bag of sandwiches and set off down the corridor, Olivia at her heels. "Be nice to me, Liv. I've got champagne chilled."

"I've got some, too."

Lauren whirled around and stared at Olivia, her head cocked to one side. "Are you all right?"

"Yes." Olivia shook her head. "No. I don't know."

"Come on, let's get you some nice cold champagne. Then you can tell me all about it."

Olivia followed Lauren into the comfortable but cluttered kitchen. She took a seat on one of the bar stools while Lauren put Olivia's bottle of champagne in the fridge before opening a bottle that sat in a bucket of ice. She filled two flutes and handed one to Olivia. "Let's sit in the living room."

Lauren's house was designed and decorated for ease and comfort. Her living room, with its large windows and view of Mt Tamalpais, was furnished with two large couches and a quantity of comfortable pillows for those who preferred to sit on the floor. Lauren set the ice bucket that held the champagne on the coffee table, topped off Olivia's glass, and sat down next to her. "Tell me. What's happened."

Olivia opened the video and handed her phone to Lauren. When Lauren hit the sound button, Olivia wanted to plug her ears. While Lauren's expression went from curiosity to realization, and finally to disgust, Olivia guzzled her champagne and refilled her glass.

"That son of a bitch. How did you find this?"

"It showed up in an email."

"Someone sent this to you?" Lauren furrowed her brow, leaned back on the couch, and watched the video again, this time with the sound off. "That woman is so young. And how could Richard be so stupid to allow himself to be filmed? What the hell. If I didn't know better, I'd say this was a set-up, a fake video."

"Could it be faked?" Olivia seized this lifeline, desperate for any explanation that exonerated her husband.

Lauren scooted close to Olivia and put an arm around her shoulder. "I think it's probably real, Liv. And I am so very sorry." Lauren set her glass down and stared at her hands for a moment. When she looked up, Olivia was struck by the flinty hardness she saw in her friend's eyes.

"Over the years I've been amazed – and impressed – by your devotion to Richard. You are a good wife; have been a good wife. But you see your husband through rose-colored glasses."

Olivia opened her mouth to argue with Lauren, but she didn't have words. There was no witty comeback, no scathing truth to be had here. Richard had cheated on her. She had the video to prove it. Had there been others?

"I'm betting this woman isn't the first." Lauren said, reading Olivia's mind in that uncanny way of good friends.

Olivia downed the rest of her champagne. "You've seen him with another woman, haven't you?"

Lauren wouldn't meet Olivia's eyes as she fiddled with her cuticles.

17

"Once. At the Fairmont. But that was a long time ago and I wasn't one hundred percent certain there was anything inappropriate going on. They weren't kissing or anything though they seemed cozy. I wrote it off to a business function. If it had been anything blatant, I would have told you. You know that. But in retrospect . . . "

Olivia pinched the bridge of her nose. How much more could she take?

Lauren refilled their glasses. "How about food, followed by more champagne? I think we should get very drunk."

"I'm supposed to be making dinner for my family tonight. How am I going to face Richard?"

"I could come with you. Stand behind you with a baseball bat, just to let him know you mean business." Lauren gave Olivia a wistful smile and pushed a box of Kleenex towards her.

"I'll never forgive him for this, Lauren. God, the idea of being in the same room with him makes me want to puke. I want him gone, out of my house." Olivia stood, wobbling on her feet for a moment as the champagne went straight to her head. "I've been so stupid. He's betrayed me in the most horrific way."

The tears came once again, spilling into hot salty rivers down Olivia's cheeks.

Olivia met her friend's gaze. "When I'm with Richard, he has this way of making me feel like I'm the only person in the world. It's like he shines on me. I've never thought about what he's like when he's not with me. I've trusted him." Olivia replayed the last few years of her marriage back in her mind, surprised at how long it had been since she and Richard had spent time together or taken a vacation together. Like most long-married couples, they had fallen into a comfortable routine. Olivia had been happy in it. After all, wasn't finding joy in that which becomes familiar the key to a long and lasting love?

"What are you going to do?" Lauren asked.

Olivia thought about this while Lauren got plates and divvied up their sandwiches, adding tabbouleh and grape leaves.

"Do you know how many times a client has sat across from me and said, 'I think my husband – or wife – is having an affair'? How many times I've said, 'Trust your instincts. Spouses always know these things.'"

Lauren handed her a glass of water. She waved it away and reached for the champagne.

"What a fool I've been. What an utter idiot."

"You have a romantic nature, Liv."

Olivia dabbed her eyes. "You've got to be kidding me. I'm a divorce lawyer! I stopped believing in romance years ago. True love isn't about romance. True love, the kind of love that withstands the test of time, is what you have when the romance wears away. True love is knowing your spouse has your back no matter what. It's about devotion and family. I thought I had that with Richard."

"You see your husband and your relationship the way you want it to be, not the way it is. The woman in that video could be his mistress. For all you know, they're shacking up together. All those nights Richard is away on business, that woman could be with him. Sorry, sweetie, but he is really good-looking. And if you don't mind me saying so, he has a bit of an ego."

"My husband is a son of a bitch," Olivia said.

"Agreed," Lauren said.

"Don't people fall in love anymore?"

Lauren, who had a rotating string of lovers, smiled. "I fall in love all the time. For a night, anyway."

Olivia laughed in spite of herself. She held up her champagne glass in a mock toast. "Screw Richard."

"Screw Richard," Lauren said. They clinked glasses and drank their champagne.

*

After they had eaten their lunch and drunk two bottles of champagne, Lauren had cleared the dishes. While she was in the

19

kitchen tidying up and putting things away, Olivia had lain down on Lauren's comfortable couch and promptly fallen asleep. She would have slept all night if Lauren hadn't woken her.

"Time to get up, Liv."

Olivia opened her eyes as the sun started to slip out of the sky, surprised she had slept so long. For a moment she wondered if the video had been part of a horrid anxiety-ridden nightmare. The events of the morning replayed in her mind's eye. Not a dream. Richard was a bastard. Now she had to face him.

"How about a cup of tea and a brownie to sober you up?"

"Perfect, and a pair of walking shoes, please. I'd best not drive. And aspirin."

"Are you sure you want to walk? It's cold outside. We can call a cab."

"I'll walk. The cold air will do me good. I need a bit of sobering, especially if I'm going to face down my husband," Olivia said.

"Coffee and brownie coming right up. Will you go through with the family dinner?"

"No," Olivia said. "I'll ask Denny and David for a rain check."

Twenty minutes later, fortified with strong coffee and the promised brownie, Olivia trudged up the hill. The days were getting shorter, and the crisp October wind pushed the alcohol-induced cobwebs away. By the time she arrived home she was sober, angry, and not at all happy to see Richard's Mercedes in the driveway. *Why was he here so early?* She was hoping she'd have time to pack his bags and arrange a locksmith. Sweaty and thirsty, Olivia let herself in the front door, hoping she could slip into her room and change out of her clothes before she confronted Richard. The house was dark, with the exception of the living room lamp. If Olivia weren't so preoccupied, she would have noticed the subdued lighting and wondered why Richard didn't turn on every light in the house, like he usually did.

"Richard?" Olivia called out. No answer. She tossed her brief-case down and headed into the living room. When she flipped

20

on the light, it took a moment for her to realize she wasn't alone. People were clustered in the corners of the room. Slowly their expectant faces registered in Olivia's brain. Denny's was the first to come into focus. Then, as if in slow motion, Olivia recognized old friends and business acquaintances. Faces beaming, everyone stepped toward her. In unison, they shouted, "Surprise!"

# Chapter 3

*Oh, God, no.* Olivia wanted to run. Like a trapped deer, her eyes darted around the room, looking for a means of escape. Richard approached Olivia, arms wide to take her into a hug. Not wanting him to touch her, Olivia started to recoil but stopped herself as she caught Denny's look of shock. Olivia Sinclair, who prided herself on keeping her cool under any circumstance, felt her composure slipping away. Someone snapped a picture, the strobe of the flash like a jolt of lightning.

Moving towards her once again, Richard said, "Happy birthday, honey." Olivia let him kiss her cheeks. Then she moved on to Denny, pulling her daughter into her arms.

"Are you okay, Mom?" Denny whispered into Olivia's ear.

"I'm okay. Just a bit shocked." Olivia meandered through the crowd, greeting people she hadn't seen in ages. She reached Wendy Betters last. Wendy had worked for Richard's law firm, Rincon Sinclair, since she was an undergrad. Over the years she and Olivia had forged a strong friendship. Wendy took Olivia's hand and said to the crowd of people around them, "I need to speak to the birthday girl for a moment." She led Olivia away and stepped close to her. "Are you all right?"

Olivia's heart thumped in her chest. All she wanted to do was scream.

"Olivia, talk to me? What can I do to help?"

"Nothing." Olivia's voice came out a whisper. "Thank you though."

"Take a minute to pull yourself together. I'll tell everyone you went to change your clothes, okay?" Wendy peered around the corner into the room where the party was in full swing. "It's okay to slip away for a couple of minutes."

"Thank you, Wendy." Eager for even a few minutes of privacy, Olivia set her champagne down and excused herself, a fake smile plastered on her face. For a moment, she thought about walking out the front door and away from the house, but she couldn't do that to Denny. Four waiters circled the room passing out flutes of Dom Perignon. The dining room table had been converted to a buffet covered in white linen. She caught a glimpse of lobster tails, salads, and cracked crab. A white-coated chef sliced a chateaubriand into thin slices. The lights had been dimmed, so the candles that blazed in the silver candelabras lent a romantic air to the whole scene. A full bar had been situated on the far wall of the dining room, and now a bartender mixed martinis for Stephen Vine and his wife.

Careful not to make eye contact with anyone, Olivia hurried down the dark corridor to her room. After closing and locking her bedroom door, she stood in the dark for a moment, wishing she could stay here for the rest of the night, alone. After slipping out of her work clothes, she put on a pair of black pants and a cream cashmere sweater. A couple of splashes of cold water on her face and she'd be good as new. There were enough people in the house so that she could tactfully avoid Richard without anyone noticing. She'd put on a brave face for a couple of hours. After the guests were gone, she'd deal with her philandering husband.

Richard was waiting for her when she opened the bedroom door, and judging by the expression on his face, he wasn't happy.

"What are you doing in here? Do you know how hard Denny and I worked to put this party together? Get out there and be with your guests. If not for me, at least for your daughter's sake."

She stared at him for a moment, this man she believed had loved her with the same fierce loyalty that she had held for him.

"Why are you looking at me like that?" Richard said.

"Why are you taking that tone with me? I don't appreciate it." Olivia shivered as she saw her Richard for who he really was. "I don't even know you anymore."

In an instant, the state of their marriage crystalized. The clarity proved an effective antidote, for all the hurt and anger dissipated, giving her strength. Olivia knew what she had to do. She made to slip past Richard and get back to her guests, back to Denny. Richard grabbed her arm and whispered in her ear, "What the hell is the matter with you?"

Olivia looked down at Richard's fingers clamped against the fleshy part of her arm. She looked up and met his eyes without fear. "Let go of me."

He let her go and stepped away.

"I'll play along. After the guests leave, we'll talk."

"About what?" Richard asked.

"Our divorce," Olivia said. And with those words she turned her back on him and headed back to her party.

The guests consisted mostly of lawyers and judges, acquaintances of Richard's. Leave it to him to use her birthday to schmooze and entertain people who had influence over his career. Somehow managing to push her feelings away, she circulated, smiled, and chatted with people who she never saw socially anymore.

Despite her best efforts, she was unable to make a connection with her son-in-law. It seemed every time she tried to speak to him, he was tucked into a corner with Richard, talking as though they were old friends. David had always treated Richard with insincere deference. Richard, in keeping with his giant ego, had lapped up the attention.

She wondered for a moment how many of these people would remain in her life after she and Richard divorced, and surprised herself by not caring. The volume of conversation increased as people consumed more alcohol. Soon the jazz that was in the background was switched to the R&B songs that Olivia and Richard had danced to in the 1980s.

Someone moved the couches and coffee table to free up the living room floor. Soon the music got loud, a blessing in Olivia's mind as it gave her an excuse not to engage in conversation. People danced. Olivia mingled. Every time someone handed her a glass of champagne or wine, she would thank them and set it down, never taking a sip. She planned on being perfectly sober by the time she confronted Richard.

When she retreated to the kitchen for a glass of water, she found Denny and David in the middle of an intense conversation. David was towering over Denny and doing most of the talking.

When Olivia said, "Everything all right?" they stepped away from each other. David gave her his usual cold smile that didn't reach his eyes and Olivia wondered, not for the first time, what Denny saw in him.

"Are you enjoying your party?" David asked.

"I am." She turned her gaze to Denny, noticing her daughter's damp eyelashes. "Thank you for planning it, Den. The catering and the decorating has your touch of elegance."

"I enjoyed it," Denny said. "Nice to know I still have an eye."

Richard and Olivia had hoped their daughter would follow in their footsteps and go to law school. As it turned out, Denny had no interest in a four-year degree. Instead, she had attended community college and studied painting. Denny was a shy, sweet-natured woman who was impeccably organized, easy to talk to, and very creative. When her best friend got married, Denny offered to organize the wedding and the reception. She did such a good job that two other brides-to-be pulled her aside at the wedding and offered her a generous fee if she would plan their weddings as well.

Denny's career was launched. She loved her job and it showed. Soon she had more business than she could handle and was on the verge of hiring an assistant and expanding, when she met David Grayson at a fundraiser for Children's Hospital in Oakland.

David – tall, dark, and handsome – had swept Denny off her feet. The romance had been a whirlwind, culminating in a marriage proposal after just six months. At the beginning, David was attentive to Denny and friendly to Olivia and Richard. Olivia had never liked him, and because she couldn't put her finger on the reason for her dislike, Richard teased her relentlessly, accusing her of not wanting to let her daughter go and of being too possessive.

David and Denny married within a year at the Marin Art and Garden Center, Denny pulling strings and calling in many favors to reserve the popular venue on such short notice. Olivia had been surprised when Denny had given up her business to be with David.

"Don't be giving her ideas," David said abruptly. "We don't want Denny to think she can get back into party planning, do we? I need her at home with me." David put his arm around Denny and pulled her close. Though he smiled, the gesture felt an act of physical domination. And there was no mistaking the flash of irritation in Denny's eyes.

"I think Denny should be able to do whatever she wants," Olivia said.

"Mom, don't," Denny said, her tone sharp like a slap across the face.

"Sorry," Olivia said, putting her hands up in the air. "Forgive me. I've had a long day."

"No worries," David said. "We were just leaving anyway. Getting ready to say our goodbyes."

"I should stay and help clean up," Denny said. "I've got my car—"

"No, you'll come with me. I'll bring you to get your car in the morning," David said.

"Okay," Denny said.

"I'll get our coats." David nodded at Olivia and left them alone.

The minute he was out of earshot, Denny said, "Don't say a word, Mom, okay? I know you think he's bossy. But he's stressed from his job."

"It's okay, honey. I wasn't going to say anything." Olivia had no business to criticize Denny's marriage, did she? Especially in light of her own situation. "You did a beautiful job on my party. Thank you." Olivia felt her eyes fill with unshed tears.

"Mom? Why are you crying?"

Olivia pulled Denny into a hug. "Because I'm so happy." She lied easily. "And because I'm very proud of you."

"I'm proud of you, too. I'll call you tomorrow, okay? If it's sunny maybe we could go for a walk."

"Okay," Olivia said. And with a wave, Denny was gone.

An hour later all of the other guests were gone too, save Richard's business partner, Andrew Rincon, and another man who Olivia didn't know. They sat with Richard in the living room, a bottle of Scotch on the table, talking in hushed whispers, oblivious to the fact that the party was over and everyone had left. Olivia took this opportunity to go into the bedroom and pack two suitcases for Richard. She took them into the hallway. That task completed, she called a locksmith, asking for an emergency change of locks.

"I can do it, but it's not going to be cheap," the man who answered the phone said.

"No problem. Can you be here in an hour?"

"See you then."

After forwarding the video to Richard, Olivia sat in her room with the lights out, waiting for the last of the guests to leave. Once she and Richard were the only people in the house, Olivia made her way to the living room, where Richard stood with his back to her, a fresh glass of Scotch in his hand. She watched him swirl the ice around for a minute before he took a sip. She waited, letting her anger build along with her anticipation. When would he notice her? There she stood, reflected in the window right before his eyes. Yet he didn't see her. Somehow this seemed a metaphor for their marriage, now that she knew it was over.

At last he looked up. From the squaring of his shoulders, she knew he'd finally noticed her reflection.

"Why did you threaten me with divorce?"

"I know."

"Know what? I'm not in the mood for games, Liv. What are you playing at?"

"Now I know why you leave the room when you make certain phone calls, why you double-check if I'm near before you check your texts. God, I've been so naïve. I'm finished, Richard. Finished with you. Finished with our marriage."

"What are you talking about?"

"Check your email."

Olivia waited while Richard pulled his phone out of his pocket and opened the email. She watched while the look in his eyes went from smug, to incredulity, to anger.

"Who's the blonde, Richard?" Olivia didn't bother to keep the disgust out of her voice.

"You've got a lot of nerve planting a camera in the studio. Jesus, Olivia. I didn't realize you'd become so desperate."

"I didn't plant the video, Richard. How dare you! I've not set foot in that studio for ages, and you know it."

"Olivia, listen—"

Richard moved close to Olivia. Instinctively she stepped away. "Stay away from me," she hissed. "Who is she?"

"She's my secretary."

"Oh, my God. What a cliché."

"She didn't mean anything to me, Liv. She doesn't mean anything to me."

"Are you serious? If I was going to cheat, at least I'd be damn sure it meant something. How many times, Richard?"

"How many—"

"Times. How many times have you cheated on me?" Although she was well aware of the white-hot rage that broiled under her skin, Olivia tucked it away to deal with later. She spoke without emotion, pretending she was in court, examining a witness. "I assume there have been others. Come on, Richard. This is the time for honesty. How many times?"

He stared at her, his surprise replaced by irritation.

"How. Many. Times?"

Sighing loudly, Richard shook his head. "Men have needs, Liv. Don't take it personally. In Europe, it's an accepted practice."

"Get out of my house," Olivia said, her voice flat and dull as stagnant water. "I've packed your suitcases. They're by the front door. You can get your other things when it's convenient."

"I don't take orders from you, Liv. I don't take orders from anyone. And this isn't your house."

"Get. Out. Of. My. House." Without thinking, Olivia moved to the fireplace, grabbed the poker, and brandished it at Richard.

Raising his hands, he backed away. "Olivia, you need to calm down."

"I could bash your head in right now and happily go to prison. Get the hell out of my house."

His fear turned to rage as he stared at her, his eyes running over her tattered jeans, her makeup-free face. Angry blotches of red bloomed on his face as he pushed past her, grabbed his suitcases and walked out the front door, away from their marriage, away from their life together. Olivia once heard someone say the best way to make God laugh was to make plans. Oh, what grand plans she'd had! And now they were gone, obliterated.

After the locksmith left, she made herself a large cup of chamomile tea and, bundled up in warm clothes, took the steaming mug out into the garden. It was pitch dark on the sloping hill behind her house, but Olivia knew the footpaths – she had built them, after all – and didn't need light to find her way to the gazebo at the bottom of the hill. The hot tea tasted good, comforting as an old friend, as she sat in the dark in the garden she loved.

She stayed outside for hours, impervious to the cold, and reflected on her marriage. Over the years Olivia had tried to create a social life for Richard and herself. She had made friends with other couples, tried to host dinner parties and social gatherings. But more often than not, Richard had ended up canceling at the last minute, using his litigation schedule as an excuse, leaving Olivia to host their social functions alone. This had happened so many times, Olivia had stopped trying.

Most women – Olivia reluctantly acknowledged – would have left Richard years ago. But Olivia had believed she understood Richard and his focus on his career. She had believed in their marriage and saw this cycle of waiting, disappointment, forgiveness as proof of her loyalty towards him. In her mind, this loneliness, this waiting for Richard to take his place by her side, was a condition of their union. Like a fool, she had accepted it because at the end of the day, she had loved her husband and the idea of a family.

Had Richard ever loved her? How smug he had been when he had confessed his infidelity to her, almost as if it were a mark of his masculinity. With a wave of sadness, Olivia realized there would be no more waiting for Richard. Her marriage was over. And much to Olivia's surprise, underneath the pain, she was overcome with a tangible sense of relief.

# Chapter 4

Richard threw his suitcases in the trunk of his car and squealed down the road, away from the house he had shared with Olivia. The memory of the smug look on her face as she issued her ridiculous ultimatum infuriated him. How dare she? Speeding up as he hit a hairpin turn, he nearly collided with another car. Forcing himself to slow down, when he got to the bottom of the hill he pulled over, put his car in park, and took a moment to get his head straight. Who had put a camera in his bedroom? Although he was furious with Olivia, he knew she would never spy on him. No. If Olivia had suspected him of infidelity, she would have confronted him about it. And because she was so intuitive, she would have gleaned the answer before Richard opened his mouth to utter it.

Either that, he reasoned, or she knew that he had taken lovers over the years and had deliberately chosen to look the other way. Didn't all spouses know when the other had strayed? Did it matter? Monogamous relationships, as far as Richard was concerned, were a bit of a joke. How could any man be expected to sleep with one woman for time immemorial?

Sandy didn't hide the camera, of that Richard was certain. Sandy was a simple-minded, hardworking young woman who

31

wanted to make a good life for herself. A good secretary to him. A passionate lover. They'd had fun together. He had told her he loved her, and had even promised to marry her. But he hadn't meant it. Surely Sandy knew that. Anyway, he hadn't heard from Sandy since he'd last seen her at the office. He'd been relieved. With Olivia's birthday coming up it had been easier not to deal with her. But now that he'd seen that video, he worried.

Like all men in his position, Richard had enemies. He could think of ten lawyers who would do anything to get their hands on Rincon Sinclair's biggest client – Countryside, Inc. – a medical malpractice insurance company that was responsible for eighty-five percent of his firm's revenue. Countryside took pride in its conservative values. If Countryside's CEO, Beth Musselwhite got wind of the video, Rincon Sinclair would be finished. Richard was smart enough to know how far he could fall. He needed damage control. He'd best put things in place before they got too bad. He took out his phone and hit number 1 on his speed dial. Wendy Betters answered on the first ring.

"Richard? I didn't get a chance to speak to you at the party. It went beautifully, I thought—"

"Has anyone heard from Sandy?"

"No. And it's not like her not to call if she was going to miss work," Wendy said.

*Where the hell is she?* Richard had been busy all week and hadn't given Sandy much thought. She was good like that, leaving him alone when he was off doing his own thing.

"Can I speak freely?" Wendy asked.

Richard's heart skipped a beat at the serious tone of Wendy's voice. *What now?*

"Andrew and I reckoned that you and Sandy had argued and stopped seeing each other, and that was the reason for Sandy skipping work."

*So they knew of the affair.* The realization shocked Richard. Hadn't he and Sandy been discreet?

32

"It was obvious from the way you two acted around each other. Neither Andrew nor I wanted to say anything. Do you think we should call the police?"

"No, but call Sandy's mother and tell her what's going on. Who knows, maybe Sandy is at her house."

"Good idea," Wendy said.

Richard wondered if Sandy had filmed them having sex after all. Had she disappeared so she could blackmail him? If so, she would have wanted money before she sent the video to Olivia. The only logical explanation was another firm, eager for the Countryside business and willing to do anything to get it, had set Richard up. If that were the case, it was only a matter of time before that video would find its way to Beth Musselwhite's inbox, just as it had wound up in Olivia's.

"Richard? What's wrong?"

"Listen. We have a problem." Richard spoke freely to Wendy. He had hired her while she was in college, and she had worked for his firm ever since. When she graduated from law school, she was promoted to managing attorney. Although she worked for both Richard and Andrew, he knew that Wendy was loyal to him. He trusted her implicitly. "Someone put a camera in my studio apartment and there's a video of Sandy and me having sex. My wife received a copy of it today."

"So that's what was bothering Olivia. Is she okay? I'm so sorry, Richard. How awful for both of you. You don't think Sandy—"

"No. She wouldn't do that," Richard said. "You know what the implication here is, right? If Beth sees this video, we'll lose Countryside." Richard exhaled, relieved to share this burden with someone else. "You're a master at fixing things, Wendy. What should we do? I need you thinking outside of the box on this one."

"Is Olivia okay?" Wendy asked.

"Olivia? Oh, she's fine. It stung a little, but she'll get over it."

"We should contact Beth Musselwhite and do damage control at the outset, tell Beth about the video before she gets a copy of it. If someone shot that video of you and Sandy in order to get Countryside, they'll make a move of some sort. We could always get an expert to say the video was photoshopped. A professional could digitally manufacture anything. That should be our position. I'll line up experts to support it when I get off the phone with you."

"Good idea."

"I'll call Beth when we hang up and set up a meeting for first thing tomorrow. And then I'll make some phone calls. Leave it with me. No need for you to worry about this. You focus on Beth, and I'll take care of everything else."

"Thanks, Wendy. Can you please text me the time of the meeting?"

"Sure," Wendy said. "Get some rest, Richard. Something tells me things are going to get worse before they get better."

# Chapter 5

*Monday, October 13*

Richard spent a hapless weekend in his studio apartment trying to stay on top of his workload, but he soon discovered he couldn't focus. He turned his attention to finding Sandy, but after going to her apartment three times on Saturday and twice on Sunday, he realized that she had gone. It wasn't like her to not tell him where she was, but he didn't worry.

Wendy called at eight o'clock Monday morning. "Beth Musselwhite doesn't want to meet with you. Says there's no need."

Richard, who had poached himself an egg, nearly dropped his plate. "She's firing us. Did you explain the situation, how the video was faked?"

"I did."

"Did she not believe you?"

"She didn't say one way or another. She said she's sending a letter with instructions."

"I'll go to her," Richard said.

"I don't think you should—"

"She owes me a face-to-face. If she's going to take her business

35

elsewhere, I want to hear it from her. And who knows, with a little luck, I can talk her round."

An hour later, Richard headed across the Golden Gate Bridge and north on 101, taking the Corte Madera exit. Countryside had its offices in a huge shopping center just off the freeway. A vast parking lot circled the entire property. Richard cruised around to the area closest to the Countryside office. There, in its reserved parking space, was Beth's silver BMW. He parked in the reserved spot right next to Beth's car and strolled nonchalantly towards the Countryside office.

The receptionist smiled when she saw Richard. Holding up her finger, she mouthed, "One second, okay?"

Richard nodded while she wrote down a phone number. "I'll see that he gets the message. Thank you." She hung up the phone and turned her attention to Richard. "Sorry about that, Mr. Sinclair. Does Beth know you're coming?"

"She doesn't. Do you mind if I just go on back?" He didn't wait for an answer. Instead, he hurried past the receptionist, into the underbelly of Beth's domain.

"Mr. Sinclair, wait."

Walking past the rows of cubicles and offices, towards the corner of the building where Beth kept her office, Richard didn't knock before he went in. In contrast to light and airy open space where the clerical staff spent their workday, Beth's office was furnished like a Victorian drawing room, thick noise-absorbing carpet, heavy dark furniture, and subdued lighting lent the office an anachronistic air that Richard never liked. Beth sat at her desk, serene and in control, as though she were waiting for him.

"I figured you'd come storming in here. I suppose I should apologize for not wanting to meet with you, Richard. That wasn't fair of me."

Richard begged, "Please don't take your business from my firm. That video isn't real, Beth. I know it looks real, but it's not.

We're investigating its origin. When I find out who is responsible, they will pay."

Beth studied Richard as she leaned back in her chair. "It's not so much the video, Richard. I understand how things like that can be manufactured."

"Beth—"

"You don't deny you were sleeping with Sandy, do you? Regardless of the video, you were unfaithful to Olivia."

"That's not the issue," Richard said.

Beth held up her hand. "Please. Let me finish. I understand that some men cheat. They tell themselves they have needs and their wife can't fill them. I've never understood the entitlement that allows men like you to break your vows, but that's not important right now. So tell me the truth. Were you sleeping with your secretary? Ah. So the answer is yes. I'm glad you didn't lie to me. And spare me the story of how the video of you two having sex is fake. It's not. You know it's not, and I know it's not. You're an investment to me, Richard. I always keep track of my investments."

"Someone put a camera in my bedroom," Richard said.

"I know. I believe that you didn't know about that. Our generation is a little different, I think. The sex films are for the youngsters." Beth took a brass paperclip out of the holder on her desk and set about unfolding it. "The issue, and what's important now, is that I no longer respect you. And I'm glad you're here so I can tell you in person that I will not be renewing our contract for representation next year. I will honor year-end bonuses, as promised. I expect you to turn over all of your cases to our new firm."

She opened her calendar. "Let's say you turn over the files by November 1. That will give you a couple of weeks to get things in order. And to make things easier for you and Andrew, I'll issue your year-end bonuses when the files are handed over to our new counsel. Does that suit?" Beth didn't wait for Richard's answer. She scribbled something in her calendar. "Very well. That's settled then."

After thirty-plus years of trying hundreds of cases before juries, not only did Richard Sinclair know how to think on his feet, he also knew how to stuff down his emotions as though they didn't exist. These skills deserted him now. Feeling as though he had been hit by a tsunami, Richard felt the room tilt. He shook his head, somehow managed to maintain his equilibrium. His brain scrambled for an appropriate response, something he could say to get Beth to change her mind. For the first time in his long and storied career as a litigator, the words wouldn't come.

"We've had a very successful relationship for almost twenty-five years," Beth said. "Your litigation skills are renowned. You'll find other work, if you want it. But why don't you retire? Take Olivia and go away for a while."

Beth stood. As if following by rote, Richard found himself standing too. Soon Beth had woven her arm through his and was ushering him towards the door. "I was very fond of you once, Richard. Now it's time for us to let things go and move on. You will survive this mess, of that I've no doubt." She patted his arm, a maternal gesture that should have infuriated him. "I'll send over a formal letter memorializing our conversation this afternoon." She pushed him out and shut the door behind him. Richard turned and stared at the closed door for a moment, a befuddled look on his face.

Sound and sights swirled around Richard as he walked out of Countryside, numb and unsure of his footing. He somehow wound up in his car, but didn't remember walking there. He tilted the seat back, and sat for what seemed an eternity as his situation sank in. Eventually his ringing phone snapped him into the present. Wendy. He girded himself for what was to come. There was no getting around Andrew. He would have to face him.

"What happened? I've been worried," Wendy asked.

"We lost Countryside," Richard said.

"Oh, no," Wendy said.

38

"Beth told me personally. Said she was going to send over a formal letter this afternoon."

Wendy lowered her voice. "Are you sure Andrew doesn't know? He's been huffing and puffing in his office since he got here."

Richard let out a defeated sigh. "He doesn't know. I'll be there in thirty minutes."

The beautiful Marin day, sunny with low-hanging clouds over the bay, was lost on Richard as he maneuvered onto the Golden Gate Bridge. His mind started to function just as he turned onto Montgomery Street. As he sat at the stop lights – of course, he hit red lights the whole way – his mind kicked into gear. Anger at Beth Musselwhite threatened to make him lose his reason, but he needed to be logical now. Rincon Sinclair would either need to reinvent itself or close its doors.

Richard thought of life as a solo practitioner. Pulling his Mercedes into his parking space, Richard checked himself in the mirror before he headed off to face Andrew. With his clout, prestige, and connections, Richard was certain he'd land on his feet. Once Rincon Sinclair announced they were closing, the offers would come rolling in. If they didn't, Richard would retire. He'd cash in and move to Hawaii or the south of France. Andrew, as far as Richard was concerned, could go screw himself.

Andrew was waiting for him in the lobby. He sat in one of the waiting room chairs, a surly look on his face.

"Where in the hell have you been?" Andrew's eyes blazed; his cheeks were mottled with suppressed rage.

"Andrew, I'm not in the mood for one of your angry tirades. We need to talk."

"Oh, that's an understatement."

"Conference room. Give me a minute." Richard felt Andrew blustering behind him. He ignored him as he slipped into his office and took off his jacket and tie. Pressing his forehead against the cold window, Richard took a second, mentally searching, without success, for a single thread of control he could latch on to.

Wendy and Andrew waited for him in the conference room. Wendy was making a list on a legal pad with the Montblanc fountain pen the firm had given her when she graduated from law school. She looked up at Richard as he walked into the room, an apologetic look on her face. Although Andrew sat with his back towards Richard, the rage undulated from him. Richard girded himself for the inevitable confrontation as he walked into the room.

Andrew turned to face him. "You've gone and lost us our biggest client?" The disgust that dripped from Andrew and hung in the air between them only infuriated Richard further. It was his cases that were the big money earners. He litigated circles around Andrew Rincon and his talent and celebrity as a lawyer had only helped Andrew.

Playing it cool, Richard took one of the bottles of water on the table. He didn't hurry, as he sat down and took a long drink. When he spoke his voice was measured and calm. "Beth Musselwhite feels that she can no longer trust me. Thus she is not giving us any more business. She wants files handed to new counsel by November 1, at which time she'll issue our bonuses. Given my past three successes, Andrew—" Richard didn't try to keep the venom out of his tone as he put the emphasis on *my* "—both of us will receive a nice chunk of change."

"Who is new counsel? Who the hell did she hire?"

Before Andrew's rage erupted, Richard said, "I don't appreciate, nor will I tolerate, this insinuation that our debacle is my fault. I didn't send that video. I've been the victim of a cut-throat hoax. Another firm wanted Countryside—"

"The hell it's not your fault. If you could have kept your pants zipped for a change none of this would be happening." Andrew stood. "Congratulations, Richard. You've ruined us. I'm this close to throttling you. Stay the hell out of my sight."

He strode out of the room, slamming the door so hard that a framed picture of the Constitution fell off the wall, the glass splintering into shards.

Once Richard and Wendy were alone, Richard asked, "Did you contact Sandy's mother?"

"Left a message. Haven't heard back from her." Wendy tiptoed over the broken glass and sat down next to Richard.

"You realize that she could be behind this video, right? I know you know think she's a sweet girl, but she could be getting ready to blackmail you. I went to law school with a guy who does skip-tracing. Want me to try to find her?"

Richard nodded. "I'm taking my files to my studio. I can't stay under the same roof as Andrew."

"Good idea. I'll report when I know something."

# Chapter 6

*Monday, October 13*

Sharon Bailey walked into her apartment, threw her jacket on the couch, and poured herself a giant glass of wine. Her day had been a long one, full of meetings about manpower and budgets and the general nonsense spouted by the people who do their policing behind a desk and have no clue what officers deal with in the field. Resisting the urge to slug back the entire drink in one go, Sharon raised the glass to her lips and was just about to take a sip when her partner, Ellie Standish, texted her. "We're up. Pick you up in five."

Sharon changed her clothes and tucked her Glock into the holster that fit under her jacket. This would be Ellie Standish's first homicide investigation, and Sharon knew she would have to keep a close eye on her young partner, while also giving her room to learn. Every homicide investigator always remembers their first murder. And there was no denying Officer Ellie Standish was ambitious, much as Sharon had been when she was a young cop starting out. Ellie had a college degree from SF State in addition to high marks at the POST academy, but high marks in school did not necessarily translate to the unique skill set an officer would need while working in the field. This case would be a test for Ellie.

Sharon checked that her door was locked and headed down the stairs, surprised to find Ellie double parked in front of Sharon's apartment, blocking the street. A brand-new gray Prius slowed to a stop behind her. The driver rolled his window down, stuck his head out, and yelled, "Move your car, you stupid bitch."

Ellie got out of the car, leaving her door open, and held her badge out in front of her, holding it like a shield as she stomped up to the car. "You have a problem?"

Sharon got in the passenger side, shutting the door so she didn't have to listen to Ellie tell off a citizen. Glancing around to make sure no one passing by had whipped out a cell phone and started to film, Sharon hunched down in the seat.

A minute later, Ellie was back in the car. "Sorry, boss. People are so impatient these days."

"Did you really have to flash your badge, Ellie? A friendly apology might have been a little easier."

Ellie rolled her eyes.

"You do that to the wrong person, and you'll get written up," Sharon continued. "For all you know, that could be the chief's son."

"Are you joking?"

"Not even a little. I can name two officers in my class at the academy who got fired for that exact same reason." Sharon faced Ellie. "This job puts you in the public eye, puts you in the position of continual scrutiny. It's important that you maintain a certain level of decorum. I know that you're an educated woman, and I know you were at the top of your class in the POST training. I respect that. I want you to succeed. My advice to you, pretend you're being watched. All. The. Time."

"I understand," Ellie said, as she navigated the traffic.

*At least she's a good driver*, Sharon thought. "This is your first murder, so let me tell you how I like to do things. We make contact with the officer who responded to the call to make sure the crime scene is secure, okay? If the ME's already there, we'll talk to him and then evaluate. Stay close to me at the beginning. Once we get the lay of the land, I'm going to bark out a series of assignments, such as canvassing and looking for CCTV. You can get patrol officers to help. If anyone questions or hesitates to cooperate fully, let me know immediately."

"Okay," Ellie said, serious now that Sharon was going to give her some independence.

They didn't talk as they drove down Geary towards Ocean Beach. The sun started to slip out of the sky, leaving vibrant streaks of pink and purple in its wake. They turned onto 48th Avenue, slowing down as they reached a cluster of black-and-white police cars along with the ME's van. Sharon was relieved when Ellie parked in a proper spot. Before they got out of the car, Ellie spoke.

"I wanted to apologize. My attitude hasn't been the best."

"Apology accepted," Sharon said.

A crowd had gathered outside the building and two uniforms had constructed a barricade. Ellie and Sharon flashed their badges. As they approached the building, Sharon grabbed Ellie's arm and pulled her to a stop. "Listen. Your job here – your obligation, if you will – is to the decedent. I know you're ambitious, and I know you're thinking this could well be an opportunity for you to shine. I hope that's true. But your career isn't important right now. The person who is lying up there dead is the most important thing, okay?"

"Understood," Ellie said. And for the first time Sharon saw humility and a tinge of fear in the young officer's eyes.

Sharon tipped her head back and stared up at the gray two-story building, with its bay windows. A curtain flickering in one of the first-floor windows indicated they were being watched.

"I saw that, boss," Ellie said.

"Good. We'll want to talk to everyone in that house."

44

The body was located in the second-story flat. Sharon and Ellie took the stairs to the front door and were greeted by two uniforms. The older man was short and thick through the middle. He had piercing brown eyes and a no-nonsense manner.

"Inspector Bailey," he said.

"Officer Watkins," Sharon said, surreptitiously glancing at the senior officer's name tag.

"The crime scene tech people are just about finished. You can go in, if you want. The ME's here, too. This is Officer Finn. He found the body. Go ahead, Finn, give your report."

Officer Finn wobbled on his feet a bit. His face and lips were pale. Sharon gave him a warm smile, trying her best to put the poor kid at ease. "Take a breath and tell me what happened."

"Sorry, ma'am. It's not my first body, but you never get used to it. I responded to a disturbance call made by the downstairs neighbors. They were bothered by the smell. This particular unit is one of those furnished holiday rentals. The owner lives off site, but after the neighbors called her, she came to find out what was going on, and that's when the body was discovered."

"Where's the owner?"

"She left. I asked for information about whoever rented the flat, but she said she had to ask her lawyer before she handed that information over to the police." Officer Finn reached in his pocket and handed Olivia a business card. "But she gave me her card. She'll be expecting a call. After that, I secured the scene and called it in."

"Did you notice anything about the body or the scene? Anything out of place or missing?" Sharon asked.

Officer Finn nodded. "Her dress is covered in red liquid. It smelled like wine. A rope's been tied around her neck, but I don't think it killed her. She's lying on the bed, with her hands clasped over her heart. It looks staged to me." He shrugged. "That's not much. I'm sorry."

"You did very well, Officer Finn." Sharon turned to Officer

Watkins. "We'll need help with canvassing and CCTV. Can you give me a minute and I'll have Officer Standish back with marching orders?"

"Yes, ma'am," Officer Watkins said.

Sharon turned to Ellie. "Ready?"

Ellie nodded.

They opened the door and were assaulted by the smell of death, a mixture of rotten meat, feces, eggs and foul pungent garlic. A thick, viscous smell that stuck to the back of the throat.

"Nothing prepares you for this, but you'll get used to it," Sharon said. Ellie's face had turned a frightening shade of pale, all eagerness gone. "Are you going to be sick?"

Ellie shook her head. "I'll be fine."

They walked into the living room, where Sharon paused for a moment, taking in the surroundings, her eyes roving the scene and memorizing the details. It was a comfortably furnished flat, the decorations impersonal and generic, typical of a furnished rental. Conveniently situated, whoever rented this flat could walk across the street to the beach, and just up the hill to the Cliff House and other restaurants. Two sofas faced the bay window, which overlooked the ocean. A dining table with seating for eight people was arranged in a nook off the kitchen. The orange and red tones of the furniture, coupled with the warm oak of the hardwood floors, made the place warm and inviting.

Two officers dressed in the protective coveralls worn by techs stood near the window, looking at photographs on an iPad. They nodded at Ellie and Olivia. The man holding the iPad said, "There's no wallet or cell phone."

"No ID?" Sharon asked.

"No. She'll be processed as a Jane Doe."

"Thanks."

"Body's in the bedroom," the man said before he turned his back on them and focused once again on the iPad.

Sharon glanced back at Ellie, who had become subdued since

they entered the house. Nothing like a dead body to shock the humility into a sassy young cop. Sharon stepped into the room just as Dr. Kristen Ward stood and turned off the tape recorder.

"Sharon. Been a while," Dr. Ward said. She stepped away from the body and pulled her hood off. "She's been here for at least a week. Looks like she's been strangled, but I'll know more when I get her on the table. You can step close. Crime scene techs are finished, and so am I. Let me know when you're ready and we'll take her."

"What's up with the rope?"

"Not sure. It certainly didn't kill her. Staged maybe? I've taken photos of it."

Sharon breathed through her mouth as she stepped close to the body. The decedent was young and blond. In life she had been attractive. Now her eyes bulged and her tongue protruded. Sharon felt the familiar clench of sadness. All murders were difficult, but this young woman appeared at first glance to be an innocent, dressed in a conservative business suit, with hair the natural shade of gold that couldn't be obtained from a bottle. She wore little makeup, but Sharon was sure she had been wholesomely pretty in life.

Unable to cope with the noxious odor anymore, Sharon led Ellie into the living room. "Get busy with the canvassing. Get the uniforms after all the neighbors, okay? Tell them to make note of those who aren't available so we can follow up. I'd like you to take the statements of the neighbors tonight, especially the downstairs neighbors who called it in. Be gentle, don't tell them anything, just ask them questions. Explain that we'll need to speak to them again. Be kind. Be tactful. Do this by the book, okay? After you do that, see if there is any CCTV in the neighborhood, check businesses in the surrounding areas. Maybe we can get a glimpse of this girl en route. See if you can track her movements."

Sharon turned to Dr. Ward. "Since there's no ID, can you run her fingerprints?"

"Will do."

"Okay, boss," Ellie said. "Do you want to take the car?"

"No," Sharon said. "I'll grab a cab. Do not discuss this case with anyone from the media. I'll make sure an order comes from on high, but don't be shy about telling the uniforms to keep it under wraps. Got it?"

"Yes," Ellie said.

"Keep me posted." Sharon waited until the body was taken from the building before she walked along the sidewalk that ran parallel to the shore towards the Cliff House, situated at the westernmost part of San Francisco and overlooking the Pacific Ocean. The restaurant was known for its panoramic views. A queue of taxis waited along the street. Sharon grabbed one and asked to be taken to 850 Bryant. She needed to see if anyone matching the dead girl's description had been reported missing.

# Chapter 7

*Tuesday, October 14*

Olivia woke up at seven o'clock feeling as though she had walked across the desert on her knees. Her eyelids felt like sandpaper, and she couldn't stop crying. Richard had been cheating on her for years. Everyone seemed to know it but her. She was a cuckold. She had spent twenty-eight years of her life being faithful to Richard, believing they had beaten the odds and had loved each other fully and completely. She laughed out loud. What a joke. What a fool she had been.

Her bedside phone rang. Without thinking she answered.

"Olivia? How did it go? Did I wake you up?"

Olivia sat up. "He had a surprise party for me. Can you believe that? I walked into this house and all of his friends were here."

"Oh my God," Lauren said. "What did you do?"

Olivia thought back to the fake smiles and phony bonhomie of the evening. "I suffered through it. Poor Denny. She did a beautiful job putting everything together." Olivia ran her hand through her hair.

"What are you going to do? What can I do to help?"

Olivia sat for a moment, grateful for Lauren who was comfortable in the silence. *What am I going to do?*

"I guess my question is really what could you do right now to make yourself feel better about things?"

"I'm going to get to know my husband," Olivia said. "I'll call you later, okay?"

She hung up without waiting for Lauren to answer.

If Richard had any secrets, they would be hidden in his study. Olivia stood at the bottom of the stairs, unable to remember the last time she had been in this room. This was Richard's domain, and out of respect and by some unspoken agreement, she had stayed out. She had trusted Richard and never felt compelled to check on his whereabouts or invade his personal space.

The room was dark due to lack of sunlight and the color of the décor. A forest green leather couch and club chair that had belonged to Richard's father, along with a dark mahogany desk, left a distinctly masculine stamp on the room. The blackout shades took away any threat of sunlight. Olivia always wondered why Richard liked this room to feel like a cave. She shivered. It was a good five degrees colder down here.

Stepping close to his desk, she ran her fingers over the leather blotter and an old Cross pen stand. Although the gold pens still rested in their place, they had never been used and the ink had dried up years ago. A credenza took up the opposite wall and it was covered with pictures of Richard. Some of them held pictures of their family, Denny as a young girl, Olivia's wedding portrait, but the photos of Richard with famous people – Dwight Clark, Ronald Reagan, Willie Mays, and Joe Montana to name a few – held pride of place. Olivia thought of Richard and Sandy Watson, of Richard and heaven knew who else, and a fresh wave of anger washed over her.

Taking a deep breath, she sat down at the desk and opened the drawers one by one. There was nothing unusual there. All the folders had typewritten labels, which held bank statements, credit card statements, IRS receipts, and the like. When Olivia stumbled across a folder whose handwritten label said TIFFANY'S, she took it out and laid it on the desk.

Opening the folder, Olivia saw a stack of receipts, current date on top, of all the jewelry Richard had purchased from Tiffany's since their marriage. Although she had never asked, the Tiffany boxes at Christmas and birthdays had become something of a tradition in their marriage. She had accepted and worn the jewelry to make Richard happy. Richard had grown up poor, had put himself through law school, and had made a success of himself by hard work and perseverance. Being able to buy fine jewelry for his wife was a matter of pride for him. As she scanned through the receipts, she recognized the pieces that he had purchased for her – this year's diamond pendant, the earrings from last year's Christmas – the invoices an historical timeline of Richard's gifts.

Olivia thumbed back to the top invoice, noticing another piece of jewelry was purchased on the same day as her diamond necklace. She thumbed through the invoices and saw that each time Richard bought Olivia jewelry, he also purchased a second piece of jewelry, a silver cuff bracelet. Thumbing through the invoices she saw that the second purchase was always the same; the only thing that was different was the name of the engraving. One year it was Nancy, and then Rachel, BethAnn, Louise, Holly, Bambi – the list went on and on. Olivia didn't need to do any investigating to know what she had discovered. When Richard had purchased a gift for her, he had also purchased a trinket for his current love interest.

*That son of a bitch.* Walking over to the credenza, Olivia stared at all the family photos. Seen through the lens of her embarrassment and shame, she was disgusted by the false tale they told. For the first time in her life, Olivia didn't hold her emotions in check. She opened her mouth and let out a blood-curdling scream that would have brought the neighbors running if they could hear. In one motion she swept her arm along the top of the credenza, sending all the photographs launching into the air before they crashed to the floor, in a cacophony of shattering glass.

Breathing heavily, she stepped over the photo of Richard with Dwight Clark and headed back upstairs.

51

# Chapter 8

The morning after the murder was a busy one. Ellie attended the autopsy, while Sharon followed up on missing persons reports in surrounding jurisdictions. She had hoped her efforts would be fruitful, but by ten o'clock hadn't discovered anything. Two hours later, Ellie returned from the coroner's office, plopping down on Sharon's couch, exhaustion etched on her face.

"How did the autopsy go?"

"I didn't throw up or pass out, if that's what you're wondering. Honestly, the smell from the crime scene was much worse. Our dead girl was strangled. Whoever killed her left clear handprints. She had a broken hyoid bone. The rope was just for show. And Dr. Ward ran the decedent's fingerprints in the criminal database, but nothing came of it. She's expanding the search to include civil servants who have fingerprints on file. She emailed you a preliminary report."

"We need to follow up with the neighborhood canvass and send the rope off for processing."

"There's more," Ellie said. "She was pregnant."

Sharon recognized the familiar wave of sorrow she experienced at the beginning of every homicide. Dealing with the emotional component of death was a necessary evil. There was no time for sentimentality during a murder investigation. Nevertheless, Sharon always felt a pang of sadness for each innocent whose life was taken too soon, even more so for children and babies.

"I'm still waiting to hear from the owner of the vacation rental. If she doesn't call me within an hour, I'm going to go looking for her. Keep me posted," Sharon said.

No sooner had Ellie left when a uniformed officer knocked twice on Sharon's office door and stuck his head in. "There's a Mrs. Milken to see you. It's about the murder in the Avenues."

"That would be the owner of the vacation rental." Sharon stood and put her jacket on. "Thanks."

"I put her in interrogation six. Oh, she's a bit of a grouch. Just saying."

*Just what I need.*

Mrs. Milken had bleached blond hair, diamond rings on all her fingers, and a snooty attitude that rankled Sharon from the outset. Forcing a smile, Sharon stuck out her hand. "Thanks for coming in, Mrs. Milken. I've been trying to reach out since yesterday."

"I don't dance to the tune of the San Francisco PD, Officer Bailey."

"It's inspector, and I didn't expect you to, ma'am. We've found a dead woman inside your rental unit. I'm trying to find out all I can about her. Now, if you could just start by—"

"Do you have any idea how difficult this is for me? It's going to cost me a fortune to get the smell out of that place. I may have to repaint the walls and replace all the furniture. Not to mention I could get a bad review. This could be a disaster for my business." As Mrs. Milken dabbed at her eyes with a tissue, Sharon wondered if this woman gave even a moment's thought to the poor girl who had been murdered.

"Can you tell me who rented the house? And when?"

The woman reached into her purse and took out an envelope,

which she set on the table and pushed towards Sharon. "A Marin County woman rented the unit. She paid with an American Express card three weeks ago when she made the reservation." Sharon's heart skipped a beat. *Bingo.* "I've printed out a copy of all the documents. They're in that envelope." Mrs. Milken stood. "When can I get a crew in to clean my unit? You realize this is my livelihood? I can't wait forever."

"So noted, Mrs. Milken. I'll see what I can do to hurry things along for you."

Mrs. Milken's face softened. "Forgive me for sounding callous, Inspector. I just find the whole thing so shocking. I've always been a housewife. It took me five years to talk my husband into letting me buy a rental unit. And then this happened and he's been rubbing my nose in it."

"Thank you for coming in, Mrs. Milken. One of the officers will escort you out." Sharon hurried back to her office. Her stomach growled. Ellie was at her desk on the phone. When Sharon walked by, she flagged her down.

"We've got a hit, boss. The dead girl – the decedent's name is Sandy Watson. She was fingerprinted when she worked at a daycare. Now she works as a legal secretary for Richard Sinclair."

"The Richard Sinclair?"

"Yes, the famous lawyer. The same Richard Sinclair who appears on the news all the time when there's a sensational legal case."

"We need to inform next of kin. After that, let's get a warrant for Sandy's apartment. You handle that. Take a techie with you. I'd like to get a look at the decedent's emails and text message history ASAP."

"Got it," Ellie said.

"Once the search is locked down, go eat a good dinner. We'll meet back here and make a plan. Something tells me it's going to be a long night."

*

Sharon took a taxi from Celeste Watson's house in the Marina District to the Financial District, getting out of the cab at Montgomery and California. Ellie had gone back to 850 Bryant to secure the search warrant and take a team to Sandy Watson's apartment. Celeste Watson had been devastated at the news of her daughter's murder. Although Sharon knew how important it was to speak to the family members immediately after notification of a violent crime, Celeste Watson had been so shaken that Sharon had treated her gently.

Sandy's mom had little information to provide about her daughter. She worked at Rincon Sinclair and was planning on going to law school. As far as Mrs. Watson could tell, Sandy seemed happy and had no enemies. Another visit would be in order, and Sharon was glad to leave Sandy's mother to her grieving.

Stepping into the busy lobby at 44 Montgomery Street, Sharon showed her badge to the security men at the desk in the lobby before she took the elevator up to the nineteenth floor. When she stepped into the office of Rincon Sinclair, she was met by a woman in her early forties, dressed in what looked like an Armani suit, with intelligent eyes and a no-nonsense way about her.

"I'm Wendy Betters. How can I help you?"

"Is there some place we can talk privately?" She eyed a young woman who was busy typing on a computer.

"Do you mind if I see your identification? I don't mean to be so particular, but we are involved in some rather tricky litigation at the moment."

"Of course." Sharon handed the woman her identification and waited patiently while the woman studied it closely. Sharon knew how important it was for a policeman to be hyper-vigilant and aware of his or her reactions to a situation, and something about Wendy Betters rankled Sharon. She couldn't put her finger on what irked her, but she made a mental note of it.

Once assured that Sharon was who she said she was, Wendy led Sharon through the spacious common area with two secretarial stations situated in front of a row of offices. One of the desks was empty. Sandy Watson's, Sharon guessed. A young woman with blue streaks in her hair beavered away at the other desk, a pair of headphones in her ears. All of the walls separating the offices from the main area were glass, which provided a sweeping view of the San Francisco Bay. They passed Richard Sinclair's office, marked by brass lettering on a heavy-looking wooden door. The office beyond was spacious and bright, with a thick rug and an antique desk the size of a cruise ship.

They wound up in Wendy's office, which was smaller than the other two, but still had a breathtaking view. Sharon wondered for a moment if she could get any work done with a view like that.

"Is this about Sandy Watson?" Wendy asked.

"Why would you ask me that?" Sharon said.

"She hasn't been to work all week. I tried to call her mother – that's her emergency contact person – and left a message. We've been worried."

"Sandy Watson is dead. Her body was discovered yesterday at a vacation rental in the Avenues."

Wendy Betters's face paled. "Oh, my God. I knew something was wrong. Can you tell me what happened? How did she die?"

Sharon shook her head. "I'm sorry. I can't discuss that with you."

"Was she murdered?" Wendy asked, her voice incredulous and unbelieving. When she started to cry in earnest, her mascara ran, leaving dark rivers down her cheeks. She grabbed a tissue from the box on her desk and dabbed at her eyes, but her efforts only made things worse.

Sharon gave Wendy a minute to compose herself before she continued with her questions. "What can you tell me about Sandy?"

Wendy hesitated, as if calculating just how candid she should be.

"It's best if you're honest with me."

56

"I know," Wendy said. "You're going to find this out anyway, so you may as well hear it from me. Sandy was having an affair with Richard Sinclair. It wasn't serious. She wasn't Richard's first affair, and she won't be his last. Richard Sinclair is a serial philanderer."

"Did Sandy have other boyfriends? Someone from her past who might be jealous of her relationship with Richard Sinclair?"

Wendy shook her head. "I don't think so. She was pretty involved with Richard, but she didn't flaunt it. She was a hard worker, an ambitious young woman. She was frugal, brought her own lunch every day, didn't buy expensive clothes, if you get my meaning."

"Where is Mr. Sinclair? I need to speak to him."

"Client meeting. I doubt he'll be back in the office today. I'll tell him to call you as soon as he is able."

She decided to go for the shock factor. "Could Mr. Sinclair have killed Sandy Watson?"

Wendy Betters's cheeks flushed red with indignation. "Of course not. Inspector Bailey, Mr. Sinclair is a well-respected attorney. He plays golf with the mayor. He is friends with the governor."

"Sorry, but I have to ask." The last thing Sharon wanted to do was alienate Wendy Betters. An investigating officer never knew when they might need a favor. Since it was early days yet, Sharon reckoned it would be best to keep the players in this drama happy. For now.

She stood. "Thank you, Mrs. Betters. I may need to speak to you again."

"Any time. It's Ms., actually." Wendy held up her left hand. "No husband for me, I'm afraid. Married to the job."

Sharon stood and handed Wendy her card. "I understand. Thanks for talking to me. If you think of anything, let me know?"

"Of course," Wendy said.

"I can see myself out," Sharon said.

Once in the lobby, Sharon approached the security desk. It was after five, and the guard on duty was in the process of pouring coffee from a Thermos. "Excuse me," Sharon said, once again showing her badge. "Could I bother you to tell me what kind of car Richard Sinclair drives? Does he have a specific parking space? It pertains to an investigation, so discretion is in order."

"Sure. He drives a brand-new Mercedes. Slate gray, convertible." The guard entered something into his computer. "Slot 147. Elevator's that way." He pointed.

"Thank you."

Sharon took the elevator down to the parking garage and wove through the parked vehicles until she found slot 147, where a gray Mercedes was parked. Sharon felt the hood. It was cold to the touch.

# Chapter 9

*Wednesday, October 15*

Olivia had been struggling with the day-to-day functions of life since she had seen the horrid video. Her bones felt as though they were filled with cement. It took everything she had to get out of bed in the morning. The idea of facing her clients and their marital issues left her with a stomach ache and a relentless desire to run for the hills.

Mary had been sympathetic and had assured Olivia she would see to things. Try as she might, Olivia couldn't shake the image of Richard and that young woman writhing naked on the video. The desire to throttle Richard, make him suffer, use their divorce to ruin his reputation, simply wasn't there. Instead Olivia was ashamed. Ashamed for Richard, the poor young woman, and for herself. She wondered if anyone else had seen it. God help them if that video was leaked to the media. And then there was Denny . . . It didn't bear thinking about.

Her bedroom faced east by design. The sunbeams warmed her face, leaving her no choice but to get up and face reality. When she sat up, stars of headache pain exploded in front of her eyes. A migraine. Groaning, she reached for the water on her bedside table. This was all Richard's fault. After taking two more ibuprofen, she stood under the hot jets of her shower, washing her hair with the organic lavender shampoo that was supposed to soothe the soul as it cleansed the hair and scalp. It didn't.

Half an hour later, showered and dressed, she still felt like death. A quick call to Mary to ensure things were going smoothly at the office, and Olivia would crawl back into bed.

She was on the phone to Mary, who was busily assuring her she had the office under control, when two San Francisco PD cars pulled up in front of her house. Two unmarked cars followed. The officers got out of their cars and Olivia watched as a cadre of police officers headed to her front door, led by a tall, middle-aged woman, dressed in a no-nonsense navy blue suit with sensible flat shoes. Dishwater blond hair framed her strong-boned face. She had the determined look of a woman on a mission.

"Something's not right," Olivia muttered into the phone.

"What's going on?" Mary asked, concern in her voice.

"There's a swarm of police converging on my house. I'm going to put you on speaker phone, okay?" Olivia put the phone on speaker and hurried to the front door, where the knocking was growing more and more insistent.

When she opened it, the blond woman said, "Olivia Sinclair?"

"Yes," Olivia said.

The woman handed Olivia the piece of paper. "I'm Inspector Bailey with the San Francisco Police Department. This is a warrant to search your premises. I'll be taking you in for questioning with regard to a homicide."

"A homicide? Who's dead? Is it Richard?" Did these people think she killed him?

Four uniformed officers and two detectives pushed Olivia aside and filed past her, invading her house. Inspector Bailey stepped into the hallway, blocking the front door as if she expected Olivia to make a run for it. "Get your shoes. I'll drive you."

"Drive me where?" Olivia asked, speaking loud enough for Mary to hear her.

"As I mentioned, we're taking you to 850 Bryant Street for questioning with regard to a homicide. We just want to talk to you."

Olivia watched one of the plain-clothed detectives go through the books in her living room bookcase. He pulled them out one by one, rifled through them, and tossed them on the floor. Unsure what was happening, unsure what to do, Olivia put her cell phone to her ear. "Mary?"

"I heard everything. I'm calling Stephen Vine. I'll tell him where they're taking you."

Inspector Bailey pulled a plastic evidence bag out of her jacket pocket and held out a latex-gloved hand. "I'll take your phone, ma'am. It's listed in the warrant."

Although she was full of questions, Olivia didn't say anything on the ride to 850 Bryant Street. By the time she and Inspector Bailey stepped off the elevator, Olivia's stomach was in knots. Her head pounded, and it was all she could do not to cry. What was happening? Why had they brought her here? She was so muddled, she didn't notice Richard, flanked by two burly police officers, his face flushed with anger.

"Olivia?" Richard called out. He started to move to her, but the uniformed officer who was with him grabbed his arm.

"Richard, what are you doing here? What's going on? The police are searching the house."

Richard gave Olivia a look of disgust. "What have you done?"

She wanted to scream that she had done nothing, that she didn't know why she was here. But someone had died. Who? And why would they think she was involved? But she couldn't find the words to speak. It was as if her mind was unable to process what was happening. Inspector Bailey led her into a windowless room, which held a table, three chairs, and a camera in the corner.

Sharon turned the camera on and gave Olivia the standard Miranda warning. "Do you understand these rights?"

"Yes, but I don't understand what's happening or why I'm here."

Inspector Bailey ignored her. "Do you know a woman named Sandy Watson?"

"No. Never heard of her. Should I know her?"

Olivia felt confidence return as Inspector Bailey scrutinized her. Every lawyer who had ever set foot in a courtroom knew police officers lied to people they were questioning. It was perfectly legal to do so, and it happened all the time. Inspector Bailey was fishing. Under the glaring fluorescent lights Olivia noticed the dark circles under the woman's eyes and the pinched tension of her lips. *She's had a tough night.* The two women locked eyes, neither looking away.

"You insinuated that I am here in connection with a homicide. I didn't kill anyone. So unless you are prepared to charge me, I'm leaving." Olivia stood.

Inspector Bailey opened the file, took out an eight-by-ten photograph, along with another piece of paper and placed them upside down on top of the table between the two women. "Are you sure you don't know a Sandy Watson, Mrs. Sinclair? Think about your answer."

"Of course, I'm sure—"

"Your husband is the Sinclair part of Rincon Sinclair, correct?"

"Yes," Olivia said.

"Do you spend much time at your husband's office?"

"No," Olivia said.

"Do you fraternize with his employees on a social level?"

"I'm good friends with Wendy Betters, but other than that, no. I used to go to the office Christmas parties, but they started having them at lunchtime, so I couldn't get away. I haven't set foot in Rincon Sinclair in over a year." The realization surprised Olivia, as if her words were a declaration of the sorry state of her marriage. Now that she knew of Richard's betrayal, the clues were everywhere.

"When was the last time you saw your husband?"

"Friday night," Olivia said. "My husband threw me a surprise party. Afterwards we got in a huge fight. I told him I wanted a divorce and asked him to leave."

"What did you fight about?" Sharon asked.

"You have my cell phone. If you look, you'll find a video saved to my photos, which I received in an email from an anonymous sender. It depicts my husband having sex with a younger woman."

"Had you ever seen that woman before?"

"No. I had no idea who she was until last night. After I showed the video to my husband, he confessed that the young lady is his secretary."

Inspector Bailey turned the photograph face up and pushed it towards Olivia. "Have you ever seen this woman?"

In the video, this woman had been young, beautiful, and full of life. Now she stared at Olivia with lifeless eyes, opaque with death, her tongue swollen and protruding from the lips that had kissed Richard. A rope had been tied around her neck, but even on first glance it seemed like a prop, a macabre piece of scenery.

"Oh, my God," Olivia whispered. She turned the picture over and tried to bite back the nausea. No luck. Pushing away from the table, she knocked her chair over as she ran to the garbage can in the corner of the room and vomited. Had Richard killed this girl? The heaving continued after her stomach emptied. When they finally subsided, Olivia felt as though she had been punched in the stomach. Hot tears ran down her face.

Inspector Bailey handed her a tissue. Olivia took it and wiped her mouth. All the while, the inspector sat across from her, still as a statue, watching and – Olivia felt quite certain – missing nothing.

"Is there something you need to tell me, ma'am?"

"Prior to that I had never seen her."

"How did your husband react when you confronted him about the video?"

"He didn't bother to deny it. Said that men have needs." Olivia shivered. *How could she have been so blind?*

Inspector Bailey pulled out a packet of papers and pushed them over to Olivia. "Is that your email address?"

The stack of papers were a printout of emails, apparently sent from olivia.lawyer@zeus.com. The addressee was Sandy.Watson@rinconsinclair.com.

"No. That's not my email. I don't use Zeus. My email comes through my office. My address is olivia@oliviasinclair.com." Olivia fished in her purse and handed Sharon her business card. "Email's on the bottom."

"Go ahead and read through those. I'd like to know if you remember sending them."

"I don't need to review them. I didn't send them. This isn't my email address."

"Ma'am, someone sent threatening emails in your name to Sandy Watson. Now Sandy Watson is dead. I advise you to read through them."

Olivia thumbed through the stack of emails, surprised at the death threats and the crude language. Surely no one would believe Olivia capable of sending such nonsense.

"Whoever sent these emails is angry, nursing a grudge against this poor girl. I didn't send these."

"But that is your email address?"

"As I said, it is not my email address. But anyone can open an email in my name. They don't check your identification, do they?"

Again Inspector Bailey didn't answer Olivia. Instead she plowed on, as if Olivia hadn't spoken. "Have you ever rented or are you familiar with a vacation rental on 48th Avenue?"

"Vacation rental? No," Olivia said.

"Come on, Mrs. Sinclair. You're a lawyer. Surely you don't think you can rent a place at the beach with a credit card without leaving a record."

"I have no idea what you're talking about. I haven't rented a beach house, or gone on vacation for that matter, in a while."

"So just to be clear, you didn't use an American Express card on or about September 25, 2014 and rent a beach house? And I advise you not to lie to me, Mrs. Sinclair."

Fear washed over Olivia all of a sudden. Inspector Bailey seemed confident, like a hunter ready to spring a trap. "Why am I here?"

Sharon Bailey pushed a photocopy of an American Express receipt across the table. "Is that your American Express number?"

Olivia didn't even look at the paper. "I don't have an American Express card. I have a business VISA and a personal Mastercard. I didn't send the emails. I didn't kill that poor girl. I've never even met her in person. The only time I've ever seen her is in a video on my phone and in this picture. Other than that, I wouldn't recognize her. Someone's setting me up. I didn't write those emails. And again, in case I didn't make it clear the first time, I don't have an American Express card."

"Your husband didn't deny his affair with Sandy?"

"No," Olivia said. "I told him I wanted a divorce. He left the house."

"What time?"

"I don't know," Olivia snapped. "You're accusing me of something I didn't do. Do you have any evidence? If not, I'm leaving."

"Sit down, Mrs. Sinclair."

Olivia sat.

"Where were you on the fifth and sixth of October?"

Olivia realized that Inspector Bailey thought Olivia had killed Sandy Watson. Olivia knew the emails and the bogus American Express charges were enough probable cause for the search warrant that was being executed at her house. She glanced at the two-way mirror and wondered who stood behind it, watching her. Had Richard killed Sandy and framed Olivia? If so, Olivia felt sure he would have planted incriminating evidence at the house. The gravity of her situation hit her.

"Someone's setting me up," Olivia said. "You have to believe me. I swear, I didn't kill Sandy Watson."

"Where were you on the fifth and sixth of October?"

"That's last Sunday and Monday? I spent the weekend at home by myself. I took a drive out to Stinson Beach on Sunday. I went for a walk and had lunch at the Sand Dollar. Other than that I worked on Monday and spent Monday evening at home."

"Anyone with you?"

"No."

Olivia swallowed the hard lump that had formed in the back of her throat. She was hot and thirsty. Her head pounded and she wanted to go home. "Can I have some water please?"

"In a minute," Sharon said. "Now, have you—"

The door to the interrogation room opened. For a moment, Olivia thought it might be Stephen, coming to rescue her at last. But it was another policewoman, younger than Sharon Bailey. Olivia guessed the woman to be in her early thirties. She had broad shoulders and a lean athletic body that spoke of hours at the gym. Her green eyes stood out against her brown skin, but there was no warmth in them. Her heart pounding in her chest, Olivia watched while the woman reached into the bag and one by one set a cheap knock-off Coach purse and an iPhone with a tawdry rhinestone cover on the table.

"Have you ever seen these, Mrs. Sinclair?"

"No, I have not," Olivia said.

"Are you sure? We found them in your bedroom closet," the young officer said.

"But I've never seen those in my life." Everything moved in slow motion as it dawned on Olivia that not only was she the prime suspect in the murder of her husband's lover, the evidence proving that she had committed the crime was quickly mounting.

When the door opened and this time Stephen Vine came into the room, red-faced with fury, Olivia nearly wept with relief.

"Don't say another word, Liv," Stephen said. He turned to Sharon. "If you've got something, charge her. Otherwise we're leaving."

Another man followed Stephen into the office. Olivia recognized him as Jonas Greensboro, an ADA with a reputation for being small-minded, media-savvy, and quick to prosecute cases without doing the most thorough investigation.

"You've got the wrong person, Jonas," Stephen Vine said. "She's being framed. I'm going to have a field day with this one."

"Do what you need to do, Stephen. Your client murdered her husband's lover." The man turned toward Olivia. "I've reviewed these charges against you, and as an Assistant District Attorney of the City and County of San Francisco, I'm charging you, Olivia Sinclair, pursuant to California Penal Code Section 187, with the murder of Sandy Watson. For the record, I'm reminding you that anything you say—"

Jonas Greensboro's mouth moved, and Olivia felt certain noise was coming out, but the ringing in her ears was so loud she couldn't hear him. White dots flashed before her eyes. When the floor started to move she felt a strong arm around her shoulder and heard Stephen Vine's voice in her ear. "Just sit here for a second, Liv." She allowed herself to be led back to a chair amid the murmuring susurration of voices.

When the voices stopped, Stephen said, "Everyone out. Now."

*

Once Olivia and Stephen were alone, Olivia said, "My God. This isn't happening." She grabbed Stephen's arm and said, "Someone went to a lot of trouble, and not inconsiderable risk in planting that evidence in my home. I'm being set up."

Stephen sat next to her. He put an arm around her shoulder and pulled her close to him. When she was close, he whispered in her ear. "They're going to take you upstairs and process you. You'll have to spend the night here. The good thing is, since Jonas already charged you, you can be arraigned first thing tomorrow. I'll get you out of here. We'll get you home and make a plan."

"I didn't kill her," Olivia whispered. "I didn't kill her." The words ran like a ticker tape through her mind's eye.

"I know. Don't worry, Liv. We'll get this sorted out."

Sharon Bailey had the courtesy to knock before she entered the room. "They need to take her now."

"I'll see you tomorrow." With a reluctant look, Stephen left Olivia to spend the night in jail for a crime she didn't commit.

# Chapter 10

*Thursday, October 16*

Olivia had never been in jail before. Although her best friend Lauren had actively protested against many a cause back in the day and had been arrested for her efforts more than once, Olivia had been the friend who posted bail and provided emotional support. She never dreamed she'd spend a moment of her life behind bars. At 10:00 p.m. the lights had been turned out. Olivia had tried to make herself comfortable on the thin mattress in her cell, but it did little to provide insulation against the hard slab it lay on. The standard-issue orange jumpsuit felt rough against her skin. Olivia was cold and hungry. She had no expectation of sleep. Not tonight.

Around her, other prisoners coughed, belched, and bemoaned their current situation. One woman kept saying, "I'm innocent. I'm innocent." Her proclamations were interspersed with pathetic tears.

This went on for hours, until finally someone said, "We're all innocent. Now shut the fuck up."

At some point – Olivia had no idea what time it was – the prison settled and the nocturnal noises took over.

\*

The next morning, with her eyes tired from lack of sleep, Olivia was allowed to use the restroom and brush her teeth with a disposable toothbrush, after which she was taken in an elevator to arraignment court, her orange jumpsuit hanging from her body, like a flag of shame.

Olivia stood next to Stephen, taking strength from him. He leaned in and whispered, "Jonas is going to try to get you remanded until trial. I'm going to ask for house arrest with electronic detention. It's expensive, but—"

"I don't care. Get me out of here."

Olivia, who practiced before the San Francisco Superior Court family law judges, had never appeared before Judge Dwight Helman. But she knew him by reputation. He was older, nearly ready to retire, stern, unpredictable, and had become well known for his rather unorthodox rulings. Olivia had read somewhere that Judge Helman had sentenced a man who had been arrested for dog fighting to ten years' community service at the Humane Society. The irony of someone who made a fortune running dog fights spending ten years cleaning kennels caught the media's attention and put Judge Helman in the spotlight.

He gave Olivia a look that said *What the hell are you doing here* before he cleared his throat and spoke. "Plea, Mrs. Sinclair."

"Not guilty." Her voice came out weak and trembly.

"Mr. Greensboro on bail?"

"This is a homicide, Your Honor. A search of the defendant's house revealed the decedent's property. Mrs. Sinclair's credit card was used to rent the apartment where the murder was committed. Mrs. Sinclair not only has means, she and her husband have friends with boats and airplanes. As such, she is a flight risk. We request remand."

*Oh, no.* White stars darted in front of Olivia's eyes. The floor tipped underneath her. She grabbed onto the table.

"Mr. Vine?"

"Mrs. Sinclair is a respected attorney who is eager to prove her innocence. Mrs. Sinclair is being framed for a murder she didn't commit. We shouldn't even be here, Your Honor. Mrs. Sinclair—"

"Mrs. Sinclair's guilt or innocence is for a jury to decide, Mr. Vine. I am going to—"

"Wait, Your Honor," Stephen Vine interrupted. "How about house arrest with electronic monitoring? I know it's unorthodox in pre-trial detention. But as you know, Mrs. Sinclair is an attorney. I need her to assist in her defense. Mrs. Sinclair will assume all costs, thus saving the taxpayers the money it would cost to detain her."

"Mr. Greensboro?"

"I still request remand, Your Honor. Mrs. Sinclair is accused of premeditated homicide. Letting clients with means to pay have house arrest sets an unjust precedent. Moreover, the egregious nature of the crime—"

"Which Mrs. Sinclair most certainly did not commit," Stephen interrupted.

Jonas kept talking. "Given the egregious nature of Mrs. Sinclair's crime, remand is required. She shouldn't be allowed to enjoy the comforts of home. I'm also concerned that she's a flight risk—"

Stephen turned on Jonas. "You think she's going to slip the bracelet, get on an airplane, and be out of the country before the police can show up? Really, Jonas?"

"Enough." Judge Helman banged his gavel. "I cling firmly to the notion that everyone who passes before me in this courtroom is innocent until proven guilty. Mrs. Sinclair, electronic detention isn't cheap. You realize the financial burden of this will rest on your shoulders?"

"Yes, Your Honor."

"You will not be allowed to leave your house under any circumstances. Do you understand?"

"Yes."

"I'm ordering Mrs. Sinclair be detained in her home under

electronic surveillance until trial. She will not be allowed to leave the home for any circumstances whatsoever. In addition to home detention, Mrs. Sinclair will post a $1 million bond and surrender her passport. I'm assuming you have Mrs. Sinclair's passport, Mr. Vine?"

"I do, Your Honor."

Judge Helman faced Olivia. "If you disobey this order, you'll be taken to jail. And I give you my personal guarantee that you'll stay there until your case is tried. I don't give second chances, Mrs. Sinclair."

*

Olivia was shuffled back to a holding cell. An hour later she was allowed to change into the clothes she had been wearing the previous day under the watchful eye of a female officer. After that, she was placed once again in handcuffs and escorted to the back seat of a sheriff's car, where she was transported home.

Olivia wasn't expecting the flocks of cameras and journalists that waited in front of her house. As they rolled to a stop, they swarmed the car.

The deputy met her eyes in the rearview mirror. Olivia sensed his curiosity, as though he wanted to ask her if she did it. "Is there another entrance to the house?"

"No. You're going to have to park in front."

Olivia almost cried with relief when Stephen Vine and Mary stepped out the front door. Mary carried the afghan from the living room sofa, the blanket she had knitted for Olivia when she was pregnant with Denny. The sheriff tooted his horn, sending the reporters scattering as he pulled up as close to Olivia's door as he could manage.

Olivia nodded and watched as the deputy, who towered over Stephen, walked up to the crowd of reporters. He said something and pointed to the patch of dirt across the street. One lone reporter tried to defy the deputy's orders. Olivia watched as he stepped close to the deputy, saying something she couldn't hear and pointing. When the deputy took his handcuffs off his belt, the man hurried across the street, where he joined his colleagues, an indignant expression on his face.

Mary opened the back door of the car and unfolded the blanket. "He's making them stay off your property." Mary's Irish brogue was back in full force, as was usual in times of stress. "Let me cover you up and I'll lead you inside."

They made quick work of getting Olivia inside the house. Mary held the blanket over Olivia, successfully hiding her face from the clicking cameras and the questions. "Mrs. Sinclair, did you kill Sandy Watson? Mrs. Sinclair, was Sandy Watson your husband's mistress?" Once they were in the house, the sheriff asked where the landline was located.

"Kitchen," Olivia managed to say.

"Are those handcuffs necessary?" Mary followed Olivia and the deputy into the kitchen, where Olivia was instructed to sit in a chair.

"She has to keep them on until the bracelet is on her ankle and we confirm it's working." The deputy set a canvas duffel bag onto the floor. Olivia watched while he installed an electronic box to the wall, hooked it up to the landline, and fiddled with it until it beeped. Then he placed the ankle bracelet around Olivia's ankle.

"You are to wear this all the time, even in the shower. You're allowed in your house and out on the back deck. If you mess with the bracelet, an alarm will sound. If you step outside the designated area, the alarm will sound. If and when the alarm does sound, you will receive a call on this landline." The deputy pointed to the phone. "You'll have ten rings to answer. If you don't answer, I'll come and haul you back to jail. Do you understand?"

"Yes," Olivia said.

"Good." The deputy removed Olivia's handcuffs, packed the tools back in his bag and left.

Stephen came into the room, along with Lauren.

"What are you doing here?" Olivia asked, embarrassed to have her friend see her like this.

"Mary called," Lauren said. "We're going to straighten up your house."

Olivia turned to Stephen. "What made you think to bring my passport?"

"Given the severity of the charges, I knew the judge would require surrender if you were going to get bail. Good thing it was at your office. Mary was able to get it for me."

Olivia stood up. "Let's go in the living room—"

"I took the liberty of having Mary and Lauren go to your house and start putting things away. The police did a number while they searched. They didn't break anything, but they were rather thorough."

"Oh, no," Olivia said.

Stephen turned to Mary and Lauren. "Would you ladies give us a minute?" When they were alone, he said, "We're going to prove your innocence, Liv. But first we need to discuss the elephant in the room."

"That would be Richard," Olivia said.

"Yep. He's the common denominator. He's got motive, means, and opportunity. Who else could have planted all the dead girl's personal items in your house?"

"Why didn't they arrest him?"

"Jonas Greensboro is a stupid man. There's no concrete evidence against Richard. On the other hand, the emails allegedly sent from you are pretty damning." Stephen moved to the window and stood with his back to Olivia for a good minute. When he turned, his eyes were steely and hard. "You and I are good friends, Liv. But I'm your lawyer now. My singular focus is keeping you out of jail."

74

"I know," Olivia's voice was but a whisper.

"So there's no misunderstanding between us, I want you to know that I'm going after Richard," Stephen said.

Olivia felt the air whirl around her. Richard. He had lied, connived, manipulated, and betrayed Olivia. Was he capable of murder? Had he strangled that innocent young girl and set Olivia up to take the fall? Was the man she had loved for most of her adult life capable of letting her to go to prison for a crime he committed? Emotions swirled around her, threatening to drive her over the brink. Her heart had grown numb, but she knew at some point, that protective lack of feeling would fade. When that happened Olivia would have to deal with her heartache and the loss of her marriage. Either that or go mad. But what of Denny?

As if reading her mind, Stephen said, "You should tell Denny. Be honest with her. Best she hear it from you rather than the media."

They talked for a few minutes, making plans. Olivia nodded and said yes when required, but the words didn't quite sink in. *I'm in shock*, she realized.

After Stephen left, Olivia stood before her kitchen window, watching as he walked up to the reporters. They swarmed him when he came to a stop. He spoke for a few seconds. When he was finished, the crowd parted for him like the Red Sea.

*

By the time Olivia had showered and put on comfortable clothes, Lauren and Mary had put the living room back in order. During the search, the police had taken down all the pictures, taken every single book off the shelf, taken the covers off the pillows and cushions on the sofa, and had left everything they touched in a heap on the floor. Mary left for a doctor's appointment, promising to come back with groceries tomorrow.

When Olivia started to place the books back on the shelves,

Lauren stopped her. "Let me do that, Liv. You need to sleep. No offense, but you look like hell." They moved to the kitchen, where Lauren put the kettle on. As she waited for the water to boil, she leaned against the counter and stared at Olivia. "Are you going to be all right?"

"I think so," Olivia said, still oddly numb. "It's the blond in the video. She's been murdered, strangled. The poor woman was found in a vacation rental in the Avenues, which was paid for by an American Express card taken out in my name." Olivia thought of the dead girl's lifeless face, her protruding tongue, and the ligature marks around her neck. She wiped her eyes with the back of her sleeve. "They found her purse and iPad in my closet, along with a pile of threatening emails from a fake email address in my name. Someone's setting me up."

"Someone's got it in for you, Liv. This is like some Lifetime movie." Lauren put a bag of chamomile tea in Olivia's mug and poured water over it.

"I know."

"Do you think it's Richard? You should change the locks."

"I did that already after my surprise party when I kicked him out." She met Lauren's gaze. At last the numbness was wearing off. "I'm scared, Lauren."

"I would be too," Lauren said.

"Sleep deprivation is affecting my courage." The effort of pushing away from the counter so she could drag herself to bed proved difficult. "I'm going to bed. You don't have to stay."

"I'll chip away at the mess in the living room before I go. Are you sure you don't want me to stay with you?"

"I'll be fine," Olivia said.

"You know I'll help you in any way I can, right?"

"I do. It means the world. Thanks for cleaning up this mess. I'll finish it tomorrow." A soft laugh. "Remind me to never get arrested again." She took her mug of tea and headed down the long dark corridor to her bedroom, where she stripped off her clothes and fell into bed. When she awoke, her bedside clock said 3:48 a.m. She had been asleep for twelve hours.

Moving to the window, she pushed the curtain aside. Across the street, she saw the glow of a cigarette and the dark shadows of the die-hard journalists who had decided to stake out her house all night. Suddenly paranoid, she went through her house, making sure all the doors and windows were locked, and all the curtains were shut against prying eyes. Only then did she shower again. Wrapped in her warm bathrobe, she girded herself for chaos as she turned on the lamps in the living room. Not a thing was out of place. Lauren had stayed and put everything away. Even under house arrest, she at least had this sanctuary. No one could take that from her.

When Olivia had designed her kitchen cabinets, she had built a small desk in the corner, with a place for her landline. Now that a landline was required for house arrest, she was glad she'd resisted the urge to get rid of it. She also had an answering machine, which Denny and Richard teased her about, arguing how obsolete answering machines were in this era of smartphones and constant connectivity. Although Olivia had a cell phone, she had yet to take the plunge and get rid of the telephone number that had belonged to her family since they moved into the house when Olivia was thirteen years old. Now the answering machine blinked with messages. Olivia took her tea and sat down at the desk. Her finger reached towards the "play" button, hovering there for just a moment.

"Mrs. Sinclair? This is Jennifer Lindstrom from *People Magazine*. I'm writing an article about Sandy Watson's murder. Would you be interested in telling your side of the story?" Olivia pressed next.

"Mom? It's me. What happened?"

*Oh, Denny. I am so sorry.*

"I'm so worried about you. No one will tell me what's happening. Please call me. I don't care what time. I'll have my phone with me. I love you."

Olivia dialed Denny's number. She picked up on the first ring.

"Mom," Denny said, her voice raspy with sleep.

"Hi, honey. I'm sorry to call at this ungodly hour. I just got your message. Tell David I'm sorry if I woke him."

"He's on a business retreat and won't be home until tomorrow. Are you okay? What happened? The news said that you were arrested for murdering Dad's secretary."

"It's a big mix-up," Olivia said. "I was arrested, but now I'm out on bail, house arrest actually. I'm confined until my trial." Eager to reassure her daughter, she plowed on. "Listen to me, Den. It's going to be okay. I didn't kill anyone."

"Of course you didn't. How could anyone think that?"

"Have you spoken to your father?"

"I tried to call him, but he hasn't called me back. He had Wendy call me to tell me he's okay and will call me tomorrow."

"Try not to believe what you hear on the news, okay, honey? Can you come visit?"

"Yes, I'll come as soon as I can."

"There are reporters everywhere. Come up the back garden, okay? You can avoid them that way, and if you'll text when you're on your way, I'll look for you. Now try to get some sleep and don't worry. I love you."

"Love you, too." Denny said.

Olivia worried that David would use the circumstances surrounding Olivia's arrest to drive a wedge even further between Denny and her. Didn't all abusers try to isolate their victims? She stopped, her mind whirling. Would David Grayson set Olivia up for murder, so he could free Denny of involvement with her once and for all? *No. Surely not.*

As she brushed her teeth, ready to get back in bed, she thought about Richard's true nature – how could she have been so blind all these years? Could he have murdered Sandy Watson? Tucking herself under the thick duvet, she wondered just how far Richard would go to protect his law firm and his precious reputation.

*

Olivia was awake when the sun came up. Fidgety and unable to concentrate, she turned on the news, flipping through the channels until she stumbled across the video clip from yesterday when she and Stephen arrived home from jail. The camera focused on her for a moment, but immediately followed Stephen after his announcement that he would like to make a statement.

"Olivia Sinclair is an innocent woman wrongly accused. She will have her day in court and she will be exonerated."

Several reporters shouted their questions at the same time.

"What evidence do they have? Isn't it true that there's video of Olivia's husband sleeping with the dead girl? Is Richard Sinclair involved?"

Stephen held up his hands. "We don't know who was involved. As for evidence, I can't comment at this time, but we are investigating other leads."

Another reporter, a man this time, spoke, "Does investigating other leads mean Olivia Sinclair is going to exonerate herself by finding out who really killed Sandy Watson? Would you say that's a correct statement?"

Olivia clicked off the television. Picking up her pen, she started making notes of all the things Mary would have to deal with. The doorbell rang just as she finished.

"Did those reporters stay out there all night? You should see the mess they've made. Coffee cups, cigarette butts, garbage all over the place. Like a bunch of children," Mary said. Olivia watched as she unpacked a grocery bag full of food.

"What've you brought?"

"Comfort food. And I don't want to hear about your diet.

You need your strength. I've brought chicken soup, fresh bread, homemade oatmeal raisin cookies, and macaroni and cheese."

"Thanks, Mary," Olivia said. "Help yourself to coffee. We can sit in the living room."

Once they were seated on the couch, Mary said, "The clients are calling. I've been taking messages. I'll need to tell them something, what with the news and all. And I'm afraid that Sheila Blanding and Will Guyton are going to get new lawyers. They talked about hiring Claire. Others will follow, I feel certain."

Olivia took a deep breath. She knew clients would leave her over this. If her lawyer had been arrested for a very sensational murder, she'd jump ship, too. That inevitable truth couldn't be ignored.

"What are you going to do?" Mary asked.

"Other than Blanding and Guyton, we only have four other active cases. I'd like you to call those clients this afternoon. Gently suggest they hire Claire. Can you get the files ready to be transferred before you leave for Ireland?"

"Easily," Mary said. "But should I cancel my trip?"

"No, absolutely not."

"I've brought a list of cases that aren't active," Mary said. "I thought we could maybe split it up and call people, maybe convince them to stay."

Olivia shook her head. "No. I'm finished. The idea of going into the office and practicing law gives me a headache, and I need to focus on my defense."

"But you won't have a practice left. How can you turn the practice over to Claire Montreaux if there aren't any clients?"

"It doesn't matter anymore."

Mary sipped her tea. "Is there anything I can do for you, Olivia? You know all you have to do is ask."

"No, thanks. I'll be fine." A pause. "You know I didn't kill her."

Concern flitted across Mary's face. "Of course you didn't. Forgive me if I'm overstepping, but have you thought Richard might be involved?"

80

"Yes," Olivia whispered. "The thought has crossed my mind."

"This is going to get worse before it gets better."

"I know," Olivia said.

*

Olivia spent the morning compiling a comprehensive list of everyone who had been in or had access to her house over the last month. In an attempt to be thorough, she included her handyman, the man who inspected her gas fireplace, the man who cleaned her windows, and anyone else who could have figured out a way into her home while she was predictably away during the day. Although she knew the list was an exercise in futility, she realized the importance of staying busy. Having something to do kept her from thinking about that poor dead girl, Richard's betrayal, and his likely involvement in her murder.

Today Stephen wore blue jeans, a burgundy sweater and a baseball cap pulled so low it covered his eyes. She watched through her kitchen window as he pushed through the crowd of reporters, his well-worn leather briefcase in one hand, a large bulging shopping bag in the other.

"You look well rested," Stephen said, as Olivia locked the door behind him.

"I'm ready to fight this," Olivia said.

"Good. Because I have a plan. Where are we sitting?"

"Living room. Coffee?"

"Please," Stephen said. When she brought them both mugs of coffee, she found Stephen with his briefcase open, spreading papers out on the coffee table in organized piles.

"What're those papers?"

He removed his glasses and rubbed his eyes. "My paralegal pulled everything she could find on Sandy Watson. Jonas gave me the preliminary police report, the emails, and a copy of the video recovered from your cell phone. That's just the beginning. I served an official discovery request yesterday. We'll get everything they have within fifteen days. I'll send supplemental requests every two weeks up until the time of trial. That way, there won't be any misunderstanding in case Jonas decides to withhold something. These are copies for you to review. Someone is framing you. I'm hoping you can go through these documents and look for something that leads us to who that person is. Are you up for this, Liv? I have two extremely competent paralegals on staff if this is too much."

"I need something to do, Stephen. If I sit around this house, I'll go crazy."

Stephen handed Olivia the shopping bag. "Here's your new laptop and cell phone. I'll let you get busy getting set up and leave those documents for you. You can review them, make any notes you think might help. Other than that, there's nothing really for you to do right now. But there will be soon. I've got an expert who will prove you didn't open the American Express card used to rent the murder scene. He'll want to speak with you. We need to hire a PI. I've got someone in mind, but I need to see if he's taking new cases. I'm going to see him after I leave here. Are you on board with that?"

Olivia nodded.

"Are you okay, Olivia? Did you speak to Denny?"

"We spoke. She's going to visit as soon as she is able," Olivia said.

"Good. You'll feel better when you see her in person."

After Stephen left, Olivia leaned against the front door, feeling defeated in every way. In the back of her mind was Richard's betrayal, taunting her at every turn.

# Chapter 11

*Thursday, October 16*

Whitfield Adam's family had been running Tamalpais Bank and Trust since its inception in 1898, ten years before the town of Larkspur was incorporated. Other than minor repairs completed over the years, the small brick building, snuggled smack in the middle of a redwood grove on Magnolia Avenue, hadn't changed since that time. Once they stepped through the glass doors, the bank's customers often commented about the timelessness of the place.

Brian Vickery stood outside for a moment, saying a silent prayer that he wouldn't lose his house, before he stepped inside. The wide-planked floors covered in what were surely original Aubusson rugs, the brass banker's lamps on the old dark wooden desks, and three teller cages all gave a silent nod to a time long forgotten. The bank catered to upper-crust Marinites, old families who had lived in the county just north of San Francisco when it was a weekend getaway and resort community for people who wanted to escape the city fog during the summer months.

If it weren't for Brian Vickery's friendship with Whit Adams, Tamalpais Bank and Trust would never approve a large loan to the likes of Brian Vickery, who lived on his police pension. But although Brian and Whit ran in different circles in adulthood – Whit ran with the yacht club set, while Brian had spent his free time at home with his wife Maureen – they were best friends growing up and this bond had withstood the test of time.

Now Brian sat in the comfortable chair across from the large antique desk, his anxiety preventing him from enjoying the warm sun as it beamed through the window.

"I'm so sorry for you, Brian. Maureen will be missed. Brenda and I were both shocked when we heard. We would have come to the funeral, but we didn't know—"

"There's no need to apologize," Brian said. "I didn't have a funeral. Couldn't bear it, to tell you the truth. And don't go blaming yourself for my financial woes, Whit. You advised me against taking such a large mortgage. You made it very clear that the repayment would exceed my pension, and I didn't listen. I just wanted to save Maureen. When the doctors said there was nothing else to be done, I couldn't believe it – didn't want to believe it. We went to a cancer specialist in Houston and finally wound up in Zurich."

Only after Maureen was gone did Brian realize the truth of the situation: Maureen had known she was dying, but she had gone along with Brian's insistence on trying everything under the sun because she loved him. He swallowed the familiar lump in this throat. No way in hell would he cry in front of Whitfield. The last thing he wanted was his friend's pity.

"I should start collection proceedings. If it were anyone but you in this position, I would have commenced legal action weeks ago." Whit opened his desk drawer and set a brochure in front of Brian. "Forgive me for being forward, but I've been trying to figure out what you could do to get out of this mess. I spoke to a Realtor. You're sitting on a goldmine, Brian. Sell the house. You'd easily fetch enough money to pay your loan and buy someplace smaller, a condo in San Rafael or something like that."

Whit pushed over the brochure with a coiffed young woman standing next to a large brick house with a "sold" sign in its well-manicured front yard.

"My house? Surely it can't be worth that much," Brian said.

They had scrimped and saved to purchase the house in 1979. It had been fashionable at the time, with its avocado green appliances and brown and gold carpeting. The avocado range still graced the kitchen. The matching refrigerator had long ago been replaced by a simple white one. Neither Maureen nor Brian cared to upgrade their house. They loved their neighborhood, with its access to miles of open space and hiking trails, but mostly they loved their huge backyard. Many happy hours were spent planting, and harvesting vegetables they grew. Maureen had drawn up the plans for the exterior garden, and it had taken ten years to plant everything they wanted.

Now the garden had filled in and was nothing short of miraculous. When they had company over, they entertained outside. Maureen had come up with the idea of building an outdoor firepit and grill, along with a covered area with a sink, which allowed them to entertain outdoors all year round.

For some reason, Brian and Maureen were never blessed with children. They talked about adoption, fertility doctors, and the like, but neither were too enthusiastic about the idea. They had each other, and although they would have liked children, their love was enough to sustain them. Their life was full with hiking, trips to the beach – they both learned to surf at a young age – and working in their garden. As the years went by and the interior of the house became more dated and shabby, the garden, as if a testament to their love, flourished. Maureen often joked that the garden was their love child.

Brian pushed the brochure back to Whit. How could he sell his house?

"Maureen is all over that house. I can't get rid of it."

Whit blew out a long puff of air as he leaned back into his chair and closed his eyes.

Brian waited, giving his old friend room to brainstorm and come up with some miracle plan that would let him keep the house he could ill afford and preserve the memories of his dead wife.

"I get it, Brian. I really do. So we need to figure out a way for you to keep the house and get me paid. I could refinance it with a long-term loan. You could make the monthly payments, but from where I sit, you're going to have to get a job, old man. Hate to say it. And at the risk of getting you angry with me, maybe a job would be a good thing. No offense, but I think something to get your mind off your troubles might be just the ticket.

"Here's what I can do right now. I can give you sixty days. But I'm going to have to ask for a balloon payment after that time. If you can get your income stream up with the sixty days, we can write you another long-term loan."

"Thanks, Whit." Brian stood and held out his hand.

"No problem. You'll need to come back and sign a mountain of paperwork. How about we do it over dinner? You look like you could use a home-cooked meal."

Brian had no interest in socializing with Whit and his charming wife, knowing full well he was incapable of the innocuous small talk and the required pleasantries. And, knowing Brenda, she'd invite a few of their other friends, people who knew Maureen and would utter their condolences. Brian shook his friend's hand. "Not ready for that yet. But rain check, okay? And give Brenda my love."

By a stroke of luck, Brian managed to walk out of the bank and make it to the safety of his car before breaking down completely.

*

Brian returned home, memories of Maureen running through his head. Knowing full well that Whit had given him the gift of

86

time, Brian girded himself to face his own horrible reality. He needed to find a way to make some money. Fast.

Around him, the musty room with its accumulated piles of mail and dust and untended business seemed to taunt him. Was Maureen watching him from heaven? He looked out the window to their beloved garden, now overgrown with weeds and dead leaves that he hadn't bothered to rake. The neighbor's cat stared at him through the sliding glass door. He knew Maureen used to feed it treats. In the kitchen, he rescued a small piece of chicken from the lone casserole dish – when had Mrs. Winkle come and cleaned out the refrigerator? – and fed it to the cat. The creature purred and rubbed against his legs, then stared at him with her steady knowing gaze. He bent down to scratch the cat's ears before letting her out.

Closing the door, he stood for a moment, surveying his wreck of a house and Maureen's once-beautiful garden. How had things gotten so run-down? He looked towards heaven and said, "I'm so sorry, Maureen." Brian Vickery was a logical man. He didn't believe in ghosts, premonitions, or anything that couldn't be substantiated by science. So when a wave of determination and resolve overtook him out of the blue, he acted on it.

Searching through the teak credenza, he pulled out a random CD and put it in the stereo. He opened all the windows, not minding the frigid October chill. The cold motivated him; it whipped through the corners and took his desperation with it. With Jim Morrison singing "Light My Fire" as loud as it could go, he tossed out the piles of newspapers that had accumulated, vacuumed and mopped and scrubbed and scoured. He switched out The Doors for Crosby, Stills and Nash, singing along to the songs he knew so well.

Each room got the same treatment. Brian worked until the house was spanking clean and he was exhausted. It was just after 2:00 p.m. when he heated up Mrs. Winkle's casserole and sat down at the table to eat.

Brian almost didn't recognize Stephen Vine when he came sauntering down his driveway, dressed in jeans and a baseball cap, carrying his well-worn briefcase. The two had had professional dealings over the years and had gone to lunch a handful of times. Stephen had cross-examined Brian on the witness stand and over the years the men had become friends. They had gone deep-sea fishing a couple of times, and Brian and Maureen always received an invitation to Stephen Vine's office Christmas party, a swanky affair held at the Corinthian Yacht Club in Tiburon. Brian had found Stephen to be a fair and ethical man, a rare quality in an attorney, in Brian's opinion.

He got up and met Stephen at the front door.

"Apologies for the drop-in, but I've got a case for you. It's big. A murder. Good money." Stephen saw the napkin in Brian's hand. "Did I interrupt your lunch? I can come back."

Brian shook his head, unable to grasp his good fortune. He chuckled and shook his head. Maybe Maureen had been watching him after all, looking down on him in his despair.

"I didn't mean to disturb you. I just thought you might—"

"I'm interested." Brian shook Stephen's hand. "Come in. You're not going to believe this, but I was just getting ready to make a list of attorneys to contact. Your timing is fortuitous, as I am in need of a job." They walked into Brian's kitchen. "Are you hungry?"

Stephen eyed the casserole. "It smells delicious."

Brian served him up a plate of Mrs. Winkle's food, and soon the two men were sitting at Brian's kitchen table – Stephen in Maureen's spot – and eating their meal in comfortable silence.

"Did you cook this yourself?" Stephen asked when he had cleaned his plate.

"No. My neighbor has been taking care of me since Maureen—"

"I'm sorry, Brian. What a tragedy. I haven't called because I figured you wanted to be left alone."

"I've let things slide," Brian said. He took their dirty dishes to the sink and refilled their coffee cups. "Tell me about this case."

Stephen reached into his briefcase and took out a thin manila folder, which he placed on the table. "Someone opened an American Express card in my client's name, used it to rent a flat in the Avenues, lured a woman to it, and murdered her. They went so far as to plant the girl's personal items and evidence of the murder in my client's closet."

"Sounds cut and dried to me, Stephen. Do you think maybe your client is guilty?"

Stephen shook his head. "She's also a friend. She didn't do it."

"What else?"

"It's Olivia Sinclair, Richard Sinclair's wife."

Brian perked up. "Richard Sinclair, the lawyer on television?"

"The very same," Stephen said.

Brian opened the folder and read the police report. When he got to the crime scene photos, his heart pounded and his mouth went dry. "Jesus," he whispered.

"What is it?" Stephen asked.

Brian met Stephen's eyes. "This knot is unique. I'm betting there's signs of manual strangulation under this rope."

"How do you know this?"

"Because I had another case just like it." Brian pushed away from the table. "Come with me."

Stephen followed Brian into an office that looked like a time capsule from 1980. A metal desk was pushed up against one wall. It boasted a rotary-dial phone, a Rolodex, an Underwood typewriter, and a Parker fountain pen, complete with an inkwell and stand.

Next to the desk, stacked in a neat tower, were four banker's boxes with the words *Janelle Maycott – May 2000* written on the outside. Brian took the top two boxes off the stack, opened the third box, took out a file and pulled out another police report, the pages worn thin with age. Opening to the photographic evidence, Brian handed the report to Stephen. "See the similarity?"

"How could I not? This girl is staged in the exact same manner as Sandy Watson," Stephen said. "Tell me about the case."

"Back in 2000, a young woman named Janelle Maycott, a college student at Cal, didn't show up for her finals. When her mother couldn't reach her by phone, she went to her apartment in the city and found her like this. Notice the knot?"

"Yes," Stephen said. "Is that significant?"

"I think it is. It's a left-handed bowline knot, used by sailors and people who know about boats. We believe Janelle was injected with something – probably propofol or something equivalent – before she was strangled."

"Did you catch her killer?"

Brian nodded at the stack of file boxes. "As you see, no. This was the case I couldn't solve. I made a promise to that girl's mother that I would find out who murdered her daughter. When I retired, I planned on reopening the case and finding out the truth. Felt like I owed that to Mrs. Maycott. But then Maureen got sick and—" Brian shook his head "—everything fell apart."

"So come to work for me, Brian. Let's find the common connection between Sandy Watson and Janelle Maycott."

Stephen didn't have to ask twice.

"Come to my office tomorrow. We'll discuss terms and make a plan. Of course, you'll have to meet my client. She will make the ultimate decision about hiring you."

"Understood. What time?"

"Meet me at my office at 8:30. Then we'll go visit Olivia at her house."

"At her house?"

"Did I mention she's been bailed to house arrest? And I should warn you that she will want to be involved. She's a good lawyer, and she could be useful."

"I'm not used to working with the clients," Brian said. "Sort of a lone operator, if you get my meaning."

"We'll find something for her to do," Stephen said. "Don't worry."

Brian didn't worry. It seemed that Lady Fate was throwing him a juicy bone. For the first time since Maureen died, Brian Vickery had something to live for.

# Chapter 12

*Friday, October 17*

The reporters were still outside when Olivia woke. They stood in the gray morning fog huddled together, seeming to conspire as they smoked and drank coffee from disposable cups. Cigarette butts and other garbage littered the grassy hillside across from her house. Had they been out there all night again? Were they on alert for any sign of movement, any opportunity to invade her privacy and go for that money shot? The best course of action was to stay away from windows and ignore them.

Denny was coming to visit today. Olivia put on a pot of coffee and put two pieces of bread in the toaster. Pulling a chair up to the sliding glass door that led to the deck, she opened it wide, letting in the cold morning air. After Denny's visit, Stephen was bringing the private detective over. With a bit of luck, they would find something for her to do, anything to keep her occupied.

This period of morning solitude spent outdoors had always been sacred to her, a few moments to herself before her busy day started. She had sat outside on the deck as a young mother, eager for the sound of her waking daughter. She had sat on this very patio the day before her first trial, nervous and apprehensive, pulling comfort from her little spot of earth. This space, with its sweeping view, her precious garden, beautiful despite her neglect of it, did not provide comfort today. Her truth was frightening. Now she was fighting for her freedom. Even more important than the potential for utter ruin was the precarious relationship with her daughter.

Olivia sipped her coffee and watched for Denny to come walking up the garden path, knowing her day would become much brighter if she could lay eyes on her daughter, assure her in person not to worry.

Olivia's breath caught when instead David came walking up the back slope of her garden. He didn't bother to stay on the path, opting instead to walk right through one of the beds, not caring that he trampled the herbs and flowers. The sight of him, so large and intimidating, caused Olivia to panic. A knot formed in her stomach. As he walked closer, his hands clenched in fists, Olivia realized she had never been alone with her son-in-law.

In her mind, there was nothing original going on with David Grayson. He was the only son of a wealthy and influential family. David worked for his family's charity, an organization that touted its strong moral compass, while it fostered causes that cut benefits for those in need and lobbied for tax cuts for wealthy people that had more money than they would ever spend.

Linda Grayson, David's domineering mother, had spoiled her only son, propping him up, telling him that he was better than everyone else, thereby instilling a sense of entitlement that never failed to take Olivia aback. She had known men like this since the beginning of her career, men who believed the wife was a commodity, that the house and the children were the husband's property by right.

At the sound of David's footsteps on the wooden stairs that led to the deck, Olivia went into the house and closed the sliding glass door. David would have to break it down to get to her.

"Olivia," David said.

"Where's Denny?"

David gave her his usual condescending smile. "Can I come in?"

"No." She made a show of dialing 911. If David became menacing, if he attempted to come into her home, she would call the police.

"I didn't mean to scare you. You don't have to call the police. I'm not going to hurt you. I'm here with a message."

"Where's Denny?" she asked again.

"That doesn't concern you. I've forbidden her to have anything to do with you. In fact, both of us would appreciate you not interfering in our marriage."

Olivia's fear morphed into a white-hot anger as her heart broke for her daughter. "How dare you. She'll find out what you're like, David. Men like you always reveal their true selves eventually."

"She's pregnant. Did you know that?

*Denny's pregnant? I'm going to be a grandmother.* A spark of joy and hope ran through Olivia, only to fizzle out when she realized her position.

"Ah, I can see she didn't tell you. Doesn't matter. You'll never see your grandchild. I know what you did, Olivia. If Denny knew that you hired a private investigator to spy on me, she'd be furious. Stay away from Denny. And just so my position is clear, if you ever contact Denny, I'll tell her how you went against her wishes and meddled in our marriage, tell her how you're trying to break us apart. Denny's mine. She'll always choose me. You should come to terms with that."

Not wanting David to see that all of his arrows had struck her heart, Olivia bit back tears. What a fool she had been to hire an investigator she didn't know. He had been clumsy, had botched the job. Now David had something concrete to use against Olivia. Never had she felt so helpless, so out of control. This monster had come into her life, had sabotaged her relationship with Denny, and there was nothing she could do about it. Not now, not if she was going to prison. David Grayson had won. Olivia swallowed

94

the lump that had formed at the back of her throat. Just as David turned to leave, she said, "This isn't over."

"Oh, but it is. I won." David Grayson turned and headed toward the stairs. Before he left, he faced Olivia and said, "Don't contact Denny again. Understand?"

"Go to hell, David," Olivia said.

"Good luck with your trial," David said before he headed down the stairs.

*

The surprise encounter with David left Olivia shaken and afraid for her daughter's safety. She spent the hours between David's departure and Stephen Vine's arrival pacing in her kitchen, fueled by pent-up energy that she would cope with under normal circumstances by working in her garden. But she was trapped in her house and there was nothing she could do about it.

Images of David telling Denny that her mother had hired a private investigator to follow him haunted her. Denny's reaction would be one of fury and betrayal. David, narcissist and master manipulator, would capitalize on Denny's anger, galvanizing the wedge between mother and daughter. Forcing herself to take a calming breath and step back from the situation, Olivia tried to console herself with the knowledge that her daughter was an intelligent, sensitive woman. Narcissists like David Grayson were attracted to woman like Denny like a shark is attracted to blood.

David had won this round. Olivia needed to retire to her corner and take comfort in the knowledge that eventually Denny would see his true colors. Deep inside she knew, in this rare instance, non-action was the best thing.

Stephen was bringing the detective he wanted to hire today. In the spirit of making a good impression, Olivia spent fifteen minutes trying to look presentable. She put on foundation, blush, and lipstick. But as she stared at herself in the mirror, the makeup looked garish against her pale skin and bloodshot eyes. The inchoate gray roots against the dark brown dye reminded her that a trip to the hairdresser was in order, yet impossible. Bending over the sink, she scrubbed and scrubbed until the makeup was gone and her skin glowed from her efforts.

As she brushed her thick dark hair and pulled it back into a ponytail, she thought that she may just take Lauren's advice and let it go gray. Why not? What was the point of trying to look young? The expensive facials, potions, lotions, scrubs, and masks all seemed like a big joke now. Certain there were no facials in prison, Olivia settled for some soothing lip gloss and scented hand lotion.

Clutching her notepad over her chest, she paced across her kitchen until Stephen's car pulled up. Through the window, Olivia watched the reporters swarm as Stephen and the other man, Brian Vickery, got out of the car. Stephen stopped to speak to them, while Mr. Vickery headed down the path to the front door, impervious to the crowd on the street. Olivia hurried to let him in.

"Good morning. Mr. Vickery, I presume?"

"Yes, ma'am," he said, as she stepped aside for him to enter.

Leaving the door unlocked for Stephen, Olivia followed Brian Vickery into the living room, studying him surreptitiously. He wore faded jeans and a well-cut sportscoat over a button-up shirt, an interesting combination of sophistication and scruff. At one time he had been a blond, but now his hair – and the whiskers on his unshaven face – were mostly gray. His eyes were a rich blue, almost azure. They reflected the man's intelligence, but Olivia saw pain there. They were just about into that awkward stage where neither of them knew what to say, when Stephen joined them. He carried a thick file, which he set on the table.

"I was able to get the first round of discovery, thanks to Inspector Bailey. I have the American Express receipt for the vacation rental and the copies of the emails that you allegedly sent Sandy. We now need to figure out a way to prove that someone

– the murderer presumably – used your name to open an email account and obtain an American Express card and rent the murder scene. That will be our first order of business. As I mentioned yesterday, I've hired an expert in this area, and he's working on your case now, Liv. He'll need some information from you. A phone call should do it. I know you need to be proactive. But let's talk to Brian first, so we can all be on the same page going forward. Brian, do you want to explain the situation or should I?"

Brian Vickery appeared to be the type of man who would let others do the talking. He took a second, as if collecting his thoughts, before he said, "Fourteen years ago a young woman named Janelle Maycott was murdered in exactly the same fashion as Sandy Watson. The killer injected her with something and strangled her. After she was dead, a rope was tied around her neck with a very specific knot, exactly like the one tied around Sandy Watson's neck."

"You think this is the same person who killed Sandy Watson?" Olivia saw Brian flash Stephen a look.

"I do, Mrs. Sinclair. If you hire me to work on your case, my plan will be to aggressively seek a common denominator between these two girls, in addition to what Stephen asks me to do, of course. I have copies of my original investigation, which I will use as a reference for your case. I know you'll want to be involved. If you hire me, I'll bring the files to you for review. In my opinion, fresh eyes on an investigation are always welcome. I'm hoping that you'll find something that can connect the two women."

"Why do you have your investigation files? Aren't you retired?"

Olivia saw the brief flit of anger in Brian's eyes and knew she had hit a nerve.

"This is the only case I didn't solve," Brian said. "I brought the files home so I could work on it during my retirement years. Janelle Maycott shouldn't have died. I made a promise – never mind. Let's just say that I'm committed to finding out who killed her."

"If I hire you, where will you start? How will you go about helping me?" Olivia asked.

"Well, I work for Stephen and you, so my marching orders will ultimately come from the two of you. My advice would be to start at the beginning," Brian said. "Someone wanted that woman dead. My job is to find out who. And why. I'm not one to mince words, Mrs. Sinclair, so I'll be straight up and tell you my first order of business will be a thorough background investigation of your husband and other members of Rincon Sinclair."

"Keep in mind, Liv, we need reasonable doubt. That's the baseline," Stephen said.

Olivia shook her head. "No. We need to find out who killed her. I can't have this hanging over my head."

"Even if the killer proves to be Richard?" Brian asked. And with the utterance of that one statement, Olivia knew he'd solve this case. Yet there was something else about Brian that nagged at her conscience. Could she trust him? She thought of Denny and how devastated she would be if Richard were accused of murder too, his name dragged through the mud, his face on the front page of every local newspaper. How much could her daughter take? Olivia reminded herself that Denny deserved the truth, just as much as Olivia did.

"Yes. Even if the killer is Richard."

"Okay," Stephen said. "So we're on the same page."

"Do you mind if I speak to my attorney for a moment?" Olivia asked. "There's a lovely view from the deck."

"I'll go get the files from the car," Brian said. Stephen tossed him the car keys, which he caught with ease.

When they were alone, Olivia said, "What aren't you telling me about Brian, Stephen? He's smart and good at his job, but there's something underneath. I need to know what it is. I am, after all, entrusting him with my future."

"I'll never understand how you do that," Stephen said.

"How I do what? I'm serious—"

"I'm serious, too. Otherwise I wouldn't have brought Brian in. I was making reference to that uncanny knack you have for sizing people up. Brian's wife died of cancer. He hasn't been coping well, okay?"

"Could you please clarify what you mean by 'not coping well'?"

"Not coping in that you'll be helping him as much as he will be helping you. And, Liv, you should know that for the ten years before he retired from the SFPD, Inspector Bailey was his partner. That connection may give us some insight that we wouldn't otherwise have."

Olivia scoffed, "Do you really think he'd take my side over his ex-partner's?"

"I think he's the best investigator for the job. I'll get you off of the murder charge. But if you want to find out who killed Sandy Watson, Brian Vickery is your man. Of that, I'm certain. He's as much of a bulldog as you are."

Olivia knew she needed a bulldog, needed to let go and trust Stephen, give him room to do this job. "Okay. I'm in."

Brian and Stephen retrieved four banker's boxes from Stephen's car. When Brian came into the house and gave Olivia a shy smile, she realized the anxiety that plagued her an hour ago had diminished. Brian Vickery, with this quiet determination, had given her hope.

"It looks like we're going to be working together, Mr. Vickery," Olivia said. Olivia sensed Stephen surveying the two of them as they negotiated their working relationship.

Olivia observed the deliberate way in which Brian collected his thoughts. *There's not an impulsive bone in that man's body.*

"I'm going to need your help, Mrs. Sinclair, but not in the way you may think. I'm sure Stephen will tell you it's best not to broadcast the fact that I'm working for you. Eventually it will come out, especially in light of the journalists outside, but let's not be so quick to show our hand. What we need to do – and what I would like you to get started on, provided it's okay with

99

your attorney – is to go through these boxes. I'd like you to be familiar with the Maycott case by the time the Watson discovery starts coming through. Our first priority will be to establish a connection, no matter how minuscule, between Sandy Watson and Janelle Maycott."

Stephen Vine spoke. "And after you've gone through the Janelle Maycott evidence, I'll need to know who had access to your house, your office, your computer, and then we need to turn our attention to Richard and his law firm. That's where Sandy worked, so it stands to reason that someone involved, even peripherally, with Rincon Sinclair could have had known Janelle Maycott."

Brian said, "I don't need to tell you, Mrs. Sinclair, sometimes the most ridiculous detail could be the snag that unravels the truth. And there's something else. You know a lot of the people we are investigating. Because you know them, you have preconceived ideas about who they are and what they are capable of. That insight will be very helpful." He stared at the Janelle Maycott boxes and shook his head. "I've got every piece of paper in these boxes memorized, so if you need to move things into a different order, feel free."

"So while I'm looking through them, I should see if there's anyone mentioned in Janelle's case that could be in Sandy's life now, like my husband? That's what we're doing, isn't it? Seeing if we can tie Richard to Janelle and to Sandy?"

"Maybe it's not your husband, but it could very well be someone who knows him, or who has crossed paths with him," Brian said. "Any connection, no matter how insignificant, could help."

She sat down and pulled one of the boxes towards her. "At least I can be productive."

Stephen looked at his watch. "I need to get back to my office." He and Brian stood, ready to leave Olivia to her own devices.

"One more thing before I go," Brian said. "Where has your husband been for the last two weeks?"

"He was in San Jose for depositions, and then he spent the weekend in Atherton with our friends the Pritchards. James and Madison host a house party every year. Outdoor activities during the day, elegant dinners at night."

"You didn't go?" Brian asked.

"Haven't gone for the past three years," Olivia said.

"Why?" Brian asked.

"Because I don't particularly care for the Pritchards. If you want me to be totally honest, I find them phony and pretentious."

Olivia didn't mention that the last time she and Richard had gone to the Pritchardses weekend party. Richard and Madison had gone on a long walk, not returning home until hours past lunch. When they had returned, Madison had given Olivia a satisfied smug grin. Looking back, the truth was so obvious that Oliva was embarrassed. They were having an affair. *Are they still?*

"Do you know where I can reach the Pritchards?" Brian asked.

"I'll text you their contact info."

Brian told Olivia his number, and confirmed receipt of the text. "Thank you. That's all I need for now."

"We'll keep you posted," Stephen said.

"Thanks. And thank you, Brian, for agreeing to work with us. I appreciate it."

Olivia watched out her kitchen window as the two men walked back to Stephen's car. She wondered what they were saying about her case, about her. As she contemplated the tasks that lay ahead of her, she wondered about the secrets Brian Vickery kept.

101

# Chapter 13

*Friday, October 17*

At 44 Montgomery, two security guards manned the desk and this time they asked Sharon to sign in. The younger of the two men gave her a curt nod and after waving her through to the elevators, went back to studying the array of monitors on his desk. His partner, however, wasn't so easily dismissed. Mr. Becket – according to the name tag – was short and barrel-shaped, with a cropped haircut that spoke volumes about his psychological type. *Alpha male, retired military.* He picked up the phone and started to punch in numbers. Sharon was certain he was calling upstairs to Rincon Sinclair.

"Put it down," Sharon said, holding out her badge. The last thing she wanted was Richard Sinclair to know she was on her way up.

He reached out his hand. "I'd like to examine your badge, officer."

*So that's how you want to play it?* "It's inspector. Inspector Bailey." She handed her badge over, waiting patiently while he examined it, checking her face against the picture in the leather wallet.

"Is this about that dead girl I read about in the papers?"

As if she'd tell him. One mention of Richard Sinclair and Sharon would bet the ranch that the overzealous Mr. Becket would hurry over to his desk and let everyone at Rincon Sinclair know there was a surly policewoman on her way up to speak to the firm's golden boy.

"I can't tell you that, sir. Ongoing investigation. I'm sure you'll understand."

He stared at her for a moment, his look a challenge. Sharon stared back. She hadn't risen up the ranks at the San Francisco Police Department by kowtowing to bullies and she had no intention of doing so now. Instead, she forced a smile and said, "Thank you for your cooperation, sir."

The man nodded and waved Sharon through. While Sharon waited for the elevator, she watched out of the corner of her eye as grouchy pants leaned into his friend and whispered something. The other guard looked at Sharon, smiled, shook his head, and went back to his monitors.

Stepping into the lobby at Rincon Sinclair, Sharon heard the murmur of voices, and instinctively moved towards them. She didn't think twice about eavesdropping. This was, after all, a homicide investigation. It didn't take long for her shameless snooping to bear fruit. Richard Sinclair, Wendy Betters, and another man were huddled together in the conference room. Sharon was going to announce herself, but instinctively stepped out of sight as the third man stormed out, retreating to another office tucked into the far corner of the suite. *Ah, I'm betting that was Andrew Rincon.*

When Wendy Betters noticed Sharon standing outside Richard's office, a look of troubled expectation washed over her face. She turned towards Richard Sinclair, and spoke to him as she moved toward the door.

Sharon had only caught a glimpse of Richard Sinclair when they brought him to the police station. It was hard to believe that he was even more good-looking in person. Thick salt and pepper hair, over a perfectly chiseled face, had rendered him even more handsome by the passage of time. *Handsome is as handsome does.* She reminded herself of this age-old credo.

From all accounts, when Richard was brought in for questioning about Sandy's murder, he had seemed genuinely shocked and disturbed by her death. But when Ellie had started to question him about his activities and whereabouts at the time of Sandy's murder, he had refused to answer and advised her in no uncertain terms that if she wasn't going to charge him with a crime, he was leaving. And he had done so.

By some fortuitous sense of coincidence, he managed to storm out of the interrogation room just as Olivia and Sharon arrived. The sparks that flew between Richard and Olivia Sinclair were telling. And Sharon couldn't help but notice that while Olivia Sinclair looked scared and seemed to be in a perpetual state of shock, Richard Sinclair had been all bluster and bravado.

Now she met Mr. Sinclair's penetrating gaze with what she hoped was a disarming smile. "I just have a few questions, Mr. Sinclair. If you don't mind?" Before he could refuse to speak with Sharon and throw her out on her ear, she said, "Sorry to barge in, but there was no receptionist—" She let her words hang in the air, unsure of how Mr. Sinclair would receive her.

He stood, smiled, and walked over to her, his hand extended. His grip was firm, brief, and perfectly appropriate.

"Don't worry about it," Richard said. "We're a bit short-staffed at the moment. And I apologize for my behavior at the police station. We're all a little shaken about Sandy's death. Of course, I want to cooperate."

Wendy came into the office with a carafe of ice water topped with thin slices of lemon. She poured it into two crystal glasses, and placed them on coasters before Richard and Sharon. "I'll just leave you both to it," Wendy said.

Richard ignored Wendy as he sipped his water, giving Sharon a few seconds to study him. Pictures of Richard Sinclair with

Joe Montana and Dwight Clark, Will Clark, Jerry Brown, Mayor Moscone, and other notable San Francisco Bay Area personalities, were a testament to his social status and reminded Sharon to tread carefully.

"This is an awful business, Sandy's murder, my wife's arrest – I just can't believe it." He puffed his cheeks full of air and slowly exhaled. "How can I help?"

Sharon took out her notebook, wishing for a second that she had brought Ellie with her to take notes. "Where were you between Saturday, October 4 and Monday, October 6?"

Richard Sinclair pulled a luxurious leather diary toward him, opened it and pushed it to Sharon. A legal pad rested on his desk. While he spoke, he wrote on the pad. "I spent the workweek in San Jose attending depositions and spent the weekend at a friend's house in Atherton."

"When did you hear of Sandy's death?"

"After you spoke to Wendy. She told me right away. I was shocked. Sandy was a wonderful girl. I couldn't believe it. I still can't."

"Did your wife know about you and Sandy?"

"I'm sure she suspected. We've been married since college. I don't think either one of us has been faithful."

*Bullshit*, Sharon thought. Olivia Sinclair didn't look like the sort of woman who would tolerate infidelity.

"Did you know Sandy was pregnant?"

At this news, Richard Sinclair squirmed. A look of surprise flashed in his eyes.

*Gotcha.* "I take it you didn't know?"

Richard shook his head. "No idea."

"Would you have married her? I'm assuming the baby is yours."

Richard gave Sharon a penetrating glance, the kind she imagined he gave to a witness who hesitated to answer a question. She met his gaze and didn't look away. "I would have taken care of the child, of that you can be sure. But marriage? I can't say.

105

Don't be so surprised, Inspector. Sandy was a modern woman; marriage and domestic things were not on her mind. She wanted to go to law school."

"The baby may have changed her mind."

"I would have done whatever she wanted," Richard said.

"Help me out here, Mr. Sinclair. Can you think of anyone who might want to murder Sandy Watson? An old boyfriend, anyone? Other than your wife, of course."

"Olivia didn't kill Sandy. And I have no idea about Sandy's old boyfriends."

Richard scribbled on a sheet of paper before he folded it in two and handed it to Sharon. "Here's the name of the law firm who hosted the depositions last week, as well as the contact information for James and Madison Pritchard. I think James is in Paris, but Madison should be reachable."

"Thank you," Sharon said. She handed Richard Sinclair her card. "Please call me if you think of anything. It's early days yet, Mr. Sinclair. I'll probably need to speak to you again."

"Whatever you need."

Sharon left Richard Sinclair standing with his back to her, gazing at the spectacular view of San Francisco Bay.

\*

As she waited for the elevator, Sharon thought of going home to her studio in the Marina, ordering in Italian food from the restaurant down the street, and pouring a very large glass of Chianti. The elevator arrived, but just as the doors whooshed open, Andrew Rincon stormed down the hall.

"Wait one second." Andrew Rincon charged her like a bull, snorting with anger and full of fury.

*Oh, hell.* Tired, hungry, and desperately in need of a break, Sharon had no desire to deal with an angry attorney. She let the elevator go, but pushed the down button again, determined to get on the next car that stopped on her floor. She braced for a confrontation. Despite Andrew Rincon's power or political clout, Sharon would cuff him and take him to jail if he so much as laid a finger on her.

When he came to a stop in front of her, Sharon didn't back away. "I've had a long day, Mr. Rincon. I'm in the middle of a homicide investigation. What can I help you with? And I suggest you move away from me, sir. I don't appreciate being crowded."

Despite his red-faced fury, Andrew Rincon stepped away.

"Thank you. Now, how can I help you?"

"You stay the hell away from this firm unless you call and make an appointment, do you understand? You are not to speak to any of my employees or my partner, without my permission. Got it?"

"No, thank you, Mr. Rincon. That's not our procedure, and I'll be conducting my investigation as I see fit. Now if you want me to come unannounced and bring your employees to the police station so they can be interrogated in an interview room, I can do that. Otherwise, I suggest you leave me to it." Sharon pulled her cell phone out of her purse and pretended to make a call. "Will there be anything else?"

"I suggest you watch your step, Inspector."

"Are you threatening me?"

"No, just speaking a truth."

Sharon let Andrew Rincon have the last word. She maintained her calm as she left the building and hailed a taxi. It wasn't until she gave her address to the driver that she realized there would be hell to pay for that confrontation.

# Chapter 14

Sharon woke up on Saturday morning at 6:30 a.m. sharp, even though she had vowed to sleep in. Peeking out the window from her third-floor apartment onto the Marina Green, she saw a crisp clear morning, devoid of fog. Die-hard runners and dog walkers were already out for their morning exercise. A senior police officer who was leading a murder investigation didn't have the luxury of weekends off. Last night she had sent her team home for a good night's sleep, and had scheduled a meeting with Ellie at 10:00 a.m.

Rather than make coffee and scavenge her fridge for a makeshift breakfast, she showered and set out into the cold October morning towards her favorite diner on Lombard Street. The coffee shop across the street, which advertised morning happy hour from 5:00 to 7:00 a.m., was crowded already. A line of physically fit young people dressed in leggings and puffer coats queued outside the building, waiting for their fancy coffee drinks.

Sharon preferred the old-school diner, with its Formica countertops, generous portions, and uniformed waitresses that knew Sharon's name. There were two spots at the counter. Sharon took one, nodding at the waitress who knew her by sight.

"Good morning, Inspector. The usual?" The waitress put down a full cup of coffee.

"Thank you, Beatrice." A man across the counter from Sharon had his nose buried in his newspaper. She flinched at a large picture of Olivia Sinclair on the front page, with the headline *Wife of Prominent Lawyer Arrested for Murder.* Sharon forced herself to stop looking at the headline. She had learned long ago that the best course of action was not only to avoid reporters – the department had a media relations person to handle those issues – but to not read the papers at all during a murder investigation. She saved a lot of grief by keeping her nose down and staying focused on gathering facts. This course of action would serve her well now, as headlines such as that one were turning Sandy Watson's murder into a rapidly escalating PR nightmare.

Beatrice set a large stack of blueberry pancakes with real maple syrup in front of Sharon. She poured a generous dollop of syrup on the top of the stack, and was just about to take her first bite when Captain Wasniki sat down on the empty stool next to her.

"Good morning, Inspector." He motioned for Beatrice, who poured him a cup of coffee.

"Will you be having breakfast, Captain Wasniki?" Beatrice asked.

*Damn.* Sharon put her fork down and said a silent prayer that her irritation didn't show. She wasn't ready to think about work yet.

"No, thank you. Just a quick cup of coffee."

"Good morning, sir," Sharon said.

"I thought I might find you here. Sorry to barge in on your breakfast, Sharon, but I wanted to catch you before you went to the office." He added cream and sugar to his coffee and took a big sip. "We'll be reopening the Janelle Maycott case."

"Okay," Sharon said, with a question in her voice. "Why does that—"

"The girl with the rope around her neck. Your first murder. The one that Brian Vickery wouldn't let go."

Sharon remembered Janelle Maycott, a young girl found in her apartment in San Francisco, strangled, with a rope around her neck, exactly like Sandy Watson. Sharon set her fork down and turned to face Captain Wasniki as the specifics of the case flooded into her memory. How could she have been so stupid? She thought of Ellie. *You never forget your first murder.* As it turns out, Sharon had. "They're exactly the same. I can't believe I didn't remember."

"Don't beat yourself up about it. It was a long time ago."

"You remembered," Sharon said.

"No, I didn't. Brian Vickery came to my house last night, if you can believe that. He explained the similarities between Sandy Watson and Janelle Maycott. I agree with him, don't get me wrong. But he was always a little crazed about Janelle Maycott's murder. Last night he told me if I didn't reopen the Maycott case, he was going to the press with the similarities."

"Oh, no," Sharon said.

"You haven't spoken to Brian, have you? I thought he might reach out to you, since you were his partner."

"No," Sharon said. "And if he does, I won't say anything."

"I'm sure I don't need to tell you that the information between the two of you should flow one way."

"You don't need to tell me, sir."

"No disrespect intended, Sharon. I know you and Brian were tight, but you need to tread carefully here. Stephen Vine hired Brian to work the Olivia Sinclair case." Captain Wasniki threw a few bills on the counter. "See if you can find a connection between Janelle Maycott and Sandy Watson. And keep your nose down on this one. Once the press gets hold of the connection between the two cases – and you should assume they will – it will become sensational."

"Understood."

Captain Wasniki stood up, changed his mind and sat down again. "I had a call from Andrew Rincon last night. He wasn't happy with your visit to his law firm. He demanded that he be notified when anyone involved in the investigation needed to speak to any of his employees."

"What did you tell him?"

"I told him in no uncertain terms that my officers don't take orders from civilians." Captain Wasniki smiled.

"Sir, I think it would be prudent to get a DNA test on Richard Sinclair. He may well be the father of Sandy Watson's baby. Olivia Sinclair wouldn't have been too happy if she'd discovered that."

"Agreed. Do you think he'd give a swab without a warrant?"

"I have no idea. He certainly wanted me to think he would cooperate."

Wasniki stood. "Carry on."

"Thanks, boss," she said.

After he left, she sat for moment, staring at the beautiful pancakes that had now gone cold.

*

An hour later, Sharon and Ellie signed for eight banker's boxes from the evidence locker that contained evidence from the Janelle Maycott case. Ellie had arranged the evidence in organized stacks and planned on spending the rest of the day reading through the documents and familiarizing herself with the case. Once that task was complete, she and Sharon would mine what they knew and look for a common denominator in the Sandy Watson case. Maybe the connection between the two cases would lead to Olivia. Or not. Sharon wondered how receptive Jonas would be if the reopening of the Maycott murder took suspicion away from Olivia Sinclair.

"You know having this case as a reference just made our job easier. Once we get through this lot, we'll be able to cross-reference the two cases." Ellie said as she dusted her hands off on the legs of her trousers.

Sharon opened the first box, which contained Janelle's bloody clothes and the rope that had been tied around her neck. Ellie looked up. "That looks like the same type of rope that was used on Sandy Watson," she said.

"Well, we don't really know that. All we know is that it's marine rope."

Ellie took the bag from Sharon and examined the rope inside it closely. "I think it's the same. Should I take this to our rope expert?"

"Is he open on Saturday?"

"His lab is in his house. Won't hurt to try and reach him."

Sharon nodded and looked at her watch. "Good idea. What do you think of this: I'll review the Maycott case, and then turn it over to you for the preparation of a detailed outline and summary. I'll prepare an outline and summary of the Sandy Watson case. From there we can look for a common denominator. Let's be sure and note every single location and person – no matter how menial or seemingly unimportant – and then we'll compare them. We'll list the connections between the two cases, and make a plan from there. Sound good?"

"Good," Ellie said. She grabbed the evidence bag with the rope in it and tucked it into her purse. "Back soon."

It didn't take Sharon long to dive into the Janelle Maycott case. She had just been promoted to inspector and been assigned to Brian Vickery, whose methods were unorthodox but successful. Brian was an old-school cop who believed in working his cases on a personal level. Although he gave Sharon some important and challenging assignments – just as she was doing with Ellie – Brian Vickery had a flair for seeing the humanity in the situation. He could have risen up the ranks. Sharon knew firsthand that he had turned down promotion after promotion because he liked being a detective and the idea of sitting behind a desk did not appeal to him. As she read through the notes she had prepared fourteen years ago, the memory of the facts and nuances of the case returned.

She got out a notebook and wrote down the date of Janelle's murder. As she read the police report, she made notes of the names of witnesses and of Janelle's neighbors.

"Inspector Bailey?" A uniform stuck his head in Sharon's office. "There's a guy on the phone. Won't speak to anyone but you. Says it's about the Watson murder, about Richard Sinclair."

"Put him through," Sharon said as she moved to her desk and picked up the phone. "Inspector Bailey."

"James Pritchard here. Is this the woman who is leading the Sandy Watson investigation?"

"Correct. This is Inspector Bailey."

"You were given my name by Richard Sinclair. I'm out front of your building. I'd like to speak to you."

"Of course, Mr. Pritchard. If you'll come to the desk—"

"No. You're to come down and speak to me outside."

Sharon didn't like being told what to do. Her mother had always been amazed that Sharon had joined the police force, where obedience to hierarchy was everything. She didn't appreciate James Pritchard's imperious tone of voice, but she bit back her irritation and responded in a professional tone. "Certainly. I'll be down in a moment."

He waited in front of the building, dressed like a banker in a navy blue suit, complete with a red power tie. He had a hooked nose and he looked down at her with beady eyes, bird-like. Sharon disliked him on sight.

"Inspector Bailey? Credentials, please." James Pritchard held out his hand while Sharon handed over her badge and waited while he studied it, eventually handing it back to her. "I've something to say to you, but I'll deny saying it if you or anyone asks, and I most certainly will not – let me repeat myself – will not testify in court. Do you understand?"

"Mr. Pritchard, say your piece. I'm in the middle of a murder investigation."

"Don't get impertinent with me, young lady. I've got friends."

Sharon waited.

"First of all, Olivia Sinclair is no killer. You're being bamboozled. Second of all, Richard Sinclair didn't stay at my house on Sunday night. He slipped away around 9:30 p.m. and never came back. That's all I have to say. Good day." James Pritchard turned to leave.

"Wait! I need more information."

He faced Sharon and took a few steps toward her. "I've given you a tip. Do your job and investigate." And with that, he turned and walked away.

# Chapter 15

*Saturday, October 18*

Brian drove south on 101, turned towards Golden Gate Park, headed down Lincoln towards the beach, finally weaving his way into the Sea Cliff neighborhood. Tucked deep in the exclusive enclave of opulent houses overlooking San Francisco Bay, Alana Maycott's abode had a sweeping view of the Golden Gate. Brian hadn't called to make an appointment, a cowardly move designed to give himself an out should he change his mind about once again making a promise to Alana Maycott that he couldn't keep.

Although Sea Cliff was a gorgeous neighborhood, it was regularly cloaked in the pea-soup fog that was San Francisco's trademark. Today was no exception. Damp tendrils clung to Brian's hair and jacket as he walked up to the front door, trying to rehearse some eloquent speech but failing miserably. The front door opened before he could knock, and a very tall man with dreadlocks and a giant ring through his nose looked at Brian with the disdain of a British butler.

"Can I help you?" The man's voice was a deep baritone, his articulation spoke of breeding and education.

"Brian Vickery to see Alana Maycott."

"One moment."

The man closed the door. Brian waited for about sixty seconds before the man opened the door once again. This time, he smiled and spoke in a friendly voice. "She's had a long morning and she tires easily. Follow me."

Brian stepped into the foyer of Alana's house, taking in the natural light and warm honey-colored wood, as he followed the man into a big living room. Under normal circumstances the furnishings would have been arranged facing the window, with its view of the Pacific Ocean and the Golden Gate Bridge. But the couches had been pushed aside to make way for the hospital bed, which had been set up near the window. All the pictures had been taken from the walls, leaving white squares where they once had hung. Now they were bunched together next to stacks on the floor.

Alana Maycott sat in a chaise longue near the bed. She wore a bright red wig, a mink coat, and a pair of bug-shaped sunglasses. Her left wrist was connected to an IV drip, which rested near her chair. She clutched a martini glass in her bony right hand. "Brian Vickery," Alana said. She set her martini on the table next to her. "I'm too weak to stand on my own, so come to me. Alphonse, get Mr. Vickery a chair."

The poor thing looked wretched, but Brian had to admire the same indomitable spirit that he remembered when Alana Maycott had suffered every parent's worst nightmare, the death of a child.

Alphonse carried over a leather club chair and set it near Alana, carrying its weight as if it were nothing.

"Thank you," Brian said. He sat down, feeling Alana's impenetrable gaze behind her glasses. "Are you moving?"

She tried to laugh but the sound that came out resembled a squawk. "You could say that. I'm dying. Cancer. Nothing to be done. Have you heard of Swedish death cleaning? It's about getting rid of everything you don't use. I've undertaken that, with Alphonse's help. I admit to enjoying giving my things away."

She looked around the empty room and sipped her martini. "Somehow I like this room in its emptiness. I'm living the life I have left to the fullest, thus the martini. Although Alphonse is stingy with his pour, says he's worried about mixing it with my medication." A pause. "I heard your wife died, Brian. I was sorry to hear that. I know you two loved each other."

"Thank you," Brian said.

She stared, not bothering to hide her scrutiny. "You've aged well, but I can see your sorrow. Tell me, why have you come? I am delighted to see you, but I'm sure your visit has a purpose."

Brian leaned close to Alana and spoke in a low voice. "There's been another murder. Just like Janelle, with the rope. I just want you to know that I haven't given up."

"Oh, you dear man. I never thought you'd given up. There was no denying your dogged diligence as you tried to find Janelle's killer. I'll be forever grateful to you for that, Brian. I felt very alone at that time, but I recognized a fellow fighter. I never lost faith in you. You'll get justice for my Janelle." Her eyes drooped. "It's the medicine and the martinis. I think I need to get back in bed."

Brian stood. "I wanted you to hear it from me personally, Alana. I'm still working on Janelle's case. The police are reopening the official investigation."

"I've come across boxes and boxes of Janelle's things. There's diaries and letters and probably thousands of photographs. My daughter was a pack rat. Shall I send them? You might find something useful. Alphonse can see to that."

Brian handed Stephen Vine's business card to Alphonse. "Can you please mail them care of this office in San Rafael? That would be helpful."

"Yes, sir. I'll do that tomorrow." He cast a concerned glance at Alana, whose head had lolled forward.

"Do you need help moving her?"

"No, we'll be fine. The medication makes her sleepy. And just

117

in case you think I'm being remiss, the martini is mostly club soda. Her medication takes away her sense of taste."

"I heard that, Alphonse."

"I'll bet you did, ma'am."

"I'll see myself out," Brian said, stepping out of the way as Alphonse swept Alana Maycott into his arms and set her gently into the hospital bed.

# Chapter 16

*Monday, October 20*

Brian slept a deep, dreamless sleep and for once he didn't need pills to do it. When the smell of coffee woke him, he lay in bed for a moment disoriented. As he came fully awake, his disorientation slipped away. He had simply set the timer on the coffeemaker, something he hadn't bothered to do since Maureen died. As he showered and made his breakfast, he realized his grief was still there, but rather than lying on his back like a bag of stones, it now sat on his shoulder, lightweight and easier to manage.

He sat in his kitchen, just as he and Maureen had done for decades, embracing the expected wave of longing that washed over him. The ache was physical and alive, but at least it came in waves now, with the time between the spasms of pain growing longer.

Just as he was walking out the door, a FedEx truck pulled to a stop in front of his house. Brian met the driver at the door and signed for an envelope from Alana Maycott, thick and jammed full of photos of Janelle. A note said, "Thought you might want these. I found them after I sent the boxes to Mr. Vine." The note was signed, *Alphonse*. Tucking it under his arm, Brian decided he would drop it off at Olivia's house later on in the evening.

He headed south on 101 into San Francisco, weaving towards the Waldo Tunnel and taking in the magnificent view of the bay and Angel Island on his left. Rush hour was long over, but the going was still slow. The lobby at 44 Montgomery was all but deserted, save the two uniformed security officers. Brian wrote his name in the sign-in book, along with time of his arrival, and the company he was visiting.

"Rincon Sinclair's on the twenty-second floor, sir," the security guard said.

As Brian rode the elevator, he planned his strategy depending on who would speak to him. He stepped into the corridor, heading towards the heavy wooden door with the words *Rincon Sinclair* in brass letters. There was a receptionist's desk at the front, but it was empty, so Brian stepped around it into the main office area.

The office plan was open and spacious. Along one wall were three offices with glass walls separating the offices from the central area, which housed two secretarial stations. All the offices had sweeping views of the city and held desks and credenzas piled with files. Banker's boxes were stacked along the walls in the conference room. Brian noticed that Richard Sinclair's clutter was organized, whereas Andrew Rincon's office seemed a bit chaotic.

The third office was occupied by a middle-aged woman in a suit, and was fastidiously organized. A neat stack of banker's boxes were tucked away in the corner, but other than that, the office was spotless. The woman worked on the computer, cast her glance between two monitors, oblivious to Brian's presence. *Good.* There were two secretary desks, one of them inhabited by a young woman with a blue streak in her hair and a diamond pierced into her nose. A pair of Bose headphones rested on her head. She listened to something and typed furiously on her keyboard. Brian spoke to her.

"Hello," he said.

She looked up startled, and took her headphones off.

"Sorry to bother you, but is there an office manager or someone I could speak to?"

Brian no sooner got the words out than the door opened and the woman in the business suit came out, a curious look on her face.

"Can I help you?" she asked.

"He was asking for an office manager," the woman said.

"That's me." The woman extended her hand. "Wendy Betters. You are?"

"Brian Vickery. I'm an investigator hired by Olivia Sinclair." Out of the corner of his eyes, Brian saw the woman put on her headphones, but she didn't hit the play button on the machine that rested by her elbow, and her hands were not on her keyboard. He noticed a trail of blood-red roses inked into the girl's arm. They crept out from under the sleeve of her white shirt, beautiful art, but something that could never be erased. He didn't understand kids these days.

"Kit, would you mind doing a coffee run? I'll buy you one."

"Sure," Kit said.

"Follow me, Mr. Vickery." After Kit was dispatched on her errand – obviously a ruse to get her out of earshot – Brian followed Wendy into her office. Once the door was closed and they were comfortably seated, Wendy spoke. "I didn't want her to hear us talk. My receptionist is out with a cold. We're in the middle of trial prep and we're also short-staffed. But never mind that. What can I do to help Olivia?"

"You don't think she killed Sandy Watson?"

"God no. Olivia's not a murderer. And just so we're clear, I can't talk to you about Sandy's personnel issues, not without a subpoena."

"Personnel issues?"

"You know what I mean. Sandy was a good employee, but I have to protect her privacy."

"I understand. I'm more after your thoughts, if you don't

121

mind. If I ask a question you don't like, you don't have to answer it. Fair enough?"

Wendy nodded her agreement.

"Did you know Sandy and Richard were having an affair?"

"Of course. Everyone did. It wasn't the first time Richard had slept with his secretary, or his court reporter, or the opposing counsel's paralegal. He likes women. Women like him."

"What about Olivia? How did she feel about Richard's liaisons?"

Wendy shrugged. "She had to have known. I don't think he's ever been faithful. I've known the Sinclairs since 2000 when I started working here as a secretary. I worked here through college and through law school. Richard offered me a job when I graduated, and the firm has been really good to me. I'm on my own here in the Bay Area and the Sinclairs treated me like family. I spent holidays with them. Olivia and I have taken a couple of trips together. I can honestly say that I am certain that neither Richard nor Olivia had anything to do with Sandy's death. It's a shame because the real murderer is out there, probably on his way to Mexico or Canada by now."

"Is it possible that Sandy thought the relationship with Richard was more serious than he did?"

Wendy thought for a moment. "I suppose that's a possibility, but she didn't change her ways. Sandy was a down-to-earth woman. She didn't put on airs, if you get my meaning."

"Do you know if Sandy had any boyfriends prior to Richard? Was there anyone who might have been jealous? Any past boyfriends with a history of abuse?"

Wendy shook her head. "Not to my knowledge. I'm sorry. I know that's not very helpful."

"How did Richard Sinclair react to Sandy's death?"

"He was devastated, of course. But he's also in the middle of a very intense case, and Richard has a tendency to keep his head in the game. He's a master at not letting his personal issues affect him. That's why he is so successful." Wendy pulled a folded piece of paper out from under her blotter. She handed it to Brian, a sheepish expression on her face. "He thought Olivia would send someone here to ask him about his alibi, so he wrote it down and gave me permission to pass it on. He also put his cell phone number down, so you could call him. He doesn't want you to think he's avoiding you. The timing of this couldn't be worse."

Brian organized his thoughts, knowing that he had to be careful with this initial round of questioning. Wendy Betters wasn't obligated to speak to him, and he wanted to leave on good terms. He stood. "I can't think of anything else that isn't privileged. When Stephen Vine subpoenas Sandy's records, we may have questions. Would you mind speaking to me then?"

"I have to get permission from Andrew and Richard, but I'm sure they'll want to cooperate. We want you to find out who really killed Sandy."

"Thank you. Oh, one more thing." Brian pulled the picture of Janelle Maycott out of his pocket. "Have you ever seen this woman?"

Wendy stared at Janelle's picture. She shook her head as she handed it back. "She's pretty. I don't know her. Who is she?"

"A woman who was murdered long ago. Thanks for your help."

The phone on Wendy Betters's desk rang. Brian waved and let himself out. In the lobby, he bumped into Kit, who carried two coffee drinks in a biodegradable tray.

"I can't be seen talking to you. Meet me at Mid-City Diner in fifteen minutes." She said the words as she passed by. Before she opened the door into the office, she called to Brian, "Fifteen minutes. Don't be late. I only get an hour."

\*

Mid-City Diner catered to the nine-to-five worker who by necessity or design grabbed their breakfast and lunch on the go. A salad bar, a sushi bar, a soup station, a sandwich station, and an all-day breakfast station provided anything a hungry person on the go could want. In addition to the self-serve cafeteria-style menu, efficient-looking waitresses were ready to serve those who wanted to eat from the grill. Brian chose a corner table, sat down, and ordered coffee. He'd offer to buy Kit lunch, figuring it was the least he could do. It seemed that the kid was taking a risk talking to him, and Brian believed in cultivating connections. Having a friend at Rincon Sinclair could serve him well as the investigation unfolded.

Kit arrived promptly at 11:29. She stood outside the restaurant, took a final drag off her cigarette and ground it into the ashtray before coming inside. Nodding when she saw Brian, she wove between the tables towards him.

He stood and extended his hand. Her grip was warm and strong. She met his eyes with a direct and forthright gaze.

"Kit Madsen." She sat down across the table from Brian and asked the waitress for coffee.

"I thought I'd buy you lunch," Brian said. When Kit smiled, Brian saw the child in her and was easily able to imagine what she would look like sans blue hair and nose piercing. His initial impression found Kit to be intelligent and hardworking.

"Thanks. I'd like a burger, please. Medium well with fries."

Brian ordered the same. Once the waitress was out of earshot Kit leaned into him.

"I wanted to tell you about Sandy, the things that they won't tell you at Rincon Sinclair," Kit said. "She was really good at her job. Got hired as a receptionist. I was working as secretary for both attorneys, but it was just too much. Richard and Andrew are both workaholics, and each really requires their own support staff. Sandy got promoted and did a really good job. She never made mistakes, okay? I'm not lying. She double-checked her work and was very thorough. We have to be. It's a busy litigation firm. There's no room for errors."

The waitress brought two waters and their coffees. Brian waited while Kit added cream and sugar to hers.

124

"I knew Richard would make a move on Sandy when they went away for that deposition in Sacramento. When they came back, it was obvious they were sleeping together. About six months after that, things started going wrong for Sandy."

"Going wrong?"

"Documents would be misfiled or go missing after Sandy worked on them. She would add footnotes to a document, and the next day they were deleted. The wrong files wound up in Richard's trial bag, stupid stuff that I know Sandy didn't do."

"How do you know that?"

"Because the same thing happened when Richard chased after me."

Brian felt a thrum of excitement, the gossamer glow of a thread that needed pulling.

"I was pretty grossed out when he hit on me, to tell you the truth. But what could I do? I sure as hell wasn't going to sleep with him. So I went to Wendy and asked to be reassigned. She knew why I was asking. I could tell by the way she reacted." Kit shivered and grimaced. "Once I started working for Andrew, everything went back to normal."

"Did you ever tell Andrew what Richard did?"

The waitress arrived with their food. Brian cut his hamburger in half and took a bite, surprised at how delicious it was, while Kit doused her fries in ketchup.

"I didn't have to. He knew – or suspected. Once I started working for him, he bought me a new computer, moved my desk outside his office. I've been getting raises and bonuses ever since." They ate in companionable silence for a few minutes. "About two months after Sandy was promoted, Andrew congratulated me on avoiding a crappy situation. He didn't like Richard sleeping with his secretaries. He also never liked Sandy. He wanted to fire her, but Richard would have been furious."

While Kit devoured her hamburger, Brian thought about office dynamics and hot-headed lawyers. He wondered what if anything these strange events had to do with Sandy's murder. If Rincon Sinclair were a bigger firm, he could understand office jealousy, especially amongst support staff. But Rincon Sinclair had five employees, three of them senior management.

"How about Richard and Andrew? Do they get along?"

"They would have killed each other years ago if it weren't for Wendy Betters. She acts as a buffer between the two of them. She's brilliant, an excellent lawyer, a savvy businesswoman, and a master at client relations. I'll miss her when I leave." Kit covered her mouth, eyes wide. "Oops."

"You're leaving?"

"Giving my two-week notice this afternoon. I'm not comfortable there anymore. And since I worked for Andrew, I had no trouble finding a job. Going to one of the big firms, working for a senior partner. More money. Fewer hours."

"Good for you," Brian said.

"I almost forgot. Richard renewed his passport. I saw the application on his desk. He did it on a rush basis. Thought that was interesting."

The instinct that had served Brian so well during his career as a cop went on full alert.

"Do you have any idea where he might be going?"

"Richard likes warm weather. He always talked about Belize." Kit shrugged. "Richard's smart, cunning, and an expert liar. He could have a plan to go somewhere completely different."

"Sounds like you don't like him."

"I don't. I can't get away from that place fast enough." She pushed her empty plate away and looked at her phone. "Thanks for lunch."

"Hey, before you go, would you mind giving me your number? I may have another question."

"Sure." Kit pulled out her phone. "What's your number, and I'll text you?"

Brian gave her the number.

"There," Kit said. "I just sent you a text."

"Thanks for talking to me, Kit. I appreciate it."

"Have a good one." She waved and was gone.

He sat for a long time after Kit left, thinking about the passport renewal. Was Richard Sinclair planning to go on the run because of Sandy Watson's murder? Andrew Rincon had a temper. Could he have killed Sandy? But why? Because she slept with Richard or because of the video? No, Brian reasoned. Sandy's murder wasn't committed by someone who had lost his or her temper. Her killer was cold and calculating, someone who took the time to plan what he was going to do.

And there was the mystery of the rope and the signature left-handed bowline knot. And Janelle. He must never forget about Janelle.

\*

After trying without success to reach the Pritchards at the number Wendy Betters gave him, Brian left a message and drove down to the Marina. Despite the brisk October temperature, runners, skaters, and dog walkers populated the path along the Marina Green. Eager to digest the hamburger and French fries that sat like a lump, threatening a ripping case of indigestion, Brian locked his car and took a leisurely stroll, embracing the wind on his cheeks and the sun on his back.

He and Maureen used to take long walks all the time, spontaneously packing a lunch and heading outdoors. Paying attention to the familiar pang of grief as it slowly shuddered through his body, he was surprised that it didn't bring him to his knees. Not this time.

He continued to walk until he reached Celeste Watson's house, surprised that Sandy, who by all accounts lived so frugally, had grown up in one of the most sought-after neighborhoods in the city. He walked up the narrow walkway, up the porch stairs, and was met at the front door by a woman near his own age. Her blond hair, now streaked with gray, was tucked into a bun on top of her head and held in place with two pencils. She hadn't taken the chain off the front door, opting to open it and peer through the crack, a surly look on her face. For a minute, Brian worried that Mrs. Watson wouldn't want to speak to him. He put on his most charming smile.

"Mrs. Watson? My name is Brian Vickery. I'm hoping you'll talk to me about Sandy."

"Are you the police?"

"No, ma'am. I'm a private detective."

"Are you representing the woman who was arrested?"

"Yes, ma'am."

"Let me see your identification."

Brian handed her the flimsy license that he had laminated.

"This doesn't have a picture on it. May I see your driver's license?"

Brian took his license out of his wallet and handed it to Mrs. Watson. He didn't blame her for being suspicious.

She handed him back his driver's license. "I'm just going to call this phone number on the license and make sure you're who you really say you are." She slammed the door in his face.

Ten minutes later, she opened the door. "Please come in, Mr. Vickery. I apologize for being overzealous, but the press . . . "

"Thank you, ma'am. I understand your caution. They are still camped out at Mrs. Sinclair's house." Brian tucked his license back into his wallet and followed Mrs. Watson into a sunny kitchen. Mrs. Watson pointed to a kitchen table tucked under a window, which looked out over a small flagstone garden lined with terracotta pots.

"Call me Celeste. Have a seat. Tea? I always like ginger tea after lunch. It soothes the stomach and aids in digestion. My daughter used to say . . . " She leaned against the counter, her back towards Brian. After a few seconds she recovered herself and

128

got busy with the kettle. By the time she set a pot of tea and a plate of cookies down, she had regained her composure. Brian couldn't help but notice her sad eyes and air of exhaustion, the telltale signs of grief. "I still can't believe she's gone. Now, what can I do for you, Mr. Vickery?"

"What can you tell me about Sandy and Richard Sinclair?"

"I think my daughter would still be alive if it weren't for that man," Celeste said. "And I wouldn't be surprised if he set his wife up to take the fall."

"Do you think he murdered your daughter?"

"I wouldn't go so far as to say he actually did the killing, but he's an unscrupulous man, uses people to get what he wants without any regard for their well-being. Of course, I saw him on television before Sandy started dating him. At least Sandy thought they were dating. To my mind they were having a tawdry affair. He struck me as a little too fond of himself, if you get my meaning." Celeste picked up her teacup. When her hand shook she set it down. "Can't keep a steady hand anymore. Since Sandy's death I haven't been myself.

"She told me she was dating someone wonderful and wanted me to meet him. I could tell by the tone of her voice over the phone that she was completely captivated by this man. When they showed up at my door, I nearly fell over. Richard Sinclair is my age. Given his notoriety, I knew he was married. She had fallen for him, and I knew nothing good would come of it. When she called on the phone to ask what I thought of him, I said she was headed for trouble. As if she would listen.

"About a month after that happened, I ordered take-out from Luigi's, just around the corner. Do you know it?"

Brian nodded, not wanting to interrupt her flow.

"It's a dark, hole-in-the-wall Italian restaurant, red and white checked tablecloths, candles in the chianti bottles – that type of place. But they have the best Italian food in town. I stopped cooking when Sandy left home. In any event, I was having a glass of wine, waiting for my to-go order when I happened to see Richard Sinclair and a woman who was most definitely not Sandy tucked into the corner. Let me assure you, it wasn't a harmless business meeting. Those two were lovers." In an angry burst of energy, Celeste pushed away from the table and stood, once again, with her back towards Brian, staring out the window, her shoulders tight with anger. When she turned to face him, the grief that she had managed to control haunted her eyes. Brian's heart broke for her.

"I could have murdered him. Would have done anything to wipe that smug, arrogant look off his face." She sighed and sat back down. "But I didn't. I quietly paid for my meal and scurried away, while my heart broke for my daughter."

"Did you recognize the woman?"

"It was too dark, but she was young, like Sandy."

"Did you tell your daughter what you saw?"

Celeste shook her head. A lone tear slid down her cheek. "I couldn't bring myself to break her heart. She was so certain Richard was going to leave his wife and marry her." She looked up at Brian, her eyes filled with a heart-wrenching sadness that broke Brian's heart. "Do you think she'd still be alive if I had said something?"

"No," Brian said immediately. "No, she wouldn't. Don't do that to yourself. The grief over losing Sandy is enough to bear, Mrs. Watson. Did Sandy have any other boyfriends who could have become jealous enough to kill her?"

"No," Celeste said. "Sandy dated some, nice boys her own age, but she had plans. She wanted to get an education and go to law school. She would have done it, too. Sandy was a determined child. Once she decided she was going to do something, there was no stopping her. Do you think Mrs. Sinclair killed my daughter, Mr. Vickery? The television reporters say there is a lot of evidence pointing to her guilt."

"No," Brian said in an instant, surprised at his own conviction. "I'm sure she didn't. She's being framed."

"Don't trust Richard Sinclair, Mr. Vickery. And be careful. He has power and influence and knows how to use it."

"I know. Thanks for the warning."

Celeste walked him to the front door.

"You'll find out who really killed my daughter?"

"I will." Although he knew from years on the police force that there were no guarantees in any investigation, he had every intention of finding out who killed Sandy Watson and Janelle Maycott.

# Chapter 17

Andrew's fury at Richard had been continual and relentless, but Richard had somehow managed to stay out of his partner's way over the weekend. Beth Musselwhite had sent her promised termination letter, along with a written guarantee that Andrew and Richard would be paid for outstanding services and would additionally receive their bonuses. Richard had gladly turned over the entire mess to Wendy. His plan was to work his cases until he handed them over, billing as many hours as possible. To this end, he was able to stay in his office behind his closed door with little disturbance.

Richard had always been able to shut off the stress and tune out the noise around him when he was focused on work. Now was no exception. He had 500-plus pages of deposition testimony to read before a trial that was scheduled to start in ten days. The case would in all likelihood settle, but Richard always prepared, just in case.

On this Monday morning, he had worked from eight o'clock straight through the lunch hour, doing his best to at least appear busy so Wendy and Andrew would leave him alone. Finally, after reading the same sentence five times, he pushed away from his desk and grabbed his jacket. He had just closed his office door when that cop – what was her name? Inspector Sharon Bailey – came into the foyer with her partner, a surly young girl who didn't bother to hide her dislike for Richard. Richard plastered a smile on his face and went into the foyer to meet the two women.

"What can I do for you today, ladies? I was just leaving."

"This won't take long, Mr. Sinclair," Inspector Bailey said. "We have a warrant to take a DNA swab."

The younger officer all but threw the warrant at Richard. He caught it as it fluttered to the ground and perused it quickly. "Very well. Let's go in my office."

Inspector Bailey stood by while the younger officer took two swabs from Richard's cheek. After she put the swabs in a plastic tube, both officers signed and dated the label, and the tube was tucked into an evidence bag, which was also signed by both officers before it was sealed.

"Why do you need my DNA?" Richard asked.

Inspector Bailey gave him a condescending smile. "Sorry. Can't discuss the investigation. Thanks for your cooperation. We'll be in touch."

And without further explanation, both women left.

Their absence created a sort of vacuum, and Richard Sinclair was acutely aware that things were happening behind the scenes over which he had no control but which could ultimately affect him. He stepped out into the hallway to find Andrew standing outside his office.

"What was that all about?"

"I have no idea," Richard said.

"Where are you going?" Andrew called after him.

"Out," Richard said.

# Chapter 18

*Tuesday, October 21*

Olivia dreamt Denny had forbidden her to witness the birth of her beautiful baby. In her dream, Denny had chosen her mother-in-law, Linda, to be at her side during this momentous occasion, a decision that broke Olivia's heart. As Denny's contractions became stronger and closer together, Olivia witnessed Denny's understanding about her husband and his family bloom. During one particularly intense moment, she reached out to Linda, grabbing her hand for support. But Linda pushed Denny away, her attention focused on the doctor, on the baby. Denny realized Linda had attended the birth for one reason: the baby.

Helpless to do anything, Olivia watched as Denny gave birth, her heart filled with joy at the sounds of her crying granddaughter. Before Denny could hold her baby, Linda Grayson took the child away, despite Denny's desperate pleas.

Olivia sat up with a jolt, drenched in sweat, her duvet in a pile on the floor. The bedside clock said 3:00 a.m. Afraid she would have the nightmare again and unable to face it, Olivia got up and headed into the living room. The banker's boxes – four from Brian and two more recently sent to Stephen Vine by Janelle Maycott's mother – and the FedEx envelope of photographs that Brian had brought to her yesterday afternoon stood in the corner, ready for her. She grabbed a fresh legal pad and stack of Post-its and opened the first box. Brian Vickery's files, folders with his neat handwriting, colored Post-it Notes, now faded with age, and the reams of reports and photographs and statements filled the boxes. Olivia was determined to study every single nugget of evidence.

At first the work was mundane, the evidence tedious and uninformative. The first folder held statements taken from Janelle's family and friends and told the story of a vivacious young woman, ambitious, intelligent, and more than a little free-spirited. By the time she finished reading, Olivia felt like she knew Janelle and was saddened by her untimely death. There was something about Janelle that got under the skin, and Olivia could understand why Brian couldn't let the case go.

She moved on to the next box to discover hundreds of photos, most of them pictures of the crime scene and surrounding area. There were shots of the interior and exterior of Janelle's apartment, and extensive photos of every item reviewed during a search of the murder scene. Olivia scanned through pictures of doorknobs, spots of carpet, and other seemingly innocuous subjects.

Nothing could have prepared her for the contents of the third box, which contained the crime scene photos and shots of the murder. "Oh, you poor girl," Olivia said out loud as she studied the gruesome close-up of Janelle's once beautiful face. In death, her tongue protruded, her eyes bulged, the rope around her neck lending a macabre sort of madness to the scene.

There was no denying the similarity between Janelle's photo and the photo Inspector Bailey had shown Olivia of Sandy Watson. Cold all of a sudden, Olivia jumped up from the couch, as if to distance herself from the lurid photos, and paced back and forth across her living room. Her heart broke for those poor young women, whose lives had been snatched away.

She padded barefoot down the hall to her bedroom, where she

put on a warm sweater and heavy socks. Catching sight of herself in the vanity mirror above her dresser, Olivia paused, surprised by what she saw. The past week had not been kind to her. Dark half-moons had bloomed under her eyes, giving her a haunted look. Her face, devoid of makeup, looked haggard and drawn, her eyes bloodshot and tired from the tears that she had shed in private. The gray roots gave her the look of a bedraggled old woman who had seen better days.

Turning her attention back to the evidence boxes, she took out every single photo of Janelle Maycott's dead body, along with all the photos of the crime scene in situ, and spread them out on the floor in a circle around her. Janelle Maycott had lived in a studio apartment, with a kitchenette and good-sized bathroom. An antique desk was tucked into the bay window, and although Janelle's mattress was directly on the floor, the floral print duvet and overstuffed pillows made the austere studio look inviting. Olivia judged Janelle Maycott to have been a woman of taste, either living on a student's salary or living a minimalistic life by design.

Once Olivia got over the initial horror of the murder, the crime scene photos were rather revealing. Whoever had killed Janelle had staged her body on the floor, folding her hands over her chest and resting them over her heart. Forcing herself to study the body, she noticed there was no evidence of a fight, no defensive marks – she had heard them called on crime shows – on Janelle's hands and arms. She skimmed through the other photos of the exterior of Janelle's apartment, but nothing caught her eye.

Olivia wondered if Sandy's hands had been folded over her chest. She had only seen a close-up of Sandy's face, so she made a note to ask about that. Feeling as though she had seen the worst and was now prepared for anything else, she moved on to the police reports, pathology reports, and reports submitted by the medical experts.

By 6:00 a.m., Olivia had gone through two boxes of Brian's

evidence. The work was tedious and time-consuming. She stood, taking a minute to stretch out the kinks in her neck and shoulders before she picked up the papers that were scattered around the living room floor and placed them back in their boxes. Had Richard and Janelle Maycott's lives intersected? After law school Richard had worked for the San Francisco District Attorney's office for three years, after which he had gone to work for a plaintiff's law firm, which had closed its doors twenty-five years ago. When he won his first big jury verdict, his career took off, and he hadn't looked back. Richard loved the limelight, loved being the center of attention.

When Richard and Andrew had started Rincon Sinclair in 2000, Richard single-handedly managed to convince Countryside Insurance into giving their sizeable block of business to his firm. In addition to Richard's public notoriety, he and Olivia had both been very active in fundraising for needy causes. Olivia took on the volunteer work in an effort to help those disenfranchised people who couldn't help themselves. Richard supported her for the publicity. Could Janelle have worked a fundraiser that Olivia hosted?

She took another box, this one from Alana Maycott, and dumped a box of photos on the floor, careful not to damage any of them. Unlike Brian's meticulous files, Janelle's mother had stuffed these belongings into the box in a hurry. The end result was chaos. There were hundreds of photos of Janelle Maycott. Sitting cross-legged on the floor, Olivia went through the photos one by one. Images of Janelle as a child, always smiling, always surrounded by friends, spoke of her easygoing manner.

Janelle Maycott grew into a beautiful young woman, with intelligent eyes and a kind smile. As the years went by, Janelle became more conservative. The print blouses and garish makeup she wore in high school and college were replaced by button-up blouses and the more tailored clothes required for internships and the reality of the adult world. One batch of pictures caught

Olivia's attention. It was taken in front of City Hall and depicted Janelle and a young man. The young man, although handsome, looked uncomfortable in a suit and tie, while Janelle looked like she was ready to take on the world, not knowing that in a few short months someone would snuff out her life.

She continued to go through the photos, almost by rote now, sure that nothing in them would help her. The photo montage of Janelle Maycott was a stark reminder of a young life ended too soon. She was near the bottom of the pile when one photo caught her attention. She recognized the location. The picture was taken at a Hope for Children fundraiser that Olivia had chaired. She'd been unable to attend because Denny had become sick with the mumps. Although Richard had volunteered to stay home and care for Denny – one of the few times Olivia could remember him making such a sacrifice – Denny had begged Olivia to stay home with her. Olivia had capitulated to her daughter's wishes, sending Richard to the fundraiser to represent both of them.

The picture she held depicted Richard and Andrew, both dressed in tuxes, standing outside the venue for the event. Two women stood between them. Andrew's second wife, Glynnis, hung on to Andrew's arm, a moment of happiness in a marriage that would end in disaster. Janelle Maycott stood next to Glynnis, looking beautiful and glamorous in a full-length dress that accentuated her lithe young body. Richard had his arm draped around Janelle's bare shoulders, while Janelle gazed up at him adoringly.

*They were lovers.*

Olivia knew it like she knew the earth revolved around the sun. She felt the cold trickle of sweat between her shoulder blades.

When the hand that held the damning photo started to shake, Olivia tossed the photo on the floor as though it were on fire. She had found the evidence that linked Janelle Maycott with Sandy Watson. That link was Richard.

Glancing at the clock, she saw it was 7:45. Ignoring social convention, she dialed Brian Vickery's number. "I'm sorry to bother you so early, but I've found a picture of Janelle Maycott with Richard."

"Okay. I'll be right with you. Give me fifteen minutes." He hung up before Olivia had a chance to respond. Flying from all the coffee she'd consumed, Olivia paced the house, not quite sure what to do with herself. Even though she hadn't much experience in criminal defense, she knew the picture wasn't enough to exonerate her, but it was a cog in the investigative machine that Stephen and Brian were co-piloting. She would have to let go and trust that they would use this photo to her advantage. When Brian's car pulled up, Olivia hurried to the front door to let him in.

"There aren't too many photographers left," Brian said, casting a glance at the gaggle of journos still camped across the street from Olivia's house. "Hopefully something more sensational will catch their attention soon, and they'll leave you in peace."

"I find I'm growing used to them," Olivia said. As they moved into the kitchen, she couldn't help but notice that just being in Brian's presence calmed her. There was something quiet and solid about him that was so different from Richard, who always needed things moving around him. Brian Vickery was the kind of man who would sit still and enjoy the peace. Handing him the picture, Olivia waited while he studied it.

Brian studied the photo for a good minute. "I'll take this to Stephen on my way to Napa, if that's okay."

"Napa?"

"I've tracked down Madison Pritchard. She's at their house in Napa. I'm going to double-check Richard's alibi." Brian tucked the picture into his pocket. "You know, this picture implicates Andrew Rincon, too."

"He's got a temper," Olivia said. "But that doesn't really fit with Sandy's murder – or Janelle's murder – does it? The crime was so calculated. Whoever killed those girls planned it. I could see Andrew getting angry and striking a fatal blow, but this crime was planned, the rope a prop in some macabre mise-en-scène. And if I'm going to be truthful, I don't see Richard committing this crime either. I know this sounds strange, but he's too arrogant to kill someone. And at the risk of sounding like a bitter, jilted wife, I see Richard for what he truly is: an egocentric narcissist. This crime just doesn't seem like something he would do."

"That's insightful," Brian said. "But there could be things that we haven't yet discovered. Like motive. What if Sandy Watson discovered something at Rincon Sinclair and threatened to go to the authorities? And what if what she found was enough to get her murdered?"

"But that doesn't explain Janelle Maycott," Olivia said.

"I know."

"Can I make you some breakfast?"

Brian's eyes softened with a hint of sadness.

"Did I say something wrong?"

"No. Reminded me of my wife."

"I was just about to make some eggs and wouldn't mind the company."

Soon she and Brian were seated with plates full of eggs, toast, butter, coffee for Brian and chamomile tea for Olivia. The grief Brian carried made him vulnerable in Olivia's eyes, and this softness made Olivia trust him. As they ate, she surprised herself by confiding in him about her run-in with David. She told Brian why she hired a private investigator to get evidence of David's infidelity, and David's threat to tell Denny that her mother had meddled so inappropriately.

"Now I need to tell my daughter what's happening with the case and how her father is implicated. I don't want her to read it in the newspapers. If I call her, David will tell her what I did. If Denny finds out what I've done, she'll never speak to me again."

Brian listened to Olivia's tale of woe without comment or judgment, his eyes full of kindness.

"What do you think? I know you don't have kids, but if you were in my position, what would you do?"

140

He got up from the table, took their plates to the sink, and took his time rinsing them. "I'd stand by my position if I were you. Call your daughter. Tell her what's happening with your family. She has a right to know."

"And what do I do when David tells her what I've done? He'll take my daughter away from me."

"You make it sound like Denny doesn't have any say in the matter," Brian said. "The truth, especially when it relates to character, has a way of wriggling to the surface. Denny will come around. Maybe not according to your timing, but she will. And all you can do is be here for her. When you talk to her, tell her that. Tell her you hired someone to investigate her husband, that you did it out of love. Tell her you will always be here for her. I don't need to tell you to own your truth. You already know that." He took his car keys out of his pocket. "I'm off. I'll report to you and Stephen this afternoon, okay?"

"Thanks, Brian," Olivia said.

*

After he left, Olivia punched Denny's number into her cell phone twice, but found she didn't have the courage to put the call through. She spent the rest of the morning cooking to distract herself. She got out her stockpot and made a huge pot of vegetable soup, not caring whether she would get to eat it. What she didn't freeze, she would give away, maybe to the journalists and photographers across the street. Would they accept food from a woman accused of murder?

Once the soup was simmering, she took out four jars of the tomatoes she canned last summer, chopped up garlic, onion, and fresh basil and made a pot of spaghetti sauce. Soon the marinara and the soup bubbled away, filling the house with the comforting smells of a warm kitchen.

She was just about to get back to the Janelle Maycott evidence, when the doorbell rang. Leaving the chain on, just in case one of the journos had decided to ambush her, she peeked through the crack in the door, and was dismayed to find Claire Montreaux standing there, looking perfectly put together and utterly professional.

"Sorry to come unannounced," Claire said. "I'm here to say how sorry I am."

"Sorry? For what?" Olivia asked.

"Can I come in?"

Not wanting Claire to see all the case evidence that was spread out in the living room, Olivia led Claire to the kitchen.

"I wanted to tell you what's been happening with your clients face-to-face. You've been fair to me and I was really looking forward to working with you. I want you to know your clients came to me voluntarily. I didn't poach them."

"It's not your fault," Olivia said. Claire fidgeted with a perfectly manicured fingernail, looking decidedly uncomfortable. "What's the matter? What aren't you telling me?"

Claire sighed. "I hope I'm not overstepping by telling you this, but given your current circumstances, I think you need to know."

*Oh, what now?* Olivia braced herself for the worst.

"Last year I attended the Bar Association Christmas party at The Spinnaker." Like an anxious child, Claire shifted her weight from one suede pump to another. "Richard hit on me. I mean, he came on pretty strong, like he wasn't going to take no for an answer. Thank goodness someone else came to talk to him and I was able to slip away."

Olivia wondered for a moment how many other women would come out of the woodwork claiming that Richard had hit on them. She wasn't quite sure how this information could help her case or help her life. For all she cared, Richard could rot in prison. If it weren't for him and his philandering ways, they wouldn't be in this mess.

Claire stopped fidgeting. "I thought you needed to know. If I were in your position, I would want someone to tell me." She hoisted her purse higher onto her shoulder. "I should go."

Out of the blue, Olivia took a deep breath and turned to face Claire. "I want to hire you."

Claire's eyes opened in surprise. "You're divorcing your husband?"

"Yes, but not for that. It's my daughter." Olivia plowed on before she changed her mind. "I'll give you a retainer. You'll need an investigator. I'll pay for that too."

Claire pulled a legal pad out of her purse and took copious notes while Olivia explained Denny's situation, her belief that David Grayson had been cheating on her, and that she had hired another investigator who botched the job so badly that David was aware of the surveillance.

When Olivia finished talking, Claire went down her notes and repeated everything Olivia requested verbatim. "I know a good investigator. I'll call him when I get back to the office. If David has his mistress with him, I'll get evidence."

"I hope it doesn't come to that," Olivia said. "My daughter loves her husband. She certainly doesn't want me meddling in her life. But David's cheating on her. Eventually she's going to find out. When she does, she'll be in need of a good lawyer."

"How long do you want me to keep eyes on him?"

"Not sure. I'll let you know. Years in this business has made me cynical."

"I understand," Claire said. "You can almost sense what's going on in these marriages, can't you?"

"I've always been good at seeing other people's troubles. Too bad I was so horrid at seeing my own." Olivia sighed. "Shall I give you a retainer?"

"No, this one's on me. I'll send a bill for expenses every month. If you could pay those quickly, I'd appreciate it. Once Denny discovers what's going on and expresses interest in a divorce, we'll work out a retainer. Is that fair?"

"More than fair. Thank you." Olivia held out her hand. Claire shook it.

"I'm sorry you have to go through all this, Olivia. You don't deserve it."

"I appreciate you saying that."

After Claire left, Olivia got back in bed, tired all of a sudden. The events surrounding her arrest and the fear that her husband was involved in the murder of two young women at the beginning of their lives, had taken its toll. She recognized her emotional exhaustion and longed for sleep, but alas it wouldn't come. She tossed and turned in her bed until late afternoon.

Padding into the kitchen, she detoured towards Richard's wine closet, where she grabbed a favorite California cabernet. She poured herself a glass and sipped it as she put on a pot of water to boil and started mincing garlic. She mixed the garlic with olive oil and a bit of butter. After slicing a loaf of French bread – courtesy of Lauren – in half, she smeared both sides with the garlicky mixture, topped that with some fresh grated parmesan cheese.

She sipped her wine while the garlic bread toasted in the oven. Soon she had a plate loaded up with spaghetti and garlic bread. She topped off her wine, and sat by herself at her dining room table. Taking her time with her meal, she realized these solitary dinners were going to be the new normal.

She thought about Brian Vickery and the kinship they shared. What would it be like to date someone like him, someone kind and not ego-driven like Richard? Life with Richard had been full of excitement and promise. Olivia imagined life with Brian would be easy and full of simple pleasures. She imagined walks on the beach with romantic sunsets, and chastised herself for being ridiculous.

Although the days of romance were over, Olivia was not ready to assume the role of retired spinster. Olivia made a promise to herself that if she managed to stay out of prison, she would find something worthwhile to do with her law degree, some sort of charity work that would afford her a modicum of freedom. If she managed to stay out of prison. If . . .

# Chapter 19

*Tuesday, October 21*

As Brian pulled away from Olivia's house, he forced himself to admit – albeit reluctantly – that he was attracted to her. Although she was nothing like Maureen, who eschewed fancy clothes and haircuts and didn't spend a whole lot of time on her appearance, Olivia and Maureen shared a down-to-earth quality that Brian found immensely pleasing. He liked women who were real and without pretense. And for all her polish and sophistication, Olivia Sinclair seemed to possess these characteristics in spades. To Brian's way of thinking, Olivia's worry over her daughter, despite her own daunting circumstances, spoke volumes about her character.

Admitting that he was lonely and in a strange place after Maureen's death was one thing. Admitting he was actually attracted to another woman left Brian feeling like an adulterer, as though he were betraying his beloved wife in death. But there was no denying that Brian had enjoyed eating Olivia's home-cooked breakfast, and – most daunting of all – enjoyed sitting across from her while doing so. He recalled the blush of her cheek, the way she moved around her gourmet kitchen like a master.

145

The idea of his arms around Olivia filled him with desire, and God help him, he was riddled with guilt because of it. He would have to keep his distance, at least until her case was completed. *Good luck with that.*

He pointed his car north on 101, towards the Napa Valley, California's premier wine-growing region, taking his time as he enjoyed the gorgeous October day, full of soft light and burnished color.

The Pritchard property was tucked among a grove of oak trees on the Silverado trail, a two-lane country road that wove through the Napa Valley and its world-class vineyards and wineries. Brian remembered what Napa was like before the California wine craze. In the 1970s, the houses were few and far between and without pretense. Since then the Napa Valley had turned into a destination vacation spot. Real estate had skyrocketed, and those who could afford it bought acres of land, which they turned around and leased to grape growers. Others even went a step further and opened wineries, eager for the prestige and the tax benefits.

Meanwhile, the teachers, policemen, and everyday working people found themselves unable to buy homes. Brian pulled to a stop at the keypad outside the Pritchard property and pressed the code provided by Madison Pritchard to open the gates.

August through late October was crush season in the wine country. Once upon a time, crush meant laborers picking grapes. Now crush had morphed into a marketing buzzword for the entire region. It was the time of social gathering, society balls, and an onslaught of visitors to the tasting rooms. Driving slowly up the winding dirt road, Brian wove towards the Pritchard house, a large stucco affair that sat atop a sloping hill. Vineyards surrounded the house, the rows of grapes flowing in uniform lines.

The driveway ended in a circular courtyard. Brian tucked his car out of the way and walked up to the front door. He knocked, surprised when Madison Pritchard – whom he recognized from the various society columns he found online – opened the door for him herself.

"Mr. Vickery?" She gave him a forced smile as she ran her eyes over him. A quick look accompanied by a flash judgment. He didn't care one way or another what she thought of him. "Follow me, please."

She led him into a cavernous foyer with a flagstone floor and leaded windows on either side of the medieval-looking front door. In the middle of the empty room a large round table held a giant bouquet of flowers. Surprised that she didn't ask him for identification, he followed her along a dark corridor into a vast library. The room was huge, with floor-to-ceiling bookcases covering all four walls. The cases were chock full of books of all kinds. Brian saw leather-bound classics, an interesting collection of atlases, and one entire bookcase devoted to old Bibles, with their gold lettering and cracked spines. He resisted the urge to peruse the titles.

One wall held two French doors, which had a view of the vineyards. Between the doors, a small wet bar and a glass-doored cabinet held an array of crystal glasses and wine goblets in varying sizes and shapes. Two couches faced each other in front of a large stone fireplace, which was lit but did little to warm the room. Each corner held its own desk, one of them made of masculine dark wood – Mr. Prichard's, maybe? The other desk was a simple table with curved legs and a Tiffany lamp on top of it. Mrs. Prichard's, he reckoned. And if the stamps and stationery scattered about were any indication, he had interrupted her while she was writing letters.

"Would you like coffee, tea, or something stronger?" Madison Pritchard was exactly as Brian expected. Perfectly coiffed hair, styled in a honey-colored bob. Flawless makeup, pearl earrings, a jade green silk blouse, and gray flannel trousers completed her ensemble. She had that look that older women get when they try to fight their wrinkles, too-tight skin covered with some mysterious potion that tried to emulate a youthful glow. To Brian's way of thinking, women and men of a certain age were supposed to have lines on their faces. Wrinkles were the glorified etchings of a life well lived. They told a story. When you let the world see them, you were sharing yourself.

"No, thank you, Mrs. Pritchard," Brian said. "I just have a few questions and then I'll be on my way."

"My husband is in Paris. He'll be back next week and will gladly speak to you then."

"Perfect," Brian said. "Richard Sinclair was with you at your house in Atherton last weekend?"

"Yes. It's an annual weekend house party where my husband hosts his college friends, a reunion of sorts. This year was the twentieth year. The men golf, sit down to lengthy formal dinners every night and discuss their money."

"No wives?"

Madison shrugged. "The wives used to come, but over the years it's turned into a men's weekend. I went to the city to do some shopping."

"What's your relationship like with Olivia Sinclair? Do you and your husband socialize with her?"

Madison Pritchard met Brian's gaze. He saw something cold there, a hint of the real Madison Pritchard, the woman without the money and the powerful husband. He wondered at her background, because what he saw in her was guttural and scrappy.

"We used to. Lately I've got the distinct impression she doesn't much care for us."

"You know Richard Sinclair is using you and your husband as his alibi for the night of his secretary's murder? Can you tell me about the weekend, when you saw him? Is there a chance he could have left your house and killed Sandy Watson?"

A look of worry flashed in Madison's eyes. Although fleeting, Brian noticed it.

"Tell me what happened, Mrs. Pritchard. If you aren't honest with me, I'll dig away until I find out what you're hiding. And don't be fooled by my humble means. I'm good at my job. If you're hiding something, I'll find out about it." Brian waited, hoping he hadn't pushed her too far. "What's it to be?"

Madison stood. "Would you like a drink?"

"No, ma'am." Brian waited while Madison walked to the wet bar, put two ice cubes in a crystal highball glass and splashed a generous dollop of Belvedere vodka over the cubes. She didn't meet Brian's eyes as she sat back down, downed the vodka in one go, and leaned back on the couch, eyes closed, as if savoring the initial flush of alcohol. Imagining Madison Pritchard did her share of day drinking, Brian waited.

"Very well. Richard Sinclair and I were having an affair. He left our house in Atherton and came to the city Sunday evening around 9:30. We met at the Fairmont. I didn't leave until after lunch, but Richard left early, before dawn. I have a feeling my husband knows of our little fling. I'm sorry if I was rude to you, Mr. Vickery." Mrs. Pritchard sighed. She looked at him with tired, beleaguered eyes. "There was no call for that. You can call me again if you need to. When my husband gets home, I'm going to tell him what happened. God knows, James hasn't exactly been a faithful doting husband."

"That's a good idea. You can bet the San Francisco PD will want to talk to you, Mrs. Pritchard. And, pardon the unsolicited advice, but it's always best to be honest with the cops. They have the resources to find out the truth." Brian stood. "I'll see myself out." He left Madison Pritchard at the wet bar, pouring herself another Belvedere.

Brian sat in his car and dialed Stephen's number.

"Any luck?"

"No. Madison Pritchard alibied Richard Sinclair."

"We're missing something."

"Agreed," Brian said.

"I'm not going to turn that photo of Janelle Maycott and

149

Richard over to the police yet. It could be interpreted as providing Olivia a motive. I think I'll wait until we have more evidence against Richard or someone else. Do you think there's a copy of it in the files at the SFPD?"

"I don't know," Brian said.

"I wanted to run something by you."

Brian waited.

"The police never printed the areas of ingress and egress to Olivia's house. In my mind, that was an oversight," Stephen said.

"They found what they were looking for and probably called off the search," Brian said.

"If someone planted evidence in Olivia's closet, they might have left a fingerprint at a window or a door. I'm going to see about getting the house reprinted."

"That's a good idea."

"Good. I'll see if I can make that happen. If the police don't agree, I'll hire an independent person to do it."

Brian hung up, more determined than ever to prove Olivia's innocence. The idea of Olivia Sinclair spending even a second in prison shook him to the core. *I don't want to lose her too.* Three aggressive taps on the window startled him out of his reverie. Sharon Bailey looked down at him, an irritated expression on her face. She waved her hand, motioning him to roll down his driver's window.

"A little lost in thought there, Brian?"

"Hey, Sharon."

"Have you spoken to Madison Pritchard?"

"Yep. Richard Sinclair snuck away from his party in Atherton and spent the night with Madison at the Fairmont. She did say that Richard snuck away Monday morning early, before dawn. I imagine you could double-check that with the Fairmont."

"Tough luck," Sharon muttered under breath.

"Olivia didn't kill Sandy Watson."

"The evidence says otherwise."

"You didn't hear this from me, but Richard Sinclair renewed his passport." Brian put his car in reverse.

"What?"

"You heard me. I think Richard Sinclair killed Sandy Watson."

"There's no proof of that," Sharon said, trying to keep up with the car as Brian backed away.

"Yet. There's no proof yet." He hit the gas pedal and headed down the driveway. In his rearview mirror, Sharon gave him the middle finger. He was close enough to see that she did so with a smile on her face.

*

Just as Brian got out of his car and wondered what he would do for dinner, Mrs. Winkle came up the walkway carrying two casserole dishes. It was 3 p.m., but he hadn't eaten since breakfast at Olivia's. Brian couldn't help but smile at the sight of his dear neighbor, with her garish housecoat, her fur-trimmed slippers, and her hot pink glasses. Mrs. Winkle and the Vickerys were the last of the residents from the old days. Their houses were the only ones that hadn't been remodeled and modernized, and they were the only people left in the neighborhood who didn't drive fancy new cars.

Brian remembered the bonhomie of the past, how the neighbors used to have barbeques at each other's houses, and speak when they passed in the street. Now the entire area had changed. Brian didn't even know his new next-door neighbors' names. He knew full well that they laughed at Mrs. Winkle behind her back. He had heard them over the backyard fence talking about her on more than one occasion. But Brian and Maureen had loved Mrs. Winkle like family. Over the years they had spent holidays together, and Maureen had loved Mrs. Winkle's grandchildren as though they were her own.

After Maureen died, Mrs. Winkle had cooked and had tried to do some cleaning for Brian, a valiant effort to stave off the chaotic downward spiral that had taken over Brian's spiritual life and physical space. By some miracle, Mrs. Winkle had helped Brian while respecting his need for space and privacy, always circling in the background should she be needed.

"Hello, Brian!"

"Let me help you with those." Brian took the casserole dishes, using one hand to unlock the front door and let them both in.

"You've been busy," she said, unable to keep the amazement out of her voice. She followed him into the kitchen. Her eyes wandered over the clean counters, the sink, and polished dining room table, a lovely antique that had belonged to Maureen's great-aunt. "I can't believe it! Well, I can believe it, but I wasn't expecting it."

"Have you eaten? I'd share my casserole."

She looked at her watch. "I can sit for a minute. I'm waiting on the cable repairman." She sat across from him, in Maureen's place. "What possessed you to do all this?"

"For some reason, I was able to see how I had let things slip, saw the house with an objective eye. And then I thought of Maureen and what she would think if she saw me living this way. So I cleaned and cleared. The physical work was cathartic. For the first time since Maureen's death, I slept through the night without taking any pills."

"That's the best news I've had all week." She looked at her watch. "I should go. You know where I am if you need me, okay?"

"You're a good friend. I wouldn't have survived these past few months without you."

She squeezed his shoulder. "You'd have done the same for me. Talk to you later."

The house, although clean and organized, still felt empty without Maureen in it. A yawning chasm remained where Maureen's life force had been. The ache in Brian's heart was still there, a familiar thing he was learning to live with. But it was more bearable today. The grief wasn't going anywhere. Not now, maybe not ever. It was on him to learn to live with it.

He didn't rush his meal. When he finished eating, he sat at the kitchen table for a long time, allowing himself to feel the pain of his loss, as though the suffering would honor it in some way. "I'll always love you, Maureen." He spoke into the void, wondering if somewhere in some other dimension, his wife heard him.

# Chapter 20

*Wednesday, October 22*

It had been nine days since Ellie and Sharon had been called to the scene of Sandy Watson's murder. When Stephen Vine had called yesterday to ask about reprinting Olivia's house, Sharon's initial reaction had been a resounding no, followed with a request that Stephen go through the appropriate channels. But he had convinced her.

"When I put you on the witness stand, I'm going to ask why you didn't print the areas of ingress and egress. I'm going to play it like you were a bit eager to charge Ms. Sinclair. If she had killed Sandy Watson, she wouldn't have brought evidence to her house. Someone planted it there. It's your job – or it was your job – to find out who that person was. I'm sure Jonas Greensboro was eager for a speedy arrest, but you have to admit fingerprinting the exterior windows and doors should have happened without my requesting it."

He was right. And when Sharon was silent, Stephen Vine knew he had her backed into a corner.

"You're the lead cop. Order a reprint of the scene. Let them think you're just being thorough." He didn't bother to say goodbye before he hung up the phone.

Sharon had been too pressed for time to run the idea by Captain Wasniki, but she was certain he would support her. In the spirit of full disclosure, she would tell him that Stephen Vine had suggested the scene reprint. As she filled her to-go cup with coffee and headed out the door, she couldn't shake the feeling that she was missing something vital, something elusive thing that her subconscious mind would reveal when it was ready.

Ellie was waiting with a worried expression on her face when Sharon stepped off the elevator.

"What's happened?"

"Jonas Greensboro came looking for you. He's furious. You're to go right up to Wasniki's office."

Sharon sighed and pressed the call button for the elevator. "Did he say what was the matter?"

"Just that he wanted to speak to you immediately." Ellie looked around to make sure no one was listening. When she spoke her voice was soft. "Has anything happened?"

"Not that I know of. But I've got doubts about this case, Ellie. I don't think Olivia Sinclair did it."

"Of course she did. She rented the murder scene. We found the decedent's property in her home. And if that's not enough, we have the emails and the video of Sandy having sex with her husband. I know it's hard to picture someone like Olivia Sinclair, with her poise and polish and good works, to commit murder. I get it. But she was jealous. And she's smart, so she planned it."

"If she's so smart, why was it so easy for us to find the evidence needed to convict her?"

Ellie met Sharon's eyes and shook her head. "Because she wanted you to do exactly what you're doing. It's not in character, right? Olivia Sinclair is too smart to leave evidence in her bedroom closet . . . That's her game. She's playing us, playing you. We're tired, boss. We've been pushing hard. That's why you're second-guessing yourself."

"What about Janelle?" Sharon asked.

155

"Don't know yet. Janelle Maycott's murder doesn't change the evidence we have on Olivia Sinclair. I'm sure we'll figure out how Janelle plays into this."

Sharon stepped into the elevator, wishing it were that easy.

*

Megan Warner, Captain Wasniki's secretary, typed away at her computer. When Sharon approached, her eyes became wary and she gave Sharon an apologetic look that made Sharon's stomach cramp. The wall between Captain Wasniki's office was glass, but today the blinds were shut and Sharon couldn't see in.

"What's going on?"

"Jonas Greensboro is out for blood," Megan whispered. "Something about reprinting the Sinclair house? You better get in there. And good luck."

Sharon steeled herself for a confrontation with Jonas, making a vow to herself that if he became verbally abusive, she would get up and walk out. She didn't care if she got written up for insubordination. She'd quit before she would be abused for doing her job. Pushing open the door, Sharon stepped into the snake pit.

"You're late," Jonas said. He was seated in one of the guest chairs in front of Captain Wasniki's desk. Captain Wasniki sat still and quiet and wore a look that Sharon had come to recognize as anger.

"I'm not actually. And I didn't know we had an appointment." She turned her gaze to Captain Wasniki. "Sir? What's going on?"

"Did you speak to Stephen Vine about running new fingerprints at Olivia Sinclair's house?" Captain Wasniki asked.

"Yes, sir."

"See." Jonas rose from his chair and pointed at Sharon. "She's gone rogue. Do all your officers make decisions of this magnitude without your clearance? Her carelessness could cost me this case."

Sharon had closed the door behind her and now stood with her back to it. When Jonas Greensboro moved close to her, she

156

met him head on. "Back away, counselor," Sharon said. "Don't force me to subdue you."

A small vessel popped out on Jonas's forehead. Sharon watched as it throbbed with Jonas's pumping blood.

"I will not tolerate insubordination," Jonas said. "You have no authority to make decisions about this case."

"Get over yourself, Jonas. You don't get to speak to me that way," Sharon said, no longer caring if she had an insubordination ticket in her file. As far as she was concerned, Jonas Greensboro could go to hell.

"If I lose this case because of your shoddy police work—"

"My shoddy police work? If you hadn't pushed me to make an arrest—"

"Enough. Both of you stop. Right now," Captain Wasniki said. "Jonas. You will not speak to Inspector Bailey in that tone. And she does have authority to make decisions about this case." He turned to Sharon. "Let's hear your side of the story, Inspector. Sit down and tell us why you agreed to reprint the Sinclair house."

Jonas glared at Sharon before he returned to his chair.

Sharon pulled the empty guest chair as far away from Jonas as she could before she sat down. She felt Jonas giving her the stink eye as she took a deep breath and forced herself to be calm.

"We brought Olivia Sinclair in for questioning and served her with a search warrant. My team was specifically instructed – per the two of you, I might add – to find evidence linking Olivia Sinclair to the Sandy Watson murder, so we could make a speedy arrest. We found evidence and we arrested her. Although the interior of the house was searched in its entirety, once we found Sandy's iPhone and identification in Olivia's closet, no one considered printing areas of ingress and egress." Sharon met Captain Wasniki's eyes. "It was a mistake. I'll take responsibility for it, if you need me to."

"And what about Stephen Vine?" Captain Wasniki asked.

"He didn't want to go to Jonas because he knew Jonas would say no."

Jonas opened his mouth as if to say something, but Captain Wasniki held up his hand. "Wait. Let her finish."

"He told me he would be obligated to put me on the stand and ask me why we didn't print the areas around the windows and doors. I would have owned the error, thereby opening the door for his argument that someone planted the evidence in Olivia's house, and if we had checked the windows and doors, we could be chasing down fingerprints, if there are any."

"That's bullshit. We've got the emails sent from her computer and the American Express card," Jonas said. "I'll get a conviction."

"Then why do you care if they reprint the house?" Sharon asked.

"I care about police officers who don't know their place." Jonas turned to Captain Wasniki. "I want her written up for insubordination."

"Not going to happen," Captain Wasniki said.

Sharon stood.

"I'll have her badge, Captain," Jonas said.

"You'll do nothing of the sort. Let me give you a little lesson about the way things work around here, counselor. You don't tell my officers how do to their jobs, got it? You do not want to make an enemy out of me." Captain Wasniki looked at Sharon and nodded at the door. "You're excused, Sharon. Please close the door behind you."

Sharon closed the door behind her, listening as Captain Wasniki and Jonas Greensboro's voices got louder and louder.

"Are you okay?" Megan asked. She got up and came to stand near Sharon, her eyes filled with worry.

"I'm fine. Thank you," she lied.

"You look a little pale. Why don't you sit down for a minute."

"I'll be all right. I need to get out of here." Sharon hurried back to her office. Once there, she shut the door behind her, closing the blinds so no one in the bullpen could see her, as she sat in the dark, waiting for her hands to stop shaking and her breath to return to normal.

She had stood up to Jonas Greensboro. Although it had felt very righteous at the time, she knew deep down that she had just made a powerful enemy. Jonas had a reputation as a holder of grudges and exacter of revenge. It would only be a matter of time before he came after her. When he did, Sharon knew her time at SFPD and the job she truly loved would be over.

# Chapter 21

*Wednesday, October 22*

When Stephen Vine showed up at Olivia's door at 8:00 a.m., she expected good news. But one look at Stephen's face put those hopes to rest.

"We need to talk," Stephen said. He followed Olivia into the living room. Once they were seated, he leaned forward, his brow furrowed. "I've come across an obstacle that I'm not quite sure how to overcome and am hoping you can help me."

"Of course. Just tell me what you'd like me to do."

"I've had two computer experts try to track down the bogus American Express card in your name. All trails lead back to you, Liv. Whoever got that card applied for it using the Wi-Fi in this house."

"But that's not possible. I never use the computer downstairs for the Internet."

"What about your laptop?" Stephen asked.

"I rarely bring it home." She thought back. "Haven't done so in months."

"Okay. Do you use a password when you log on to the Internet at home?"

"I do."

"Okay. We're still waiting to get your laptop from the police. I'll work on that. No worries."

Olivia said, "I realize the picture of Richard and Janelle Maycott could be construed as a motive for me. I'm sure Jonas Greensboro is going to paint me as a jealous wife who murdered Richard's lovers." She stood and walked into the dining room, coming to stop at the glass window with its dramatic view. Gazing out at King Mountain and her neglected garden, the realization that she was well on her way to spending the rest of her life in prison nearly took her breath away. When she sensed Stephen behind her, she turned to face him. "I should prepare myself for the eventuality that I could wind up in prison and get my affairs in order, shouldn't I?"

"Don't think that way. We're not there yet. I admit to being a little concerned, as I thought getting evidence to prove your innocence would be a slam dunk." He gave Olivia a sheepish smile. "That'll teach me to be too sure of myself. But, again, all we need is reasonable doubt. And I do have some news that could potentially help us."

Stephen took her hand and led her into the living room, back to the couch. "I'm operating under the theory that someone – other than Richard – got into this house and used your computer to obtain an American Express card in your name. That same someone came in after he murdered Sandy Watson and planted evidence. This person had to have access to this house. We know they didn't smash a window and there's no evidence that any lock had been picked, right? You'd notice that."

"Right." Olivia thought about her surprise party and wondered how long the guests had been mingling before she arrived home. "And what about my party? It's just possible that one of my guests—" Olivia couldn't finish the sentence.

"I've made arrangements for the police to bring their finger-print team out again and specifically look for fingerprints at all

161

places of ingress and egress. In their eagerness to find evidence that you killed Sandy Watson, they neglected to dust for prints on windows and doors. When the person who planted evidence entered the house, it's very possible they left a print."

"If they weren't wearing gloves," Olivia said.

"True. But not printing the windows and doors was an oversight. It speaks to a quick investigation, cutting corners to make an arrest. We're going to remedy that. And maybe we'll find a fingerprint that shouldn't be there."

"That helps?" Olivia asked.

"Reasonable doubt. That's all I need." When there was a knock at the door, Stephen patted Olivia's knee. "That's probably Brian. I need to talk to him. The police fingerprint team will be here in half an hour. Are you up for continuing to look through evidence? We have a couple more boxes from Alana Maycott, if you're up to it. And I'll understand if it's too much."

"No, I'll do it. I need to keep busy. Just bring the boxes in when you can."

After Stephen left, Olivia found she was too restless to concentrate, so she moved all the boxes of evidence pertaining to Janelle's case into the dining room, putting the boxes she had yet to look through on the top of the stack. After that, she busied herself arranging the photos, police reports, pleadings, and witness statements in such a fashion that she could look at her handwritten index and retrieve anything listed there within seconds. She showered, drank too much coffee, and sat down once again to the box of pictures received from Janelle Maycott's mother, only to be interrupted by the ringing of her doorbell. Peering through the peephole, she saw Wendy Betters standing outside.

"Wendy, come in."

"Have those reporters been there long?" Wendy asked.

"Since the day I was released from jail. There used to be five times that many."

Wendy was dressed in yoga pants and a Cal Bears hoodie.

Her hair was pulled back in a ponytail and, for the first time that Olivia could recall, Wendy's face was devoid of makeup. "I am actually going to a yoga retreat in West Marin. That's why I'm dressed like this."

"It's good to see you. I'm surprised Rincon Sinclair can function without you," Olivia said.

"I am taking a much-needed day off." Wendy set her purse on the counter and pulled out a sealed manila envelope, which she handed to Olivia. "There's a list of every contractor, repairman, computer salesman, phone repairman, and electrician who has set foot in Rincon Sinclair since Sandy started working there. I erred on the side of caution and listed absolutely everyone. Many are a long shot, but you never know. Is there any news about your case?"

"No. The police are coming back to take new fingerprints," Olivia said.

"Did they get a warrant?" Wendy asked.

"No. This is being done at our suggestion."

Wendy moved into the dining room, drawn to the evidence that was spread over the table like a moth to a flame. "Is this your evidence?"

"Yes. And my investigator has more boxes for me. I'm trying to find a connection between Sandy Watson and another woman who was murdered fourteen years ago in a similar fashion. Her mother sent us boxes of old photos, and I've been charged with the task of going through them looking for a connection between the two cases."

"You only need reasonable doubt, Liv."

"I need to find out who did it, Wen. If the jury convicts me, I'll keep looking."

"The jury won't convict you," Wendy said. "Stephen Vine is a good lawyer. You didn't kill anyone. Do you have anyone in mind as a suspect?"

"Richard," Olivia said not bothering to hide the sarcasm. "But

I don't think he did it, plus he has an alibi." A fresh thread of anger at Richard and his infidelity threatened to invade Olivia's psyche. She pushed it back.

"I need to go. Do you want me to come and stay with you for a couple days? If you don't want to be alone . . . "

Olivia thought for a moment how nice it would be to have Wendy around, a trusted friend to talk to, someone to cook for. "Thanks. I'll be fine for now. But maybe you'd come stay with me when the trial starts?"

"Of course," Wendy said.

"The trick is to not turn on the news," Olivia said.

"I'd say that's good advice. Hope the fingerprint people find something to help you. Call me, okay? Anytime."

"Thanks, Wen."

\*

The fingerprint people arrived just as Wendy drove away. Olivia watched while Stephen led them around the side of the house. Once they were out of sight, she spent the rest of the morning trying to ignore them as she trudged through the rest of the photos of Janelle Maycott. The photos were similar to the others, a chronological depiction of a vivacious woman before her life was cut short. A picture of Janelle at Fisherman's Wharf holding a live crab made Olivia smile before she felt the sting of tears. She liked Janelle and wished she'd known her.

"Is that a picture of Janelle?"

Olivia jumped. She hadn't heard Stephen come into the house.

"Didn't mean to startle you. I knocked, but I guess you didn't hear."

"It's all right." She tossed the photo down on the dining table. "That's Janelle. So sad. Her poor mother."

Stephen walked the length of the dining table, pausing now and again to thumb through the piles of evidence Olivia had arranged there. "There's a lot to go through here. I like the way your mind works."

Olivia handed Stephen the envelope that Wendy had dropped off.

"What's this?"

"Wendy Betters brought me a list of all the people who had access to Rincon Sinclair since Sandy Watson started working there. Maybe we could cross-check the names with Janelle Maycott's case."

"Let me get my paralegal on this. You've plenty to keep you busy here."

Olivia hesitated, not trusting a paralegal when she could do it herself. Her life was in jeopardy, she should do the sleuthing. Turning her back on Stephen, Olivia felt an unexpected wave of panic. She wasn't accustomed to depending on others to fix her problems. Lauren was right. Olivia needed to be in control. "But we're no closer to finding out who really killed those poor girls, are we?" she asked.

"Olivia, we're going to find out who killed Sandy," Stephen said, his voice full of certainty. "It might not be until after your trial, but there's nothing to be done about that. You want to find out what really happened. Brian Vickery will help you do that. My only concern is keeping you out of jail.

"We'll dig into the connection between Janelle and Sandy. That's the key, I'm sure of it. Whoever killed these poor girls is feeling very sure of himself right now. He thinks he got away with murder. Twice. I am going to find that person." Stephen put his hands on Olivia's shoulders and stared into her eyes. "Liv, that's a promise."

Olivia nodded, wishing she had Stephen's confidence.

Brian Vickery stepped into the dining room. "Sorry to barge in. The front door was open. Stephen, a word?"

Stephen and Brian stepped into the hallway, leaving Olivia to pretend she wasn't straining to hear their murmured voices as they whispered. Outside, Inspector Bailey and three more men in blue windbreakers with SFPD emblazoned across the back walked through Olivia's garden and under her back deck. She craned her neck to see what they were up to.

"Olivia," Stephen said. "They've found a handprint on the wall near the window under the deck. It seems as though someone leaned against it, using their hand to prop them up. It's a clean print and it's very fresh."

Brian nodded at both of them and slipped out the front door.

"What does that mean?" Olivia asked.

"Well, have you leaned against the downstairs wall within the last six or eight weeks?"

Olivia cast her mind back to the many times she had spent her day in the garden, often not coming indoors until after the sun set in the summer sky. Although the downstairs basement had windows, Olivia had never landscaped the area under the deck. Every couple years she would have someone throw some bark over the dirt to keep the weeds at bay, but that was it. Her garden shed was tucked under the eaves on the side of the house, and as far as she could remember, she had never put her hand on the wall. "No. Not that I recall."

"Your husband?"

"No idea," Olivia said.

"I need to go down there and talk to them. They'd like to see if they can find a matching print on the interior."

"Dare I hope?"

"Hope is good, Liv. Always hope. This could be a good thing. I'll let them in. Brian and I will stay with them the entire time, okay?"

"Of course. You can see yourselves out and lock up behind you. I'll continue to go through this lot." She nodded at the stacks of papers and boxes of photographs on the dining room table. Once Stephen left her alone, Olivia went into her bedroom. Kicking off her shoes, she sat on her bed, took out her cell phone and dialed Denny's number.

Denny answered right away, but Olivia could tell from her tone of voice, that David was in the room. She envisioned him hovering nearby, listening to their conversation.

"Hi, Mom." Denny's voice of devoid of emotion.

Olivia said, "David told me not to call you, but I thought you should know what's been going on."

"I know what's going on. I've spoken to Dad." Olivia heard David murmuring in the background. "David told me what you did, how you hired a private investigator to follow him. How dare you!"

"I wasn't trying to meddle, Den. I just wanted you to see—"

"No," Denny snapped. "You don't get to talk your way out of this. Why do you always need to push yourself into situations where you're not wanted? You have no business involving yourself in my marriage. David says you've been trying to drive a wedge between us since the beginning. I didn't want to believe it, but now I can see he's right."

"That's not true and you know it. He's not good for you, Den. He's a liar—"

"Don't you dare speak about my husband that way. You can't control me anymore, Mom. That's your problem. You need to be in control of everything and everyone. And when you're not, you can't cope."

The sound of crashing waves filled Olivia's ears. She held the phone away from her, staring at it, a look of disbelief on her face.

"I'm tired of your abusive husband and tired of your disrespect. You know what, Den. I love you, but I won't be spoken to this way. I've tried to help you because I love you and I think you made a huge mistake. You owe me an apology."

"I owe you nothing," Denny said. "You've been meddling in my marriage since the beginning. It's unhealthy, Mom. It's like you have this relentless obsession with breaking us up. We'd be happy if it weren't for you. Stay away from me. I don't want to hear from you and you need to butt out of my business and my marriage. It's no concern of yours." Denny hung up the phone.

*Damn it.* Olivia threw down her phone. She was tired of acting strong, tired of feigning confidence in Stephen Vine's ability to prove her innocence. She had lost her job, had lost her sham of a marriage, and now she had lost her daughter. Someone had done a very thorough job of framing her for murder, and if they didn't get a break, Olivia could very well spend the rest of her life in prison.

Olivia glanced at the clock. Six-thirty. Another day gone. She could hear the murmur of Stephen and Brian's voices as the fingerprint techs packed up. Soon they came upstairs.

"I'll see you soon," Brian said. His eyes caught hers and lingered there. "Are you okay?"

"I'm fine," she lied.

"No you're not," he said.

*I've nothing to live for.* These words popped in her mind. The reality of them took her aback.

"Seriously. You look a little pale. Do you have someone who could come and stay with you?"

Olivia forced a smile. "I'm okay, really. Just tired."

"Try and get some rest. I'll text you once I know something."

Once he and Stephen were gone, she turned the deadbolt, walked into her bedroom, pulled the curtains and lay down on her bed. Her grief erupted in sobs that came from someplace dark and deep. Helpless to do anything else, she cried until she soaked her pillow and used piles of Kleenex to sop up the tears. An hour later, her mind and body limp with emotional exhaustion, Olivia slept.

# Chapter 22

Brian headed back home after the fingerprint team left Olivia's house. The days were getting shorter and the air held a noticeable chill. Brian had been surprised when they had found a fresh fingerprint that might indeed help Olivia prove her innocence. The evidence against Olivia was rock solid, and even though he never said it, Brian sensed Stephen Vine was growing more concerned each day. Brian and Stephen had both been surprised when the computer expert hadn't been able to say definitively that someone else had opened the American Express card in Olivia's name.

Yet the morning session with the fingerprint team had given them a solid lead. Even though the results weren't ready yet, there was no denying that someone had entered Olivia's house through the study window. And they had found five matching prints on the interior of the window, indicating by their position that someone had climbed inside. Unfortunately, no unusual fingerprints were found in Olivia's closet – where the cell phone and purse were recovered – but that simply meant that their perpetrator had put gloves on or had remembered to wipe them away.

169

It didn't take a psychology degree to see that Olivia was two steps away from a complete and utter breakdown. When Brian had first met Olivia, he was surprised at the calm way she viewed her situation. Most people accused of murder would be distraught, overwhelmed, and completely unable to function. Olivia Sinclair had rallied with a steely determination that Brian had found impressive. He hadn't doubted for a second that she wouldn't give up until she had found out who killed Sandy Watson and cleared her name.

Today he had come to the realization that Olivia's sangfroid was an act, a fragile protective shield held in place by an ever-weakening thread. Today that thread had snapped. Today he had understood her struggle. She reminded him of a wild bird in a cage, helpless and at the whim of something over which she had no control.

Stephen Vine had been dismissive when Brian mentioned his concerns.

"She'll be okay, Brian. Once we get a handle on the evidence and I tell her my plan, she'll rest easy. She didn't do it. I'm going to get her off." He patted Brian's shoulder, one of those hail-fellow-well-met gestures that was so out of character Brian nearly laughed out loud. When Stephen noticed the skepticism on Brian's face, he said, "I'm going to get an acquittal. Don't you doubt that for one minute."

Brian pointed his car towards home. All he wanted to do was sit in his newly organized kitchen, eat a bologna and cheese sandwich, and think about Maureen.

Distracted by his thoughts, Brian didn't notice the furls of black smoke climbing into the air near his house until a fire truck with its sirens blaring roared up behind him. He pulled over to let it go by, surprised when it turned onto his street. He followed the fire truck, only to be held up by barricades and a gaggle of onlookers standing by. Two young police officers – they all looked young to Brian nowadays – walked up to his car.

"What's going on?"

One of the officers, a kid with blond hair and intelligent blue eyes, leaned toward him. The young man's mouth moved, but Brian couldn't hear the words. In his mind's eye, he calculated the relationship between the curling tower of smoke and his house. He pulled his car over in front of the barricade, got out, and started to walk around it. The officers approached him. One of them grabbed his arm.

"You need to wait here, sir," the officer said.

Brian shook loose from his grasp and stepped away holding his hands up, as if in surrender. "My house is number 642. Where's the fire?"

The two officers looked at each other. The taller one once again stepped close to Brian.

"Is the fire at 642?" Brian shouted.

"It is, sir. Let me call the chief . . ."

Brian reached into his pocket and tossed his keys to the officer who had moved close to him. "Here are my keys in case you need to move the car." As the officer caught the keys, Brian jumped over the barricade and took off at a run, towards the smoke and the sirens and the chaos. Ignoring the officers shouting for him to come back and the biting cramp in his side, he sprinted and didn't stop running until he reached the crowd that had gathered near his house. He pushed through the wall of people until he had a clear view of the inferno that raged inside. Unable to do anything, he stood, numb, as the hot hungry monster hell-bent on destruction ravaged Maureen's house.

A crew of firemen watered down the roofs of the houses on either side in an effort to prevent the fire from spreading. His neighbors had gathered around, mostly people who had moved into the neighborhood within the last ten years or so. He didn't know any of them. Not a single soul. Brian stood helpless as the windows in the front of the house exploded in rapid succession raining shards of glass. The noise of the fire was deafening.

Unable to do anything else, Brian watched, helpless, as his life with Maureen went up in flames.

He must have stood for a good hour, his fists clenched so tight that his fingernails dug into his palms, impervious to the dark clouds that had formed. When they opened and the sky delivered a torrent of rain, Brian wondered if Maureen had seen the fire, if her ghost had had made the heavens open. Soon the fire was under control and Justin Branson, the fire marshal, made his way over to Brian. Justin was three years younger than Brian. He had gone to Redwood High and had been an all-star water polo player. Now he looked wary.

"Justin." They shook hands. He thought maybe he should say something, ask a question, but he couldn't. Try as he might, Brian couldn't string a sentence together if he had to. "I don't know – Maureen – I need to get inside. See if there's anything left."

He must have walked toward the house because Justin put a strong hand on his arm, holding him back. "You know I can't let you go in there. Come sit in my car with me, okay? We can talk."

Brian followed Justin to his car. Where was Mrs. Winkle? Visiting her grandkids? He felt wet tears run down his cheeks and was so surprised that he touched them, examining his fingers.

"I'm right here," Justin said, pointing to a red SUV.

Once they were in the car, Justin turned on the ignition and blasted the heater. Brian realized that his hands were numb and his ears tingled from the cold. Justin pulled a dented Thermos from the back seat. He reached into his glove box and took out an extra plastic cup, which he filled with coffee and handed to Brian. "Drink that."

Brian sipped the coffee. All he tasted was smoke.

"This fire was no accident, Brian." Justin looked straight ahead as he broke this news, as if he wanted to give Brian his privacy.

"My life with Maureen—" Brian's voice caught as he bit back the tears.

"Hey, buddy, it's okay," Justin put his hand out, as if to pat

172

Brian on the shoulder, but pulled it back at the last minute, clearly uncomfortable with the display of emotion. After a few minutes Justin said, "Do you know anyone who would want to burn your house down?"

"I'm working with Stephen Vine's office defending a woman – Olivia Sinclair – who's been accused of murder. I have a feeling this arson is tied to our case. Someone framed Olivia for murder and she is hell-bent on finding out who. We've discovered that the murder Olivia is charged with is tied to a cold case that I worked on before I retired. But I don't know why someone would burn my house down." *Unless they thought I had evidence about the Janelle Maycott case inside.* Overcome with a desire to get out of this car and away from the smoking wreckage of his house, Brian wiped his eyes and opened the door. "You have my cell. Call me if you need me."

Brian walked towards his car, not sure where to go or what to do with himself. He knew one thing for certain. He would find the person who had destroyed his memories of Maureen, and he would make that person pay.

# Chapter 23

*Wednesday, October 22*

Olivia awoke from her nap to the sound of rain pelting on the roof and a car pulling up in front of her house, her pillow still damp from her tears. Through the approaching darkness she saw the last of the journos encamped across the street had left, either to flee the cold rain or to follow the forensic team, ever searching for something new and sensational about the case. *Good riddance.* Between bouts of reviewing evidence she had taken to wandering aimlessly around the house, not quite sure what to do with herself. She went into the kitchen and poured herself a glass of water.

Through the pounding rain she saw Brian Vickery sitting in his car, his forehead resting on the steering wheel. From the safety of her dark kitchen, she continued to watch until he finally got out of the car and headed towards the front door. He hurried through the rain, but his gait was clumsy, as though his back hurt. Pulling the shades down, Olivia turned on the kitchen lights and hurried to let him in. Something was wrong. When she opened the door, Brian Vickery stood before her, smelling of smoke and ashes.

"Brian?"

When he met Olivia's eyes, she saw a devastation there that twisted in her heart.

"Somebody burned my house down. I didn't have anywhere else to go . . . "

"Come in." Olivia stepped aside and once Brian entered she locked the door and threw the deadbolt. "I've got plenty of room. Richard's study downstairs has a fold-out sofa. You'll have privacy down there."

"Thank you, Olivia. I smell of smoke. Any chance of a quick shower?"

"Of course. Everything you need is downstairs. And you can borrow some of Richard's clothes until you get something new."

"I feel a little awkward borrowing your husband's clothes."

"Okay. You can borrow my bathrobe while you wash your clothes," Olivia countered. "It's pink and fluffy and might just fit." The idea of Brian Vickery in her pink fluffy bathrobe made Olivia smile.

"Point taken. I'll borrow some sweat pants, if that's okay, just until mine are clean."

Olivia led Brian downstairs, showed him the washer and dryer, and got him situated with a pair Richard's old sweats and fresh linens for the fold-out sofa. She left him to shower, with the promise of leftover spaghetti and a glass of red wine. Was it a coincidence that someone burned down Brian's house after he started investigating Sandy Watson's murder? These thoughts distracted her to such an extent that she almost didn't notice the dining room lights were on. Certain she had turned them off before her nap, Olivia stood still, trying to quiet her breath. She sensed another heartbeat.

Over the sound of the rain and her hammering heartbeat, she could just make out the sound of footsteps and the shuffle of papers. Someone was in the house, and they were rifling through the documents she had spread out on the dining room table.

Grabbing the fire poker, she rushed into the room, poker raised, ready to strike.

When she saw Richard, she skidded to a stop, nearly falling backwards. He turned to face her, throwing his hands in the air. When he saw the poker in her hand, his face went from surprise to irritation.

"Put that thing down. It's me for crying out loud." He smirked and nodded at the poker. "You think you could overcome a full-grown man with that?"

"How did you get in here?"

"Since I could no longer use my key? I wriggled the bedroom window loose. I told you to fix it, Olivia."

"What do you want, Richard?" Olivia didn't drop the poker.

"I want my things. This is my house, too. There are documents in my study that I need. And I've come for my clothes."

Olivia swung the poker up over her shoulder. "Now isn't a good time. You need to leave. Call me tomorrow and we can make arrangements for you to come back."

Richard laughed. "I don't think so, sweetheart. You don't tell me when I can come into my own house."

"Richard, you need to go. If you don't, I'll call the cops."

"And tell them what? I've come to my own house to get my personal property? You've ruined my career and my reputation. You realize that, don't you?"

His words should have triggered a torrent of rage. Richard had not shown her a scintilla of consideration at the embarrassment of being arrested and the difficulties of being a prisoner in her own home, never mind that she had been accused – and may well be convicted – of a crime she didn't commit, not to mentioned the cheating . . . But the rage didn't come. Olivia didn't have the energy for any more emotion.

"I want you to leave."

"Too bad. My God, when did you become so selfish?"

"I know about you and Janelle Maycott," she replied. "So do

the police. I found a picture of you together. Did you kill those girls, Richard? Tell me, you son of a bitch, did you kill those girls? Did they get in your way, threaten to ruin your reputation? Inconvenience you?"

For the first time Olivia saw behind Richard's mask. Gone was the charm and soulful earnest concern that had been her husband's trademark. If the eyes were the window to the soul, Olivia realized – for the first time in her decades-long marriage – her husband didn't have one. All Olivia saw was emptiness and anger. In one step Richard overpowered her and took the poker out of her hand. She tried to move away from him, but he grabbed her by the wrist, pulling her against his body, rendering her helpless.

"You're hurting me," she cried out, surprised at Richard's violence.

"I'm going to get my things. Do you understand?" He wrenched her tighter against him. A sharp shooting pain shot up her arm into her shoulder.

She nodded, helpless to do anything else. When he let go, he gave her a push, which sent her sprawling just as Brian Vickery, hair wet from his shower and dressed in Richard's sweatpants, stepped into the room.

"Did you just push her?" he asked incredulously, his voice tinged with surprised indignation. "Did he push you, Olivia?"

Olivia's heart pounded as she stared up at Brian, surprised at the quiet menace in his tone. Richard stood with his hands clenched into fists. Olivia wondered at the violence she saw there.

Brian held out his hand and pulled Olivia to her feet. "Are you all right?"

She nodded.

"This is my house too, Olivia. You know as well as I do that California is a community property state," Richard said. He chuckled, a low throaty sound that infuriated her. He crossed his arms over his chest and cocked his head at Olivia, a condescending smile on his face. "You really want to fight me?" Richard turned to face Brian, as if seeing him for the first time. "Who the hell are you?"

"You should go." Brian positioned himself between Olivia and Richard.

Richard gave Brian the same self-righteous smirk he gave Olivia. "You know those are my clothes, right? You're in my house. How about I strip you naked and throw you out on your ass?"

Olivia watched, goggle-eyed, as Richard stepped towards Brian and tried to push him. In one fluid motion, Brian had Richard pinned against the wall, his arm twisted behind his back at an angle that had to be painful. When Brian spoke, his voice had an edge to it that gave Olivia pause. "I'm going to walk you out the door now. You're going to get in your car and drive away. Understand? Because here's the thing. Someone burned my house down today. I'm not in a very good mood. If you so much as look at your wife, I'm going to enjoy beating the shit out of you. Got it?"

Richard nodded. Brian let his arm go.

Richard turned to Olivia and said, "I'll be back for my clothes and my wine."

"No," Olivia said. "You're not to come back here. Not ever. I'll send your things to you at the studio."

Richard started to respond, but Brian interrupted. "Goodbye, Mr. Sinclair."

The minute Brian was back inside, Olivia locked the front door.

"Do you think he'll come back?" Brian asked.

"I have no idea."

"Did he hurt you?"

"My shoulder hurts where he wrenched it." Adrenaline coursed through Olivia's body, fueling her anger at Richard. "He's never been violent before."

"He's desperate," Brian said.

Olivia sat on the couch, more upset than she cared to let on, while Brian fiddled around in the kitchen. With a shaking hand, she took the glass of wine Brian handed her.

When Brian sat next to her, Olivia felt the connection between them. She wondered if he felt it too. How easy it would be to lean into Brian now, let her body rest against his. But she didn't want to burden him with her emotional baggage, not after he had suffered such a loss. She sat back on the couch, relieved that the necessary confrontation with Richard was behind her now. She'd draw up divorce papers. All she wanted was her house. Of course, he'd hedge and try to intimidate her, but in the end, he would sign. "I'm going to put his belongings in garbage bags, and drink his wine cellar."

"And I'm not going to lecture you about vengeance," Brian said.

"I'm so sorry about your house, Brian. Do you think it has to do with my case?"

"It could very well," Brian said.

"That confrontation needed to happen. I needed to stand up to Richard, let him know he doesn't control me. I've never seen him so violent, so without feeling. Maybe he's always been that way, and I was too blind to see it." She closed her eyes, hoping to stave off the headache that threatened. "I think of all the things I didn't do because I was waiting to do them with Richard. I've wasted most of my adult life on that man."

"Best not think that way."

Overcome with a sudden wave of longing, Olivia thought of Denny, the one good thing in her life. She missed her daughter so much it hurt.

"When this is behind you, you can start over. Do the things you've wanted to do." Brian refilled their glasses. "I didn't plan on losing Maureen. Twenty-five years of my life were spent working when I could have been with her. We were so happy, you know? We scrimped and saved so I could retire. We were going to travel . . . " He shook his head.

"She was really strong, spiritually I mean. So tough during the chemo. I think I knew somewhere deep inside that I was going to lose her. I took early retirement when the treatments didn't work as well as we hoped. I wanted to be with her, to take care of her." Brian set his fork down. He didn't meet Olivia's eyes and he continued with his sad tale. "I nursed her myself. I bathed her and fed her and gave her medicine. She had a port on her chest for chemo, and I took care of that. She called it my tragic labor of love."

"Oh, Brian, I'm so sorry for your loss," Olivia said. She couldn't help but compare Brian to Richard, realizing for the first time the kindness that had been missing in her own marriage.

Brian's involvement with her case had brought about the destruction of the home he had shared with the wife he loved. The burden for his latest loss lay with Olivia. She would somehow have to find a way to make things right with him.

*

Olivia woke up on the morning after her confrontation with Richard despondent and feeling sorry for herself. She tried to shake off the dark cloud that seemed to follow her. She knew she needed to get back to the tedium of reviewing documents so she could find the link between Janelle Maycott and Sandy Watson. As she showered and dressed, she thought about the boxes received from Alana Maycott that she had yet to go through and found she had little motivation to do anything.

Brian had already left the house, but he had left her a carafe of coffee. Olivia had just poured a cup for herself when Lauren came walking up the path, dressed in hiking boots, looking like Medusa with her hair in a mass of tangled curls. When Olivia opened the door, Lauren stared for a moment.

"Something's different. What happened?"

Olivia poured Lauren coffee. "I had it out with Richard yesterday. He came by the house unannounced to get his things. I told him to call first. He didn't like it."

Lauren sipped her coffee. "So the rose-colored glasses are off at last?"

"You should have seen him, Lauren. He was violent. I hardly recognized him." Olivia sipped her coffee. "I need to talk to you about something."

Lauren watched Olivia over the rim of her glass. "Your tone of voice is making me nervous."

"I need to make plans in case I wind up in prison."

"Oh, God, Olivia. Please don't say that. You're not going to prison."

Olivia shook her head. "Juries can be fickle. I'm going to plan for the worst-case scenario. I am asking you, as my best friend, to manage my assets in the event I am unable to do so. I'll set everything up to make it easy, but I need to protect Denny. I don't want that husband of hers commandeering everything I've worked for. Denny and David aren't doing well. They're going to wind up divorced. I can feel it my bones. I want her to have a place to go when that happens. And if I wind up in prison, I'll probably need money . . . I don't know. But when I find out, I'd like you to help me."

Lauren's eyes shimmered with unshed tears. Worry lines tugged at the corners of her mouth. "I can't believe we are having this conversation."

"Hopefully it won't be an issue. But I would be remiss if I didn't make some sort of plan." Lauren listened raptly while Olivia told her about Brian Vickery, the Janelle Maycott murder, and how they were hedging their defense on finding a connection between the two women. "The evidence against me is damning. Stephen's experts can't find any evidence that I'm being set up. Whoever framed me for this murder did a very expert and thorough job. And Brian's house. Burned to the ground. It's all my fault."

"Are you telling me that fire yesterday was your investigator's house burning down? And that the arson could be connected to your case?"

"It's a possibility," Olivia said.

"You could write a book about this," Lauren said. "I'm serious, Liv. I couldn't make up a story like this if I tried. Aren't you frightened? Do you think whoever burned down this guy's house could come after you?"

"I can't think like that, especially since I'm trapped at the moment. Richard's at the root of this, I can feel it in my bones."

"Richard's a self-absorbed ass, but I don't think he'd kill someone. Do you think he's capable of murder?"

"I don't know. You should have seen him yesterday."

"Olivia, listen to me. I know you're scared. God knows, I would be too. But you need to pull yourself together. You're innocent. You need to prove it. Figure out what you need to do and get your lawyer and your investigator to do their jobs. You are not going to prison. And that's final."

Olivia looked at the boxes stacked in the corner of the room. Her mind flashed on Richard, and the smirk on his face when she picked up the poker. She had lost everything she treasured, her husband, her daughter, her job, and potentially her freedom. The only thing Olivia knew for certain was that she was innocent. Lauren was right.

"I know you like to be in control, Olivia. You like things to go according to plan, to fit into their box. Life isn't like that. Your relationship with Richard has proven that you can't control those around you. Once you find out the truth, you can repair the relationships that you care about. I understand you feel defeated, but you need to get out of this maudlin state of mind and get back to work."

They walked to the door. "Thanks, Lauren."

"Go find your evidence, Liv. Save yourself," Lauren said before she turned and walked away.

# Chapter 24

*Thursday, October 23*

After the previous day's confrontation with Jonas Greensboro, Sharon had spent her workday locked in her office, sending a message to all and sundry that she did not want to be disturbed. The rope analysis had come back with confirmation that the rope found at the scene of the Sandy Watson murder was an exact match to the rope from the Janelle Maycott murder. Sharon sighed, trying to ignore that frisson of doubt in the back of her mind, that feeling that something important was right under her nose but she was too stupid to see it. She picked up the dossier Ellie had prepared on Olivia Sinclair and read it for the second time.

Olivia had been born into a fourth-generation Marin family. Her father taught political science at College of Marin until he died suddenly of a heart attack at age sixty-three. Her mother was an accountant and had passed away four years ago.

Young Olivia had an aptitude for math and science and did well in school. Her parents expected her to become a doctor, but Olivia surprised everyone and opted for law school instead. She played piano and was enthusiastic about the arts. Over the years, Olivia had been interviewed by various newspapers, had won awards, and had been honored by her peers for her outstanding work. She donated selflessly to the local abused women's shelter, and had hosted her share of fundraisers for its benefit. Her law practice was small, her client list exclusive. A handful of discreet phone calls to Sharon's attorney friends revealed Olivia's reputation as a hardworking litigator, who often represented the underdog spouse and worked to get them their equitable distribution of the marital assets.

If Olivia Sinclair had committed a murder, she'd toss the evidence, hide it so no one would find it. The woman wasn't stupid. If she put her mind to murdering someone, she'd cover her tracks. Sharon's gut instinct had reared its head and wouldn't leave her alone. This wasn't the first time Sharon had experienced a sensation like this. Under normal circumstances, she would try not to overthink and let her subconscious mind do its thing. But time was of the essence now. Once Sharon was off the Sinclair case, she would be hard pressed to do any follow-up work, but she knew this unresolved issue would bug her until she figured out what it was.

When her phone rang, Sharon reached for it, welcoming the distraction. "Inspector Bailey."

"Boss, I didn't want to barge in there, but Wendy Betters is here. She wants to speak with you."

Sharon sighed and looked at her watch. It was three-thirty and she had skipped lunch. "Okay. I'll be out in a minute. Can you put her in one of the interrogation rooms?"

"Okay. Should I record?"

"May as well. And I wouldn't mind you listening in, maybe standing behind the glass. Pay attention to her body language."

"Will do."

Sharon found Wendy Betters seated at a table, a manila envelope on the table in front of her. When Sharon walked into the room she gave her a smile that seemed genuine. "I feel like I'm about to be interrogated."

184

"Sorry about that." Sharon sat down opposite Wendy. "We really don't have any place else to meet."

"I understand." Wendy pushed the envelope towards Sharon. "I found something that I think you should know. Neither Andrew nor Richard know I'm here, so I'd appreciate it if you could not tell them how you came across this information."

Sharon's heartbeat quickened as she reached for the envelope. Inside were computer printouts of statements from the Bank of the Caymans. The name on the account was Rincon Sinclair Investments. At first glance Sharon saw the account had a whopping $3 million on deposit.

"What are these printouts?"

"Our firm doesn't have a traditional 401(k) retirement account. Instead, Andrew and Richard agreed to fund this investment account when they first opened Rincon Sinclair. Each year the firm puts $150,000 into a stock account, which I manage. I have an eye for new companies and my strategy has been to invest short-term and cash out when I hit a certain percentage on return. When I cash out, the funds are transferred to this account in the Caymans. It's an unorthodox way of playing the market, but it's worked for us."

"And why are you telling me this?" Sharon asked.

"Because someone – I think it was Andrew – helped themselves to $1 million out of the fund." She pushed a strand of hair behind her ear. "Andrew and Richard each own forty percent of this account. Twenty percent belongs to me. All the paperwork is there." She tapped the envelope. "I don't know if it has anything to do with the murders, but I thought you should know. I have an interest here."

"Okay. Is there anything else you can share?"

Wendy stood. "No, that's it."

Sharon stood too. "Can I keep these statements?"

"Yes. Again, I'd appreciate it if you didn't tell Andrew and Richard you got this information from me."

185

"I can't make any promises about that, but I'll try."

"Thanks," Wendy said.

Sharon followed Wendy outside the interrogation room. She called to one of the uniformed officers and said, "Would you please show Miss Betters out?" Once Wendy was gone, Ellie joined Sharon. They watched as Wendy Betters walked away.

"Well, Ellie, what do you think?"

"I don't think Andrew Rincon murdered that girl," Ellie said. "It's just my gut. I could be wrong. Richard Sinclair is the one who renewed the passport. Richard Sinclair is one sleeps with every woman who crosses his path."

"Have someone put eyes on Richard Sinclair."

With a nod to Sharon, she hurried off.

Sharon tucked the bank statements under her arm and made her way to Captain Wasniki's office. She took the elevator to the executive floor. Megan was away from her desk, so she let herself in. "Boss? A word?"

"Have a seat. One second." Captain Wasniki didn't look up. He had a spreadsheet open on his computer and was copying down figures on the latest budget. Once he was finished, he turned the paperwork over and gave Sharon his full attention.

"You've got that look on your face. What's happened?"

"I don't know what you're talking about."

"The look that says your intuition is telling you we've screwed something up, someone else screwed something up, or we've arrested the wrong person. Go ahead, tell me. After dealing with budgets all afternoon, I can take it."

"I don't think Olivia Sinclair killed Janelle Maycott or Sandy Watson," Sharon blurted.

Captain Wasniki threw his pen down. "Jonas Greensboro has this case locked down. He has enough evidence for a conviction, and I'm pretty sure at this point he has zero interest in your intuition. Admit it, Sharon, the evidence against Olivia is pretty damning."

186

"Something's wrong. And Olivia wouldn't be so stupid as to keep Sandy's phone and purse in her closet. Nor would she rent the place she intended to murder someone with her own credit card. Another thing that bothers me, there's no doubt that Olivia received the video after the murder. So she didn't have a motive at the time the murder was committed. Wendy Betters just stopped in to tell me that the Rincon Sinclair bank account has been looted. She thinks Andrew did it and he's going to run."

"Andrew Rincon?" Captain Wasniki stared at her. Sharon tossed the envelope on his desk and sat down across from him. "Everything's in there. I have to follow this up. Can I just have another week?"

"What about Richard Sinclair's alibi?"

"I know. But something's not right."

"You have until Monday. After that, we'll turn this evidence over to Jonas. He has a team of investigators who can deal with it and you and Ellie are going back into the rota. There are other cases that need your attention. Understand?" Wasniki said.

"Thank you." Sharon stood.

Sharon was just about to leave when Megan knocked and entered. "Boss, the Larkspur Fire Marshall just called. There's been a fire connected to the Sinclair case." Megan looked at the message. "Someone torched the house belonging to Stephen Vine's investigator."

# Chapter 25

Richard drove down California Street, thinking that today would be the last day he would venture into the office space that had been his home for the past twenty-five years. He expected to sign his name, receive his share of the investment account, and be on his way. Inspector Bailey's warning not to leave town bothered him. So did the picture of Janelle Maycott and him that he saw on Olivia's dining table. Did the police have that picture? The last thing Richard needed was more attention from the police. In an abundance of caution, he thought he'd hire a lawyer so he could at least have someone on standby, someone ready to sort out any messes without too much bother to Richard.

As he pulled into the parking lot under his building, he allowed himself a momentary reflection of pride. He had plenty of money socked away. After today, he could do anything he wanted.

Sitting in his car, Richard called Frank Johnson, one of the best criminal defense attorneys in the city. Frank took his call, of course, and after Richard explained the situation about the two murdered girls, his relationship with Sandy Watson, and the photo that could connect him to Janelle Maycott, Frank agreed to meet with Richard at eleven o'clock. If he played his cards right, he'd be on the road by noon.

"You're smart to be cautious," Frank had said.

"Thanks, Frank. See you in a couple of hours."

As he rode the elevator to his office, Richard congratulated himself on hiring Frank. Feeling once again like he owned the world, he stepped into the office of Rincon Sinclair for the last time. Soon he would be done with Andrew and his unpredictable tirades. He was even tired of doe-eyed, loyal Wendy.

To Richard's surprise, everyone was waiting for him in the conference room. Boxes were stacked into neat piles, waiting for the microfilm people to come. Wendy gave him a startled look. *Something's wrong. Damn it.* Andrew sat with his back towards Richard, but there was something about the set of his shoulders that gave Richard pause. For the briefest moment, he thought about turning around and leaving, blowing off the meeting entirely, but his ego put that thought aside. Richard Sinclair didn't run away from anyone, especially Andrew Rincon.

"Good morning." Richard forced a smile as he stepped into the conference room.

Andrew whipped around and flashed Richard a look so full of violent hatred that Richard recoiled and stepped back without thinking. Andrew stood, his hands clamped into two meaty fists. He rushed toward Richard, who in turn hurried around to the far side of the conference table and wheeled one of the high-backed chairs between them, effectuating a barrier. Andrew took a breath, shook his head, and stepped away.

"What the hell did you do with it?"

"It?" Richard had no idea what Andrew was talking about.

"I've called the police. They're on their way. If you put the money back, I won't press charges. I'm giving you an out. I suggest you take it."

"What are you talking about? What money?" Richard asked.

"Don't you play me for a fool." Wendy, eyes wide and face

189

noticeably pale, flinched as Andrew roared at Richard. "You cleaned out the investment account and transferred the proceeds to an account in the Cayman Islands. I was able to trace it, you stupid ass." Andrew paced back and forth, while Wendy looked down at her hands, an uncomfortable witness in this drama.

"You're being ridiculous, Andrew. You know damn well I didn't steal money from this firm. I would never do that."

Andrew tore open a manila envelope that had sat on the table. With shaking hands he pulled out a stack of papers and threw them at Richard, who caught them before they went flying. "Your signature is right there in black and white, you son of a bitch." Richard was surprised to see unshed tears shimmering in Andrew's eyes. "I've trusted you all these years, Richard. Did you take other money too?" Andrew shook his head. "Never mind. I don't want to know." He took out a handkerchief and wiped his eyes. "What is your intention? Are you going to make me press charges?"

"I don't have any money to give back," Richard said, managing somehow to keep his voice calm and steady. "As God is my witness, Andrew, I swear I didn't steal from our firm. I came here to sign documents and get money."

Richard thumbed through the documents. Andrew was right. There in black and white was his signature agreeing to the transfer of the entire proceeds of the Rincon Sinclair investment account to an account on Grand Cayman. The first transfer was made several days earlier, but the account had been cleaned out as of this morning at 5:30 a.m. Richard tossed the sheets of paper down on the table.

Knowing there was no reaching Andrew through his fury, he spoke to Wendy. "I swear to God, I didn't do this. Can you help me find out who did?"

"No, she can't," Andrew said. "She is an employee of this firm and I am going to forbid her to be involved with you. The police will be here any minute. We'll let them sort this out."

With one fell swoop, Andrew knocked the coffee pot, the cups, and the food onto the conference room floor. He stormed out of the room, slamming the door to his office. Richard turned to Wendy. "I swear to God, I didn't do this. Do you believe me?" A hint of disbelief washed over Wendy. Gone in an instant. "You think I'm capable of stealing from Andrew?"

"Of course, I don't. But the evidence is pretty damning," Wendy said, not meeting Richard's eyes.

Richard knew how these things worked. Once the police were involved he would likely be arrested. He needed to lay low until he met with Frank. Without a word, Richard hurried to the elevator, Wendy on his heels.

"Where are you going?"

"To meet my lawyer. After that, I'm going to find out what the hell is going on around here," Richard said. Wendy got on the elevator with him and followed him to his car. Just as he opened his car door, Wendy grabbed his arm and looked at him with pleading eyes.

"Wait. Think about what you're doing. If you go on the run, the police will start looking for you. Andrew has called them. He's going to file a report. You need to be careful right now."

"I wish I could say thank you for believing in me, Wendy." He didn't give voice to the insults that would have reduced her to tears.

"Richard, stop it. It's not that I don't believe you. You have to admit the evidence is pretty damning." Wendy stepped close to Richard. "Look at me, Richard. Look at me in the eyes and tell me you didn't make that wire transfer. Make me believe you."

Richard sighed. He met Wendy's eyes and said, "You know damn well I didn't steal from this firm."

Wendy nodded. "Okay. The bank has to have phone records or some proof of who did this. Let me call them and speak to one of my contacts. I've made a few friends there over the years."

"I'd appreciate that."

Richard had had enough of Wendy. He jumped in his car and pulled out of the parking garage just as two police cars stopped in front of the building. Through his rearview mirror, Richard watched the officers get out and head into the lobby.

*Close call.*

# Chapter 26

*Friday, October 24*

The smell of smoke and destruction hung in the cool October morning as Brian walked down the driveway towards the burnt-out shell of rubble that was once his home. His eyes roamed the property, taking in the wasted and bedraggled garden and the ruined house. One lone five-gallon bucket Maureen had used to water their tomatoes had survived the inferno. Other than that, utter destruction reigned. Everything that Brian held dear was gone.

"Morning, Brian," Justin said. "I figured I'd find you here. I wanted to let you know that we've shared our information about the fire with your old partner at the SFPD."

"Have you found out anything?"

"It was started with an accelerant – no surprise there. A witness has come forward with a promising lead. She saw a young man – juvenile delinquent, were the words she used to describe him – lurking around your house with a can of gas."

"I need to speak to this witness," Brian said. "Please, Justin. I'm asking as a friend."

Justin looked at Brian with sad eyes. "You need to step away. I can't let you get involved. Surely you can see that."

In the old days, Brian's neighbor would have come straight to him with that nugget of information. In the old days he and Maureen had known all of their neighbors. But the old families had cashed in, sold their houses for incomprehensible sums of money, and moved someplace without high taxes and commuter traffic.

"Okay. Well, that's all I wanted to tell you. You know where to find me if you need my help with your insurance claim. I should have a report ready in a couple of days. Do you have a place to stay?"

"Yes, I'm fine," Brian said. The two shook hands and soon Brian was once again alone, among the ashes and his memories of Maureen.

After Justin's car pulled away, Brian grabbed the bucket, turned it over and sat on it, eager to be alone with his thoughts. He heard the crunching of footsteps behind him and turned to see Sharon Bailey approaching.

"Brian?" Her voice was tentative. "I was hoping I'd find you here. I'm not supposed to share this, but you should know that we are operating on the assumption that this fire is tied into the Sandy Watson and Janelle Maycott murders. We'll find out who did this. Maybe we'll even be able to solve the murder because of it."

"I didn't realize there was so much inter-departmental cooperation these days," Brian said.

Sharon flashed him a look.

"I'm sorry. I shouldn't have said that." Brian stood and kicked the bucket he was sitting on away. "She didn't kill anyone."

"I know."

Surprised at her response, Brian met Sharon's eyes and saw the fatigue there.

Sharon added, "I'm starting to think that way too. I shared my feelings with Captain Wasniki, and he's given me four more days."

194

"What made you change your mind?"

Sharon shook her head. "I can't, Brian. I'm sorry. I've told you too much already." She waited a beat before she said, "Why didn't you take my calls after Maureen died? I wasn't trying to pester you. Just thought you could use a friend."

"You should go," he said.

"I'm not going anywhere, Brian. You never called me back. I'm not sure why, but that doesn't matter. You and I have too much history. We were partners for over ten years. I thought we were friends. Maureen was my friend, too. She shouldn't have died. You've every right to feel cheated, and I've no idea what hell her death must have been for you. That doesn't explain why you shut me out."

Brian wanted to shout at Sharon, but he realized the anger he felt wasn't directed at her. He was angry at the world, at God, at the universe. In an instant he knew there was nothing to be done about it. His wife was gone. His house was gone. But that didn't mean he would forget Maureen. He'd never forget her. If he closed his eyes, he could remember how she smelled, he could conjure the feel of her arms around him. That was something he could keep.

He looked at Sharon. "You're a pain in the ass, Bailey. You know that?"

"Yes, sir, I do." Sharon was focused on her cell phone.

Brian's cell phone vibrated as the pictures started coming from Sharon. The first one was taken when Maureen and Sharon had won the three-legged race at the policeman's picnic. The Maureen in Sharon's pictures was young and healthy and full of life. His heart swelled. Brian stared at the picture for a long time, remembering the day as though it had just happened. Another picture popped in, this one of Brian and Maureen, with Maureen standing on her tiptoes kissing Brian's cheek.

"Shit," he said as he wiped at his eyes.

"I need to go. I've got tons of these and will get them all to you, okay? We won't forget her, Brian." Sharon squeezed Brian's arm before she turned to head back up the driveway.

"Thank you." Brian's voice was thick with emotion. And gratitude.

# Chapter 27

Richard left Frank Johnson's office at 1:00 p.m. on the nose. The attorney had gladly taken Richard's retainer, but other than that, nothing had gone as planned. When Richard had asked if he could leave town, Frank hadn't minced words.

"You'll look guilty of stealing the funds from the Cayman account, especially in light of the evidence that Andrew has. We need to find out what happened to that money. If you didn't take it, someone did. I'll find out who, don't worry about that. The photos with you and Janelle Maycott and your relationship with Sandy Watson could be an issue. Let me put out some feelers at the SFPD and see what they've got. Once I know what we're dealing with, we can make a plan."

Richard waited while Frank finished handwriting his notes. When he put his pen down, Frank said, "It's strange being on that side of the table, isn't it? All I can tell you is not to worry. Don't mean to sound like I'm bragging, but I am rather good at my job. Keep your cell phone with you. When I know something, I'll call, okay?"

The two men stood and shook hands. Richard stepped outside

of Frank's office onto California Street. He tipped his head back at the skyscrapers, this part of San Francisco that he considered his kingdom, his territory. He longed to slip into one of the obscure bars in the financial district for a burger and a stiff drink. But didn't want to drink alone. Did he?

"Andrew Rincon can go to hell," Richard said out loud. If Andrew wanted to throw around false accusations, Richard would reciprocate in kind. There would be war. A clash of the Titans. Richard would make it his singular obsession to win. Andrew didn't stand a chance. Feeling better now, Richard spotted a bar across the street.

"Richard?"

He turned, startled to find Wendy hurrying after him.

"Wendy?"

"Forgive me, Richard. I followed you. I was worried."

"I just met with Frank Johnson. Have you had lunch?"

Wendy stepped close to Richard and spoke in a whisper. "I've found something that could prove you're innocent. I think Andrew is setting you up. What if Sandy discovered what he was up to? I think he killed her, Richard. And he wants you to take the blame."

"I don't believe it."

"After what he did to you this morning?" Wendy rolled her eyes in irritation. "Okay, fine. You can try to figure this out on your own. Sorry to bother you." She turned on her heels and walked away. Richard went after her.

"Wait. I'm sorry. I overreacted."

"You need to stop reacting at all. You shouldn't have run out of the office, Richard. That wasn't like you."

"Agreed. Now tell me what you've got."

"I searched Andrew's desk and found a list of what I think are passwords, you know, long numbers with the occasional letter. The money that is missing from Rincon Sinclair was transferred to an account in the Caymans, right? If one of these passwords can access that account, we can prove that Andrew is setting you up."

"This changes everything. I need to give this information to my attorney. Right now. Would you mind giving me that list? Or come with me, if you'd like." Richard reached for his phone, but it wasn't in his pocket. Had he left it in his car?

"Of course. But it's on my boat."

"In Sausalito?"

She gave Richard an exasperated look. "Surely you didn't think I'd keep evidence proving Andrew is a murderer at the office, did you?"

"Okay. Let's go to your boat. I'm ready for this to be over," Richard said.

"Me too," Wendy said.

# Chapter 28

*Friday, October 24*

Inspired by Lauren's pep talk, Olivia plowed through the rest of the Janelle Maycott murder evidence before turning her attention to the relevant documents regarding Sandy Watson. The only evidence she found connecting the two women was the photo of Richard and Janelle, a double-edged sword in that the picture could cast Olivia in the role of the jealous wife, who had murdered two of her husband's lovers. Sitting cross-legged on the living room floor, she had read through everything twice, but nothing had caught her eye.

Throwing her pen down in frustration, Olivia stood and stretched. As she worked the stiffness out of her knees, her eyes strayed to a picture of herself taken after her first trial. The photo sat in a silver frame on her bookcase, and she hadn't given it a thought in years. Someone had snapped a photo of her walking out of the courtroom, briefcase in one hand, waving at whoever took the picture. She was radiant from her victory, high on adrenaline after a grueling courtroom battle.

Olivia's recent troubles had caused her to forget who she was and what she was made of. This picture of her, fighting strong and victorious, served as a stark reminder of who and what she was. A litigator. A fighter. A wave of determination flooded Olivia. Her freedom was on the line. She was innocent. Who better to find proof of that than herself? Who else would be more motivated for the task? She picked up one of the second round of boxes received from Janelle Maycott's mother. In one fell swoop, she dumped all the photos – there were hundreds – in a pile on the floor.

Two hours later, Olivia had finished sorting. She hadn't found anything yet, but she was still determined to keep going when Brian Vickery came home, carrying a bag of groceries and a bottle of wine.

"I thought maybe I could cook for you tonight," he said. "Are you sure it's okay if I stay? I don't want to put you in an awkward position. And I can get a hotel—"

Olivia set her cup in the sink and helped Brian put the groceries away. "I prefer it, actually. I appreciate the company. You're the only one who doesn't look at me with pity. Did you get things sorted with your insurance?"

"Yes. The claims adjuster seems reasonable."

Olivia shook her head. "I'm so sorry for all of this."

"It's not your fault." Brian washed his hands before he put cloves of garlic on a small cutting board. Using the flat end of the blade, he crushed the garlic before he mixed it with a bit of olive oil. "It's 4:30. Start grilling around six o'clock?"

"Perfect."

"I need to work on my insurance claim. Do you mind if I log on to your Wi-Fi?"

"Of course. You can use Richard's desk. The Wi-Fi password is on a slip of paper in the top drawer. I'm going to finish sorting through this box of pictures and then I'll make us a salad."

Brian followed Olivia into the living room, where the pictures lay scattered about on the floor. "Finding anything?"

"Not yet," Olivia said. "But I've got these to sort through, plus those boxes in the corner."

"I'll leave you to it." He paused for a moment. "Thank you again, Olivia, for letting me stay here."

"It's the least I can do. If it weren't for me, you'd still have a house."

Back in the living room, Olivia sat on the floor and continued to go through Janelle Maycott's life in pictures, taking comfort in Brian's presence. He was so different from Richard, seemingly so gentle and passive, yet so physically strong when Richard tried to threaten him. Although she hadn't known Brian Vickery long, Olivia trusted him. With Richard, she had to worry about keeping up appearances, living up to what Richard deemed *our standards*. There was no stepping away from Richard's self-manufactured rat race.

Olivia remembered one time long ago when Richard had caught her on a Saturday afternoon gardening without makeup. He'd been mortified. "What if someone drops in?" Olivia had brushed off his concern and had continued to garden makeup-free in her grubby jeans. She realized now how telling that little drama had been. If she had seen that behavior in a client, she would have recognized it immediately.

*God, I've been so blind.*

She was thinking about steak and salad and – she was surprised to find – Brian Vickery as she started putting the photos she had looked at back in the box. One photo caught her eye. Actually, she had looked at it before, but hadn't noticed something about the picture that struck her now. Were her eyes playing tricks? She carried it into the kitchen, where the light was better.

*

Brian came upstairs at 5:30. He was just headed into the kitchen, when Olivia stood up, lithe and supple as a schoolgirl, and waved a photo in the air.

"What have you found?"

202

Olivia shook her head. "I'm such an idiot."

"What is it?" Brian asked again.

"Let's go in the kitchen where the light is better."

Brian followed her, pushing away the guilty pleasure he felt when their arms touched as she set a picture down on the island. She pointed to one of the faces. "Do you recognize anyone in this picture?"

Brian studied the photo of Richard, Janelle Maycott, and another woman who looked familiar but whom he couldn't place.

"Picture this woman fourteen years older with dyed blond hair."

"It's Wendy Betters." Brian recognized the woman immediately. The photo depicted Richard in the middle of two young women, his arm around both of them. Janelle Maycott was dressed in a business suit and despite her serious expression, she still managed to look fresh and beautiful and full of life, while Richard posed for the camera. Brian's eyes lingered on Wendy Betters's image. He set the photograph on the table, and covered the images of Janelle and Richard with his hands, leaving Wendy in stark relief. She was the only person in the picture who wasn't looking at the camera. Her body was pressed up against Richard Sinclair's. Her head was tilted back, and although Brian could only see her face in profile, there was no mistaking the adoration in her eyes.

"My God," he said.

"She's in love with him," Olivia said. "I can't believe I didn't see it. God, what a fool I've been. When I had computer trouble last year, Wendy fixed it for me. I gave her my password. She told me to change it afterward, but I didn't. I trusted her. I've always trusted her. Implicitly."

Brian took a screen shot of the photo and texted it to Stephen Vine with a brief explanation. Stephen called back almost immediately. Brian put the call on speaker and explained the situation.

"I was just about to call you both," Stephen replied. "It seems that Richard has stolen funds from Rincon Sinclair and seems to have gone missing. The cops are looking for him. This could bode very well for you, Olivia."

"Richard stole money?" She had a hard time believing that her husband would steal, but reminded herself that a few weeks ago she would never have believed Richard capable of cheating on her either.

"Brian, when we meet we can decide to whom I should take this photo. I have a feeling Jonas will just dismiss it. Let's meet at my office first thing in the morning, okay? We should move on this."

"Sure," Brian said. "What time?"

"Is seven o'clock too early? This could be the break we are looking for."

"See you then," Brian said. After Brian hung up, he found Olivia standing in the living room, gazing out the window, like a bird in a gilded cage. Brian moved towards her.

"What's wrong?" Something made Brian stand close to her, too close.

"I have to call my daughter and tell her that her father has stolen money and run away." She wiped her eyes with the back of her hand as she turned to face him.

"This isn't your fault. Your daughter will see that."

Olivia shook her head. "She'll blame me."

Brian wasn't thinking about Maureen when he opened his arms, and Olivia stepped into them as though it were the most natural thing in the world. His arms engulfed her, pulling her close to him as though he could protect her from all the things that bound them together: murder, arson, her husband's betrayal. They had both suffered, were suffering. This pain bonded them. When she tilted her face up to his, he kissed her.

204

# Chapter 29

*Saturday, October 25. Late morning.*

The clock was ticking for Inspector Bailey. Evidence from both murders and half-drunk cups of coffee lay strewn around her office. Unable to sit any longer, she gathered the coffee cups and tossed them in the garbage. For a moment, she thought about getting even more caffeine, but her better judgment prevailed. Any more coffee and she'd start shaking in her boots. She'd reread the Maycott file. Again. No joy there. Her stomach growled and she was just about to go for food when her phone rang.

"It's Wells from Tech."

"I didn't know you worked on Saturdays," Sharon said.

"We're backlogged, and I'm getting overtime. I have your fingerprint reports from the Sinclair house." Sharon had worked with Welford Bexley for years, and knew that although he was definitely happy working on the evidence analysis side of police work, there were times when he wished he could be out in the field. Over a beer one night, Sharon had teased him, suggesting he watched too much *Law and Order*.

Dared she hope? "Is there a match?"

"Since your case is chock full of lawyers, I ran a comparison to the Cal Bar live scan. Did you know the State Bar just required all lawyers run a live scan? Which means their fingerprints are taken electronically and fed into all statewide databases?"

Sharon knew that attorneys often got DUIs and didn't report the arrest to the bar association, as they were required to, and had wondered over the years if the bar association would ever do something about it. She recalled reading somewhere that the live scan was designed to remedy this situation.

"The handprint – which was surprisingly clean, I might add – belongs to a Wendy Betters."

Sharon made a quick gasp.

"Surprised at that? Good news?"

*Wendy Betters?* Sharon stopped for a moment, replaying the facts of the case in her head, letting everything fall into place, relishing that feeling of knowing. She'd been such a fool. Wendy Betters. Of course. Why hadn't she seen it? Wendy Betters was the jealous lover.

"Sharon?" Wells asked.

"I'm here. Wells, you just blew my case wide open. I owe you a beer. Hell, I'll buy you dinner. Thanks for rushing it through."

"No problem. And I'll take you up on that dinner. You can tell me all about the case."

Rummaging through the folders on her desk, Sharon found the background information Ellie had gathered on Wendy thus far. Ellie walked into the office just as Sharon muttered, "I can't believe I didn't see it sooner. It's Wendy Betters. Her fingerprint is on the outside of the house."

"We have a problem," Ellie said. "Richard Sinclair's gone missing."

"When?"

"Yesterday. Around 2:00 p.m. The team keeping eyes on him followed him to an office on California Street. They were in a car, and when he took off on foot, they lost him."

"And we're just hearing about it now?" Sharon shook off her

anger. "Never mind. Just get him found, please. Upgrade the BOLO to an APB. When you've done that, I want you to drop everything and reach out to the police department in the town where Wendy grew up. If she's killed two people, there's a slight chance she'll have been in trouble with the police as a delinquent. Or at least they might know her and give us something. Meanwhile, I need to update the captain. And, Ellie, have uniforms bring Ms. Betters in for questioning. We can let her sit while we get our ducks in a row." The last thing Sharon wanted was for Wendy Betters to go on the run. "I'll bet she planted the evidence at Olivia's. I wouldn't be surprised if she stole the money from the Rincon Sinclair slush fund. Everyone trusted her," Sharon said.

"Do you think she burned down Brian Vickery's house?" Ellie asked.

Sharon thought of Wendy's petite stature and the description of a juvenile delinquent. "I'd say that's a distinct possibility. Maybe she thought there was evidence there that she didn't want to get out." Leaving Ellie to her task, Sharon hurried to Captain Wasniki's office.

"He's got people in there. It's going to be a while," Megan said.

"Sorry, Megan. I need to talk to him now." She barged into the office, startling Captain Wasniki and the two men. "I'm sorry, sir. But I need to speak to you. Now."

The men stood and shook hands. Once Sharon and Captain Wasniki were alone, Sharon said, "Richard Sinclair is missing. We're looking for him, but that's not why I barged in here. Wendy Betters did it. She killed Janelle Maycott and Sandy Watson. I know it."

"Wendy Betters the attorney?" Captain Wasniki, usually so supportive of Sharon's gut feelings, didn't bother to hide his skepticism.

"The one and only."

"Do you have any evidence to support this theory?"

"I'm sure she's in love with Richard Sinclair. Why else would

207

she stay at his law firm all these years? She was law review at Cal, graduated at the top of her class, and turned down a handful of more lucrative and prestigious jobs to keep working at Rincon Sinclair. She makes good money there, but she could have gone far, had a brilliant career. Why? Because she wanted to be near Richard Sinclair. She loves him. And I didn't see it."

"Evidence, Inspector."

Sharon gave Wasniki a smug smile as she handed him the fingerprint report. "Wendy Betters's handprint is on the wall outside Olivia's house."

"But she was friends with the Sinclairs. Didn't I read in one of the reports that they treated Wendy like family? You need to be prepared for her to explain away her handprint. There could be a legitimate reason why her handprint is on the outside of the house."

"Maybe." Sharon stood. "There'll be other evidence. Now I know where to look, who to focus on, I'll find it."

"Do you think she and Richard Sinclair were working together?"

"Don't think so, but maybe."

"Find out. Keep me posted," Captain Wasniki called to Sharon.

Ellie was at her desk, the phone cradled on her shoulder as she furiously wrote notes. When she saw Sharon, she waved, an excited look on her face. "Thanks, so much, Sergeant. Do you think Mr. Buford would mind speaking to my boss directly? Sharon Bailey. Can you tell him she'll be calling? Okay, great. I'll tell her to call in ten minutes. Appreciate it." Ellie hung up the phone. "You'd better sit down for this."

The desk next to Ellie's was empty. Sharon scooted its chair near Ellie and sat down.

"Wendy Betters grew up near Seattle. Her father was a welder, but his passion was sailing. Apparently Wendy learned to sail at a very early age. Her dad died of a heart attack when Wendy was fifteen years old. When Wendy turned eighteen, her mother died. The guy I spoke to said the cop who investigated the mom's death swore up and down Wendy murdered her mother." Ellie wrote down a name and phone number on a piece of paper and handed it to Sharon. "His name is Willis Buford. Apparently he loves to talk about this case. It's the one he couldn't solve."

"Good work, Ellie. Follow up on the APB, please." Sharon pushed the chair back to the desk next to her. "I'll just go call Mr. Buford."

"Boss," Ellie said before she hurried out the door in a flash.

Sharon refilled her coffee before she shut her office door. Sitting at her desk for a moment, she collected her thoughts and cleared her mind before she dialed the number on the message slip.

"Buford here." Willis Buford had the gruff voice of a street-worn cop. Sharon had images of him sitting in a small house, eating his dinner from a TV tray, not quite sure what to do with himself in retirement.

"Hello. This is Sharon Bailey from the San Francisco Police—"

"Been expecting your call," he said. She heard the rustling of papers and a muffled groan. "Got the file in front of me. Not that I need it. Know what's in it front and back."

Sharon said. "Are you aware of what's been happening here in San Francisco? The murdered girl? A Marin County attorney arrested for the crime?"

"I only know what I've seen in the news."

"Mr. Buford, I think Wendy Betters committed the murder. Anything you can tell me about her would be appreciated. And, of course, held in the strictest confidence."

"How much time you got, ma'am? Because I think the best way to tell this story is to start at the beginning."

Sharon leaned back and put her feet on her desk. "I've got all the time you need, Mr. Buford."

"Wendy and her family lived in a small cottage on Puget Sound. This was before the real estate boom, mind you. The Betters didn't have a lot of money. Bob was a welder. He did all right. When Seattle real estate started to skyrocket, the Betters got offers to sell their cottage every day. But Bob and Milly dug their heels in. Bob and his friends built that house themselves right after he and Milly married. They had memories there, and they weren't selling.

"When Bob died, things became difficult for Milly. Taxes went up, and she had a daughter to raise. But she still refused to sell. She managed to put food on the table and Wendy always had nice clothes. But the car eventually broke down and couldn't be replaced, and it looked like Wendy would have to attend community college in Seattle. She was a good student and had her heart set on going to college in California. Her mom couldn't afford out-of-state tuition, but Wendy was determined.

"Something changed in Wendy when her father died. My son went to school with her and he used to come home with stories. Said she got mean. Bullied other kids. Became withdrawn. We wrote it off as grief. My wife and I reached out to the family, took a basket over with cakes, muffins, coffee, things like that. When we arrived at the house Milly wasn't home. Wendy opened the door, told us in no uncertain terms that they didn't want nor need charity. When she told us to get off her property and never come back, that's when I saw that emptiness in her eyes. You're a cop, so you'll know what I'm talking about. An empty soul, remorseless. My wife just thought the child was suffering due to her circumstances, but I saw something different in Wendy's eyes, a cruelty that shook me. I admit when we left there, I was very worried.

"Bob Betters had a small sailboat. He and Wendy were both big sailors. Milly didn't go with them. She couldn't swim and had no interest in learning. Imagine how surprised we all were when Wendy called in a mayday when her mom went overboard. Somehow she had managed to get Milly out on the boat. How Wendy managed that is a mystery because Milly Betters was scared of the water. Wendy said she was down below and when she came up her mother was gone. The circumstances were made even more suspicious because the day was fine, sunny and clear with calm water. Poor Milly's body didn't wash up until a week later."

"And you think Wendy killed her mother?"

"I am sure of it. Could never prove it. My captain was furious at me for suggesting that Wendy, a young woman who had suffered mightily, could murder anyone. She was just a kid, after all. The coroner ruled the death accidental, but I never believed it. Milly Betters was a good woman. She didn't deserve to die. I defied orders and investigated Wendy anyways. Nearly lost my job over it."

"I imagine there wasn't any evidence to prove Wendy pushed her mom," Sharon said.

"Her story didn't make sense. She said that Milly had on a life jacket, but when Milly's body was found, no life jacket."

"Could that be a result of time in the water?"

"Maybe, but her clothing and shoes were intact. I can tell you this with certainty, Wendy Betters is a sociopath. Always has been. If you pay attention when you're near her, that mask will slip off and you'll see what's underneath. There's that look in the eyes . . . I'm betting you know exactly what I'm talking about. You're a homicide investigator. Wendy Betters is an empty soul. Didn't show a lick of grief when her mom died. She walked around town, not speaking to anyone, with a surly attitude. Most of the folks around here felt sorry for her. Not me. I was glad when she sold up and got out of here. But I had a feeling she'd hurt someone along the road."

"Did you continue to follow Wendy over the years?"

"Tried to. I was hell-bent on finding out the truth. Felt like I owed it to Milly. But I had a heart attack. My doc gave me a choice: walk away from stress or die. I've got grandkids, so I chose to walk away."

"I'm going to get Wendy Betters. That's a promise. I may need to call again, if that's okay? Maybe we could get Milly Betters's case reopened."

"Anything I can do to help, young lady," Willis Buford said. "About time Milly got some justice."

Sharon hung up just in time to intercept Ellie's text.

*Wendy not at Rincon Sinclair. Instructions?*

Sharon texted back: *Does Wendy still have a sailboat?*

Ellie called, rather than texting. "Thought it would be easier to call. Yes, she does. You think maybe she's there?"

"Not sure."

"It's berthed in Sausalito. Want me to check it out?"

"You go to her apartment, if she's not there, come to Sausalito. I'll go to the boat. She did it, Ellie. Be careful. If you see her, don't approach her without backup, understand?"

"Yes, ma'am."

Sharon went back to Captain Wasniki's office and filled him in on her conversation with Willis Buford. "I'm going to Sausalito to see if she's at her boat. Can you inform the Sausalito PD and get me some backup? Don't want to step on toes."

Captain Wasniki reached for the phone. "Report in when you get there, okay? Don't do anything by yourself."

Sharon hurried out of the office, that familiar thrum of excitement pulsing through her veins.

# Chapter 30

*Saturday, October 25*

Brian Vickery's stolen kiss was the first thing Olivia thought of when she awoke.

The jolt of pleasure at his touch had surprised her, but the comfort she felt took her aback. The few seconds she let herself go, surrendered to the feeling of being kissed, being safe, had been lovely. But they had caught themselves and had laughed away the awkwardness and carried on as if nothing happened. There had been a lot of stolen glances during the evening, and Olivia admitted to a little regret that they had laughed off the connection. When the phone rang, Olivia was pleased like a teenager with a crush to see that it was Brian who called.

"Hey, Brian."

"Good morning. I just wanted to check in and see what you were up to."

"I'm going to look into Wendy's background. Don't worry. I won't do anything foolish, but I am going to see what I can find out about her."

Brian was silent on the other end. Finally he said, "Call me or Stephen and let us know what you find out."

"What's Stephen doing?"

"He's calling Jonas Greensboro. We're going to turn the picture over to him, so the police can investigate."

"Why didn't you just give it to Sharon? She was your partner."

"Not my call. Stephen has his reasons."

"Fair enough."

Glad for something to do, Olivia set off down the research rabbit hole. She knew that Wendy grew up in Seattle, near Puget Sound. Other than that, Wendy had always been tacit about her childhood and personal life. Olivia assumed it was painful, so she had never pushed for details. Backtracking, Olivia reckoned Wendy graduated from high school in 1995. Looking online, she discovered the *Seattle Intelligencer* had digital archives going back to 1992, which were available with a digital subscription. Olivia subscribed and began searching by entering Wendy's name. No luck. She was about to move on and figure out another way to look into Wendy's childhood when a headline caught her eye. *Unsolved Murder Rocks Sleepy Community.*

The article gave little information, other than Millicent Betters fell overboard in a boating accident while out sailing with her daughter. In 1995 a final article appeared about the lead investigator on the Millicent Betters's drowning who was on paid leave pending an investigation. Scanning the article, Olivia made a note of the policeman's name. It took her another minute to discover his telephone number.

"Mr. Buford? I'm calling from San Francisco. My name is Olivia Sinclair. I know this may sound a little odd, but I'm looking for information about Wendy Betters and came across a newspaper article mentioning you."

"Are you with the police?"

In a split second, Olivia decided the best course of action would be to tell Mr. Buford the truth.

"No. I'm currently awaiting trial for the murder of my husband's mistress. I didn't kill her, Mr. Buford. But I think

Wendy Betters did." Olivia heard Mr. Buford's breath, in and out, while her words hung in the air. "I'm fighting for my freedom, Mr. Buford. Anything you can tell me will be appreciated."

Olivia half expected the man to hang up on her. After all, she wasn't a police officer and he was under no obligation to speak to her. When he started talking, she took notes on the computer, but was soon so captivated by his story, and Wendy's history, that she stopped writing altogether.

"What I've just told you is basically the same thing I told that police officer from San Francisco. Wendy Betters was a dangerous child. I'd bet my pension she's grown into a dangerous woman. You be careful, young lady. Take an old man's advice and let the police handle this."

"Which police officer did you speak with?"

"A woman. An Inspector Sharon Bailey. I spoke to her not thirty minutes ago. I'll repeat my story, if you want to hear?"

"I do, please," Olivia said.

Thirty minutes later, head reeling from Mr. Buford's story, Olivia hung up the phone. She paced her house, chastising herself for being such an idiot. Not only had Richard completely bamboozled Olivia, but Wendy had betrayed her in the most horrific way, capitalizing on their friendship to get close to Richard. Olivia thought of the Thanksgiving and Christmas dinners Wendy had spent with them, how close Olivia thought they were. She had always prided herself on her understanding of people, the way she intuitively knew how to care for her clients, but here she was, a fool in her own marriage.

And Wendy. Wendy had been Olivia's confidante. She thought of the intimate details she had shared with Wendy over the years, recalling how Wendy had been interested in Richard's quirks, what he did and didn't like. Olivia wondered if Wendy had made a play for Richard. Had he rejected her and pushed her over the edge?

A plan to trap Wendy formed in the back of Olivia's mind. She did laps in her house, playing the scenario over and over in her head, taking it apart to look for flaws. After using the bathroom and splashing cold water on her face, she took her cell phone into the living room and made herself comfortable on the couch. She had an app on her phone that recorded phone conversations. Taking a deep breath, she hit record and dialed Wendy's cell phone number.

"Hello, Olivia," Wendy answered. "I reckoned you'd be the first one to figure everything out. You always were the brightest of the bunch."

"What are you talking about? I just called to thank you—"

"Liar. You know what I did. I can hear it in your voice. You're sitting up there, locked in your castle, your mind busy trying to save yourself. Well, darling, you're too late."

"I talked to Willis Buford." Switching her strategy, Olivia plowed on, not giving Wendy a chance to interrupt. "He is convinced you killed your mother."

"Willis Buford is a stupid man. I needed to sell our house to pay my way through college. She didn't want me to go. Wanted me to go to community college and get a job at the local bank, if you can believe that. A bank."

Wendy's voice had a manic quality to it. *I'm talking to a sociopath.* The reality of the situation hit Olivia hard.

"Ah, you're surprised. Well, how were you to know? So yes, I killed my mother. I killed Janelle Maycott – she nearly took Richard away from me, you know. And then Sandy Watson. He was falling in love with her. Can you believe that? Janelle was a beauty, so I could see the attraction, but Sandy? She was a simpleton. Richard told me he appreciated her gentle nature." Wendy laughed. "He would have grown tired of Sandy eventually. But the little bitch got pregnant. That would have tied her to Richard forever, so she had to go. Anyway, in case you're wondering, I also burned your investigator's house down – a miscalculation on my part. I figured eventually that picture of Richard, Janelle, and me would surface. Thought it was at Mr. Vickery's."

216

"What are you after, Wendy? Richard and I are getting a divorce. I don't want him. You can have him."

Silence. For a second Olivia was sure Wendy had hung up on her.

"What am I after? All I'm wanting is credit for all I've done for Richard, a little acknowledgment for the sacrifices I've made for him. Without me he'd be a two-bit personal injury attorney, chasing ambulances and scrambling for his next DUI case. I made Richard Sinclair what he is. I got him the television appearances, I covered for him all these years."

"I know," Olivia said. "I know what you've done for Richard over the years, Wendy. He took advantage of you. Meet me, so we can talk about it in person."

Wendy laughed. "Nice try, Olivia, but I'm not falling for it. You're not my friend. I've always hated you. Did you know that? You were so stupid, so blind to what Richard was up to. Everyone knew he cheated on you. He'd buy you jewelry from Tiffany's – which I picked out, by the way – and at the same time, he'd have me pick out something for his current mistress. What a joke. I would have paid dearly to watch you open that video of Richard and Sandy going at it like rabbits. I was Richard's true partner. You don't even know who Richard really is."

"What are you going to do?"

"Leave, of course. I'm not going to jail. I've got the money and the man. I don't like it when people get in my way, Olivia. Don't make that mistake and I won't come for you."

"You put the camera in Richard's studio?"

Wendy laughed. "I did. Admittedly, it was difficult to watch Sandy in bed with him, but I needed to set you up for the murder. You're an old woman now, Olivia, a shriveled old spinster. It must be horrible to realize your marriage was a lie and the chance for you to find love has passed. And I can hear your little brain trying to figure out what to do. My advice is to back off. I have

217

Richard. He's sleeping now, thanks to a magic cocktail of drugs. We're sailing away from here."

"So you're going to hold him hostage?"

"He'll come around to my way of thinking," Wendy said. "I've got the $3 million from the Rincon Sinclair investment fund. Richard's got some cash stashed away. We'll be very happy on some tropical island."

"Wendy—"

"Shut up, Olivia. I don't want to hear what you have to say about Richard. You don't know him. Not like I do."

"Let me speak to him."

"Tell your wife goodbye," Wendy said.

"Liv. Help." Richard's voice slurred.

Wendy came back on the line.

"Don't worry, Olivia. Richard is safe and sound. I'll take good care of him."

"Wendy, wait. Think about what you're doing."

"It's a little late for that, Liv. Call the cops and I'll dose Richard with propofol and dump him in the bay. His death will be on you. Got it? Goodbye, Olivia." Wendy hung up.

Olivia dialed Brian's number. He answered on the first ring. "I was just getting ready to call you. I'm at Stephen's office now. You're on speaker phone."

"Wendy is at her sailboat. It's in Sausalito."

"How do you know this?"

"I called her. Listen to me. She confessed to everything, Janelle's murder, Sandy's murder, the fire, everything. I recorded the conversation. And she's got Richard."

"I'll call the police right now," Stephen said.

"I'm going there," Olivia said. "That'll draw the police as well."

"Olivia, damn it, don't you dare," Brian said.

Olivia ignored Brian's warning. "I'm sending you the recording of the confession right now. Send it to Sharon Bailey, please. Wendy's boat is at Schoonmaker Point. Hurry up."

Olivia sent a copy of the audio recording of Wendy's confession to Stephen and Brian, along with a backup copy to herself. She stepped into a pair of slip-on shoes and hurried out the door, car keys in hand. When the alarm started beeping, she moved even faster, ignoring the sound of her ringing phone as she jumped in her car and hurried to Sausalito.

# Chapter 31

Impatient with the Saturday traffic, Sharon pulled into Schoonmaker Point, heading to the parking lot reserved for boat owners. She had the slip number for Wendy's boat. Now all she had to do was find it and manage to take Wendy by surprise. Her cell phone rang. Ellie. Sharon answered the call and turned the ringer on silent.

"Boss, Olivia Sinclair has violated her house arrest. Her GPS tracker says she's on her way to Sausalito."

"Okay. She's probably headed here. Can you get someone to intercept her? I don't need Olivia Sinclair in the middle of things."

"Sure. I'll be with you as soon as I can. Captain Wasniki is on the phone with Sausalito PD. You should have backup soon."

Sharon had the feeling she was stepping onto a pile of kindling doused in gas. Olivia Sinclair's presence in this situation was the ignition required to blow the whole thing sky high. Removing her Glock from the glove compartment, she tucked it into its holster before she set off to find Wendy's boat.

Wendy's boat, *Easy Money*, was berthed at the very end of a long dock, far out into the water. *Convenient for a quick getaway*, Sharon thought. Grateful there weren't many people around, she approached the boat, the dock swaying under her feet. She

220

crouched low, in an attempt to remain unseen. The boat was uncovered; the door leading below deck was open. Sharon waited awhile but didn't hear anyone moving about. Creeping up to the side of the boat, she raised her eyes and peered into one of the portholes.

*Oh, crap.* Richard Sinclair had been arranged in a fold-away deck chair, his arms and legs secured with duct tape, a gag in his mouth, his head rolled forward. He was either unconscious or dead. On the small table near the galley, she saw a large duffel bag. So Wendy was going to try to escape on her boat. Sharon wondered what she planned on doing with Richard. She waited five minutes, but Wendy was nowhere to be seen. Reluctant to board the boat without backup, Sharon resisted the urge to go to Richard Sinclair. She could only hope the poor guy wasn't dead.

*Where is my backup?* Sharon turned her back on the boat long enough to look to the parking area. Nothing. She held her breath and listened. Sirens. Getting closer. She stood up on creaking knees, pulled her Glock out of its holster, released the safety, and stepped onto the deck. Certain that help was on its way, she started down the short flight of stairs that led below deck.

"Mr. Sinclair? Police."

Richard Sinclair groaned, but he didn't lift his head. She hurried over to Richard and had just reached out to remove the gag, when she felt a painful thud on the back of her head. Everything went black.

*

When she awoke, Sharon was lying flat out on a berth in the bow of Wendy's boat. The gentle swaying made her nauseous, but she combatted the sensation with deep breaths and a prayer. From her position she could see Wendy Betters as she sat next to Richard Sinclair, who was semi-conscious. She watched as he struggled to hold his head up but his eyes had an unfocused

221

look to them. His head lolled forward as he slipped once again into unconsciousness. All the while, Wendy hovered over Richard raving like a madwoman.

"It's really going to be okay, darling," Wendy cooed, as she stroked Richard's cheek. "I did it all for us. Killed Janelle Maycott, Sandy Watson. I've got lots of money and we are going to be very happy."

Sharon bore witness as Richard looked up at Wendy, startled at her revelation. When Wendy caressed Richard's face, running her fingers over his cheek, he tried to pull away from her touch.

"Now, now, that's no way to respond." She kissed the top of his forehead. "From now on it's going to be just the two of us. I'm going to take your gag off, okay? If you scream or shout, I'll sedate you so deeply you won't wake up until we are in Mexico. Understood?"

Richard nodded. Wendy took his gag off.

"What the hell have you done? Is that Inspector Bailey?" His voice was raspy as he spoke through dry lips.

"She got in the way," Wendy said, her tone petulant like a child's.

"Is she dead?"

Sharon closed her eyes, hoping Wendy would think she was still unconscious.

"Of course not. I hit her over the head. She'll be fine."

"They'll come looking for her."

"Don't you worry about that," Wendy said. She squatted down in front of Richard. From Sharon's vantage point she had a perfect view of Wendy's adoring gaze. "We'll be together. Finally."

"I don't love you," Richard said.

"Don't say that," Wendy shouted. She stood up, her face mottled with pent-up rage.

*She's well and truly mad.* Careful not to make any movements that would garner Wendy's attention, Sharon surveyed her surroundings for a way out. Nothing. The bow was tiny, cramped, and the only exit through the door that led into the galley and cabin area. Sharon closed her eyes. *Think.* No grand plan presented itself. All she could do was hope that backup arrived. Sooner rather than later.

"Wakey wakey," a soft voice said.

Sharon's eyes popped open and she looked into Wendy Betters's smiling face. Wendy had taken Sharon's Glock. She now pointed it directly at Sharon's heart. "I could shoot you now and be done with it, but that would be a mistake, wouldn't it? I'd attract too much attention."

"Why did you kill them?" Sharon asked, hoping to get Wendy talking so she could stall for time.

"Trying to stall for time, Inspector Bailey? Come on, let's get you some fresh air."

With the Glock pointed at her, Sharon rose slowly, catching herself as the boat seemed to tilt. On wobbly legs she moved through the cabin and up onto the deck.

"Lie down," Wendy ordered.

Sharon should have tried to wrestle the gun away from Wendy, but she couldn't seem to move fast enough. *I've got a concussion. Where the hell is my backup?* Unable to lift a finger to defend herself, she sat still and submissive as Wendy Betters bound her wrists with duct tape.

Through the glinting sunlight, Sharon watched as Wendy held up a syringe.

"It's propofol. I'm going to inject you with it before I throw you overboard. You'll drown, but you won't feel a thing."

"So you're going to kill me and sail off into the sunset?"

"Exactly. Richard and I are going somewhere far away and very warm."

"Tell me why you killed Janelle Maycott. What did she do to you?"

"Richard had his eye on her. She was so beautiful. And while Richard slept with every woman he met, I could tell Janelle was going to be different. He was besotted with her. I couldn't lose him. Janelle Maycott threatened to come between Richard and me, so I had to kill her. It's very simple, really."

"And Sandy Watson?"

"She discovered my little scheme. You see, I've been slowly leaching the money out of the Rincon Sinclair investment account. I'm very talented at playing the stock market. While I left some of the profits in the investment account, I took what I like to think of as a commission. Sandy discovered it quite by accident. That was my money. I earned it. Why should I settle for a measly twenty percent? And the little bitch got pregnant, didn't she? She would've had the child, which would have tied her to Richard for life. I couldn't let that happen. So here we are." Wendy smiled when she looked at Richard and stroked his cheek. She turned toward Sharon. "Goodbye, Inspector Bailey."

Sharon didn't stand a chance. Wendy moved close and pushed the needle through Sharon's trousers into her thigh and pushed the plunger.

# Chapter 32

Olivia drove like a bat out of hell and made it to Sausalito in record time, despite the weekend traffic. Avoiding the marina parking lot, she found a metered spot on the street, which actually put her closer to Wendy's berth. Although she hadn't been out on the boat with Wendy in years, she had the benefit of knowing where she was going. A tall cyclone fence protected the boats that were moored at Schoonmaker Point from the general public. Olivia loitered by the gate until an older man carrying a six-pack of beer and a fishing rod approached.

"I'm meeting my friend," Olivia said. "I was supposed to text her when I got here, but my phone is dead."

"Which friend?" the man asked, suspicious.

"Wendy Betters. We work at the same law firm. She's taking me sightseeing. I just moved here—" The segue into small talk worked. The man punched in a code and held the gate for her. "Thanks a lot," she said, walking slowly towards Wendy's boat, as if she had all the time in the world. Each berth came with a large tackle box bolted to the dock, so items such as extra rope, life jackets, and the like could be safely stored. Once the man who opened the gate was out of sight, Olivia ducked behind one. It wouldn't do for Wendy to see her coming.

In the distance, approaching sirens confirmed the police were en route. Time was ticking. A wave of panic threatened, but Olivia pushed it back. Why had she come here? To save Richard? To show Richard what a brave woman she was?

Her eyes on Wendy's boat, she scurried down the dock, her legs quickly adapting to the gentle sway of the water. Every few berths, she would duck out of sight, careful to remain unseen. As the sirens got louder, Wendy appeared on the deck of her boat. She listened for a moment before she untied the boat and slowly backed out of her berth. Pulling her cell phone out, Olivia called Brian's number. He answered on the first ring.

"Olivia, what the hell do you think you're—"

"She's getting away. Richard's on that boat. Tell the cops."

"Okay. We can see you ducking down. She won't get away. You need to come here and turn yourself in."

"I know." Olivia stood, ready to accept the consequences for her reckless act of attempted heroism.

"It'll be okay," Brian said. "Stephen's given the recording . . ." His voice trailed off.

"Are you seeing this?" Olivia whispered.

After untying her boat, Wendy disappeared for a few seconds. When she came back into view, she carried Inspector Bailey's limp body over her shoulder like a sack of sugar. In one fluid motion, she dumped the policewoman over the back of the boat as if she were disposing of garbage. Olivia heard the engine rev as Wendy took the helm of her boat and headed towards the Golden Gate Bridge and out to sea.

Glancing back, Olivia saw a cluster of bystanders. More than one person had their phones out and were filming the whole scenario. Three uniformed cops – Sausalito PD by the look of them – were running towards her. She ignored them, sprinted to the end of the dock and dove in. The shock of the frigid water nearly took her breath away, but she was close enough to see Inspector Bailey's body floating face down. Numb from the cold and driven by adrenaline, Olivia swam towards Sharon, her stroke strong and sure.

It took her about thirty seconds to reach her. Remembering the water safety class she had taken when she was a teenager, she flipped Sharon on her back, put an arm across her chest, and dragged her towards shore.

Paramedics waded into the water just as Olivia reached the shore, took Sharon from her and immediately started mouth-to-mouth resuscitation. Numb and cold, Olivia staggered out of the water, too weak to walk. A paramedic put an arm around her, holding her up so she could walk to one of two waiting ambulances. She sat in the back of the open ambulance, a wool blanket around her shoulders as the paramedic checked her vitals. From this vantage point, Olivia watched as the other paramedic turned Inspector Bailey on her side as she choked up bay water, coughed and gagged and sputtered until she eventually was revived.

Once she could breathe on her own, Inspector Bailey was loaded into the ambulance parked next to Olivia's. As the paramedic headed for the driver's side, he said, "You got to her just in the nick of time. You saved this woman's life."

Olivia turned her attention to the drama as it unfolded out on the water. Two policemen had commandeered what looked like a Boston Whaler with an outboard motor. The boat rushed towards Wendy's sailboat, quickly catching up to it. One of the cops stood and held a megaphone up to his mouth. A hush fell over the crowd as Wendy turned to the approaching boat. She held a gun, which she trained on the officers.

Both of the officers drew their weapons and ducked down as Wendy fired three shots. The officers returned fire. Wendy didn't bother to duck. Olivia saw her topple just as a sheriff's deputy arrived at the ambulance to take her back to jail, Brian Vickery and Stephen Vine trailing behind him.

"What were you thinking?" Brian asked. He pulled the wool blanket tighter around Olivia's shoulders.

"I had to clear my name," Olivia said. "Richard's on that boat. She's going to kill him."

"The Coast Guard will see to him," Brian said.

An eager young reporter ran towards Olivia, a microphone extended.

"What happened here, Mrs. Sinclair," she asked. "Why did you break house arrest?"

"To prove my innocence."

The reporter motioned for her cameraman to move closer. "Did you do that, Mrs. Sinclair? Did you prove your innocence?"

Before she had a chance to answer, a deputy positioned himself between Olivia and the camera and turned his back on the reporter. "You need to come with me, Mrs. Sinclair."

# Chapter 33

And just like that it was over. Stephen Vine called in a myriad of favors to get Judge Helman involved on a Saturday. Judge Helman, who was looking at his phone, gave Olivia a look that was full of fury as she was led into his chambers, clutching a wool blanket around her shoulders, wearing a standard issue gray sweat suit, her wet hair matted against her scalp. She smelled of San Francisco Bay and couldn't seem to get warm.

Jonas and Stephen sat opposite the judge's desk. Olivia took an empty chair between them as the court reporter set up her steno machine. Once she had everything situated, the judge put his phone down and stared at Olivia. "We're on the record. I hear you broke the conditions of your house arrest, Mrs. Sinclair."

Stephen stood before addressing the court. "Your Honor, there are extenuating circumstances, if you would indulge—"

"Mr. Vine, I'm here at your behest on a weekend. Do not try me. I'll speak to your client directly, if you don't mind."

Stephen sat back down.

It took all of Olivia's might not to cower under Judge Helman's look. *He's going to throw me back in jail.*

"Mrs. Sinclair, what were you thinking?"

Olivia waited, not sure if the judge actually expected a response.

"Do you not understand the question?"

Olivia glanced at Stephen, who gave her an encouraging nod.

"I discovered that Wendy Betters had Richard. She confessed to killing Sandy Watson, Janelle Maycott, and her own mother. She also confessed to burning my investigator's house down." Olivia wiped her tears. "Wendy told me she had Richard. I figured if she was going to try to escape, she would do so in her boat. I needed the police there. I knew they would come for me if I left my house."

"Why the urgency?" Judge Helman asked.

"When I spoke to her on the phone, she sounded—" Olivia hesitated "—unstable, for lack of a better word. It was just a gut feeling, Your Honor."

Olivia was crying now. The tears rolled down her cheeks. Her knees threatened to collapse. Stephen stood and put an arm around her. "You can sit, Liv." He helped her ease back into her chair.

"Your Honor, if I may?" Stephen asked.

Judge Helman nodded.

"During the course of preparing for trial, we discovered a connection between Wendy Betters and Sandy Watson and a young lady named Janelle Maycott, who was murdered in 2000. Mrs. Sinclair discovered evidence that would have exonerated her of all charges, but in the process of doing so, forced Miss Betters – the real murderer – to play her hand, if you will. She may have acted rashly—"

"You don't by chance have any proof of this confession?" Judge Helman asked.

"We do, Your Honor," Stephen said. "My client recorded her phone call."

"Let's hear it."

Olivia's heart pounded in her chest. She felt like she was going to be sick and, try as she might, she couldn't stop the tears that flowed down her cheeks. They listened to the recording, and on

230

hearing it a second time, Olivia was even more surprised at the crazed madness in Wendy's voice.

When the tape recording finished, Judge Helman turned to Jonas. "You're awfully quiet, Mr. Greensboro."

Jonas stood, and out of habit started to button up his sportscoat. When he realized he was wearing a zip-up jacket, he shook his head. "We've heard the confession and seen the video."

"Video?"

Stephen stood. "Olivia Sinclair saved Inspector Bailey's life, Your Honor. Wendy Betters injected the inspector with some type of drug, bound her hands and ankles, and threw her in the bay. Mrs. Sinclair dove in after her. She pulled her to shore, where the paramedics performed mouth-to-mouth resuscitation. Another minute and the inspector would have drowned."

"Where is the inspector now?" Judge Helman asked.

"She's in the hospital being treated for a concussion. They are expecting a full recovery," Jonas said. He pulled out his phone and handed it to Judge Helman. "Here's a video of events."

The judge took Jonas's phone and watched the video. Did Olivia see a flicker of compassion in his eyes?

Judge Helman reached under this desk and pulled out a box of Kleenex. "Mr. Vine, give your client a tissue."

"Based on this evidence, Your Honor, we move that the charges against Mrs. Sinclair be dismissed with prejudice," Stephen said.

"The People join in this motion, Your Honor," Jonas said.

Judge Helman faced Olivia. "Given the evidence presented to me, the defendant's motion to dismiss the charges against Olivia Sinclair with prejudice is hereby granted. Jonas, prepare an order and I'll sign it. Use your influence to get Mrs. Sinclair out of here. She needs to be home."

# Chapter 34

Weeks went by and October turned to November. Denny called when she heard about Wendy Betters and Olivia's role in solving the case against her, but their conversations were stilted. Olivia felt certain David lingered in the background, supervising their talks, ever in control. Christmas decorations went up on Magnolia Avenue; the days got shorter.

After helping Olivia clear up the boxes of evidence in her dining room and taking them to Stephen Vine's office for storage, Brian had rented a studio apartment in San Rafael. Although they spoke on the phone occasionally, they never discussed their kiss. The unspoken words between them made things awkward, and after a while the phone conversations became few and far between. Olivia found she missed his quiet ways and hoped their kiss hadn't damaged their friendship. She'd give Brian some time and then she'd reach out, invite him for dinner or suggest they go for a walk together.

Worries of Brian took a back seat to the sadness over her rift with Denny. Olivia withdrew into herself. The grief of losing her daughter wouldn't let go, and Olivia found she had little interest in socializing. She savored the physical labor of her garden and rattled around her empty house, knowing she couldn't go on this way forever. Every couple of days she would go for a long walk or a drive with Lauren. Other than that, she didn't really see anyone. Eventually she found comfort in her solitude.

During the week before Thanksgiving, Olivia sat in Lauren's kitchen, a towel around her shoulders while Lauren snipped away at her hair. Olivia had approached her own hairdresser about cutting her hair short and letting her gray hair grow in, but her hairdresser had balked at the idea. "You'll look like an old lady. I can't let you do that." The response had made Olivia so mad, she'd left the salon and had no plans to go back.

"Why do women have to expend so much energy looking young?" Olivia asked Lauren. "I mean think about it, we're so conditioned to stay thin, wear makeup, keep up appearances, and for whom? Men?"

"Aside from the fact the promise of youth is a billion-dollar industry," Lauren said, staring critically at Olivia's hair. "I don't think men even notice. We do it for other women. Women judge each other, compare themselves to each other. That, my friend, is the tragedy. Now that you don't have a conventional job, you can be free. Embrace your wild side. You can reinvent yourself and do and be whatever you want. What do you want to do, Olivia?"

"Something useful. I want to help people. Beyond that, I have no idea. I don't even know myself anymore."

"You've got lots of time to figure things out."

"I wonder how many innocent people are in prison for crimes they didn't commit. I had a good lawyer – I should say I could afford a good lawyer. What about those who can't? How many Jonas Greensboros are out there, ruining the lives of innocent people to advance their career or political agenda?"

"You can be a criminal defense attorney and hire that hunky detective. I could get used to feasting my eyes on him every day." Lauren put her scissors down and stepped back, a pleased smile on her face. "Come with me." She took Olivia's hand and led her into the bathroom. The two women stood side by side, looking at each other in the mirror. Lauren with her long gray hair, which curled in wild tendrils, and Olivia, her hair a mixture of gunmetal gray and white, cut short like a man's.

Olivia barely recognized herself. She saw a woman who had lived and loved and lost, a woman who looked every second of her sixty-two years.

"Your metamorphosis is complete, my friend. Now you can go out and meet a man who deserves you."

"I don't need a man to be happy," Olivia said.

"Agreed. But that doesn't mean you can't be open to the possibility, Olivia. All men aren't like Richard, and I know it's going to take some time to get over everything that's happened, but you don't know what your future holds. You've said that yourself. Be open-minded. Good things are coming to you. I can feel it." Lauren rubbed her hands together. "Let's have some champagne and plan our Thanksgiving feast."

# Chapter 35

After the Sandy Watson murder case came to its sensational conclusion, Stephen Vine and a handful of other attorneys started throwing Brian more work than he could handle. Unable and unwilling to deal with rebuilding, Brian had sold his lot in Larkspur for way more money than it was worth and had moved to a small studio apartment. He had signed a one-year lease, thinking of it as a self-imposed commitment. After that, he'd have to make a decision, either start over someplace else where no one knew of his past or stay in Marin County. If he stayed in Marin, he'd have to work. Maybe he'd rent an office and hire someone to help him. He trusted things would sort themselves out in good time.

On this particular Monday morning, Brian braved the commuter traffic, sitting on 101 southbound, prepared to spend a good hour driving ten miles into the city. When The Eagles' "Life in the Fast Lane" came on the radio, Brian turned it up, letting the memories of Maureen come as they may, feeling the pain of what he'd lost and the sorrow of what would never be. When the song came to an end, all that was left was nostalgia. What a life they'd had. What a love they'd shared. That's what mattered.

Brian made a mental note to replace the records he lost in

the fire. When he felt lonely for Maureen, he could blast Eric Clapton, The Eagles, and a dozen other records that would bring Maureen to life. He could remember being young and going dancing with her at Uncle Charlie's. Those memories needed to be saved and tended to, in the same way that Olivia Sinclair tended her garden.

Sharon was waiting outside of her apartment as Brian drove up, two large cups of coffee in a tray. She had lost weight and had a worried look in her eyes that Brian had never seen before. "Good morning. Got you some coffee."

Brian took a sip from his cup. "Thanks."

They headed towards Alana Maycott's house in Sea Cliff.

"I remember when it was foggy out here almost every morning," Brian said.

"Me too. Climate change, I reckon," Sharon said. "Are you keeping busy?"

"I am," Brian said. "Stephen Vine and a couple other attorneys are giving me more work than I care to deal with."

"Maybe you'll hire me," Sharon said.

"You're not thinking of leaving are you?" Brian asked.

"Not yet. But soon. Twenty more months and I'll have done my twenty-five."

"I thought you were a career cop, one of those people who would stay on the job until they kicked you out."

Sharon stared out the window, quiet with her thoughts. Brian let her be, and after a few moments she turned to him and said, "I could have died if Olivia Sinclair hadn't been there. There was no way someone from shore could have reached me in time to pull me out of the water. I screwed up big time going on that boat without backup. Now I don't trust myself to make good decisions, and I'm scared of my own shadow."

Over the years Brian had seen Sharon overcome the obstacles faced by all women cops with a stoic grace that had not only amazed him but also earned his respect. He had seen her browbeaten by obnoxious officers who outranked her; he had seen her physically attacked on more than one occasion when making an arrest. Throughout it all, Sharon had been strong, both psychologically and physically. So when she wiped her eyes now, Brian was surprised.

"This will pass, Sharon. You need to give yourself some time."

"I wish I could believe that." She turned her gaze away from him and fell silent, her subtle way of saying *conversation over*. After a while she said, "The last time I saw Alana Maycott she wasn't terribly kind."

Brian remembered Alana Maycott storming into the police station, bossy and imperious, demanding to know exactly what was being done to catch her daughter's killer. The team investigating Janelle's murder had dismissed her. She was a mother suffering immeasurable grief. But Sharon, the pretty young blonde who looked like she should have been a fashion model, had caught not only Alana's eye, but Alana's ire.

"Do you remember how she lashed out at me? Asked me if I was qualified to do this job?"

"You handled her well, Sharon."

Sharon snorted. "I wanted to die. Felt like a deer in the headlights."

They parked the car and walked up to the house. When Alphonse opened the door to let them in, he said, "She's not doing very well, but she's anxious to see you. I'm asking you to not stay long, if you don't mind."

"Of course," Brian said.

Alana lay in the hospital bed, the view hidden by swirling fog.

"I know I look like death. I'm just about done here, I think. Now I can die in peace, thanks to both of you." She looked at Sharon. "Young lady, I remember back when you were a slip of a woman investigating Janelle's murder. I wasn't terribly kind to you then. Will you forgive me?"

A look of surprise flashed in Sharon's eyes, as though she

wasn't expecting humility. "Of course, Mrs. Maycott. You were in a horrible state of shock."

"That's no excuse, but thank you for trying." She focused on Brian. "And you, Mr. Vickery, what are your plans?"

"I'm adjusting to being without my wife. And, yes, I've got a few clients."

"And what about the Sinclair woman, the one who was being framed for the murder? I watched her dive into the water. Are you going to date her?"

Brian chuckled. "Hadn't really given that much thought, Mrs. Maycott."

"Nonsense." She grabbed his hand and held it with surprising strength. "She's a warrior spirit, just like you. Don't let her get away. Do you hear me?"

"Yes, ma'am," Brian said. She let go of Brian's hand. "My morphine is kicking in."

Sharon and Brian stood.

"Goodbye, you two. Thank you from the bottom of my heart."

As they drove away, Brian thought of Alana's comment about Olivia Sinclair. He had to admit that he missed Olivia's company. He pulled up to Sharon's studio.

"I'm glad we did that, Brian. Thanks for bringing me." She got out of the car and tapped on the window. When Brian rolled it down, Sharon leaned inside and gave him a sly smile. "And I agree with Mrs. Maycott. You should date Olivia Sinclair. I can see you two together. Don't look at me that way. You don't have to marry her, just spend some time with her."

"Goodbye, Sharon. See you at Thanksgiving." Brian pointedly ignored Sharon's comments, but as he drove away, he found himself smiling at the thought of Olivia Sinclair. Maybe he'd take Alana's advice and give her a call. There was no harm in going for coffee. Was there?

238

# Chapter 36

It rained on Thanksgiving Day. Olivia and Lauren ate Dungeness crab, accompanied by an iceberg lettuce salad with homemade bleu cheese dressing, and crusty French bread, on the floor in Olivia's living room, before a roaring fire. For the first time since her marriage, Olivia didn't host a giant sit-down formal dinner.

"That was delicious." Lauren took their empty plates into the kitchen, returning with the cold champagne. "How does it feel, not having all the responsibility of entertaining Richard's clients on the holidays?"

"I don't miss Richard or his clients one bit." Olivia scooted up to the couch.

"Have you spoken to him at all since you saved his life?"

"He's been calling. I've been avoiding him." Olivia sat back on the couch. "I'm worried about Denny. I'm afraid I've lost her."

"You're going to have to fix things with her somehow and do so without interfering."

"And just how do you propose I do that?"

"Tell her you're sorry. Promise not to meddle again." Lauren put her glass down and gave Olivia an inquisitive, all-knowing look. "Liv, what have you done? Tell me right now."

Olivia closed her eyes, wishing things weren't so complicated,

239

wishing Lauren didn't know her so well. "I hired Claire Montreaux to represent Denny."

"You what?"

"Please don't judge me. David's cheating on her. The PI I hired was close to getting proof of that."

"After she specifically asked you to stand down? That's so disrespectful. I can't believe you would do that." Lauren moved closer to the fire, holding her hands out to its warmth.

"There are things you don't know."

"Okay, enlighten me."

"After my arrest, Denny was supposed to come here. I was all set to apologize to her, throw myself on the sword, and swear to never involve myself in her life without an express invitation." Olivia shivered, cold all of a sudden, as she remembered the day David Grayson had come walking up her garden path. She told Lauren of their conversation, how David had mocked Olivia that day. "He told me that he forbade Denny from seeing me. How he had won and Denny would always choose him. He's a sociopath. And I'm not just saying that because I don't like him. He enjoys power."

"I had no idea." Lauren sat next to Olivia on the couch.

"I explained the situation to Claire and hired her to represent Denny. She has a PI following David. This time David won't know. And before you say anything, Claire is Denny's lawyer, so she won't be reporting to me. If Denny stays married to David, nothing will happen and Denny won't need to know what I've done. But if she shows up on my doorstep, which I believe she will, she'll be well equipped to take on David and his family."

"I can't believe she married into that family." Lauren patted Olivia's hand. "If this all comes out, explain to Denny what you just said to me. She'll understand."

"I'm going to be honest with her. And if she doesn't like it, I've no one to blame but myself."

*

240

Denny came at 5:32 the following morning. Olivia was deeply asleep when she heard a soft rapping at the door, but mothers know things, even if their children are long out of the house. She jumped out of bed and hurried down the hall. "Denny? Coming." She threw the door open, and there stood Denny, pregnant, bedraggled, and exhausted.

Olivia stared at her daughter, trying to figure out what she could say to repair their damaged relationship. "I'm so sorry for meddling in your marriage. Can you ever forgive me?"

"Mom? What have you done to your hair?"

"I've cut it off and set myself free. Now come in out of the cold." Olivia stepped aside, her heart full, as her daughter came into the house.

"I drove straight through. I'm starved and exhausted."

"Of course. I'll make you something. Eggs? Pancakes?"

"Both?"

For a brief second, Olivia saw Denny as a little girl, with her towheaded curls and chubby legs, smiling gleefully at the flower-shaped pancakes Olivia used to fix for her. While she mixed the batter and heated the griddle, Denny talked.

"I spoke to Dad. He told me about the divorce."

"Sorry you had to hear it from him."

"I've no one to blame but myself for that. David wanted me to stay away from you. He convinced me that you were a toxic influence in our relationship and that if I wanted to make our marriage work, I would need to get out from under your control." She ran her hand through her hair. "And I was stupid enough to believe him. But we were talking about Dad. He said he's been trying to call you. Why haven't you been taking his calls?"

Denny watched as Olivia scrambled eggs and flipped pancakes. "I'll speak to your father when I am good and ready, on my terms, not his. I'm done dancing to his tune." She served up the pancakes and set them before Denny.

"You're different. It's not just your hair. You're – I don't

241

know – tougher, maybe. Like you've got some street smarts. The privileged Marin County lawyer has some grit to her schtick."

Olivia laughed out loud. "Nice, Den. Have you ever thought of writing?"

Denny's face grew serious as she loaded maple syrup onto her pancakes. "It turns out you were right all along. David basically stopped coming home at all after he forbade me to speak to you. His absence made me suspicious, so I got one of those GPS trackers and put it on his car. Like an idiot, I followed him right to the no-tell motel. Caught him in the act with his secretary."

"You don't seem too upset," Olivia said.

"I was at the time. I cried for a week. David swore up and down it would stop, but then he got tired of what he called my emotional outbursts. When I told him that I could no longer trust him, he promised to put me out on the street with no money."

Olivia bit her tongue as she flipped another batch of pancakes. "When he threatened to take my baby, I saw him for who he really is. You were right, Mom. I should have listened to you. I lied to him, acted like I understood why he cheated on me, told him I loved him and would do anything to make our marriage work. He had a business dinner. The minute he left the house, I packed my suitcase and left. I drove all night and here I am. Anyway, you were right all along. I know I said some horrible things to you, and so did David. I apologize. Now I need you to help me because I swear to God I'll run away and go into hiding before I'll let David Grayson take my baby."

"You might want to hold off on your apology because I did something, and you might not like it." Olivia pushed her plate of pancakes away. "I hired an attorney for you. Her name is Claire Montreaux. She's good, a fighter. I gave her a retainer to hire a private investigator – a good one this time – to follow David and find out what he was up to."

"Jesus, Mom," Denny said, the look on her face an equal measure of admiration and disgust. "Did she find anything?"

"I don't know. She doesn't work for me. She works for you, so she won't discuss your case with me without your permission."

"So her PI doesn't work for you either?"

"No, honey. They work for you. And you can fire her, if you want. I'll pay for another lawyer if you need me to."

Denny continued to eat. Olivia didn't press her. Finally Denny took her plate to the sink and rinsed it. "I'll meet her. Do you think she can see me this afternoon? David will be on my heels. I didn't tell him where I was going, but he'll figure it out."

"I'll call her right now," Olivia said.

"I'm going to shower, put on my pajamas and sleep for a couple of hours." Denny stood and wrapped her arms around Olivia, resting her head on her mother's shoulder. "I should have listened to you from the beginning."

"And I should have let you figure this out on your own," Olivia said.

"There's going to be hell to pay," Denny said. "David is very sure of himself."

"You have a good lawyer, Den. You need to sit back and let her do her job."

Denny rested her hands on her stomach. "He's not taking this baby."

"We'll fight," Olivia said.

"I know." She ruffled Olivia's hair. "I like it. It suits you."

\*

Olivia, Denny, and Claire Montreaux were ready when David showed up at Olivia's house the next morning, full of anger and self-righteous indignation, ready to drag Denny by her hair back to the cave. After Claire and Denny had met for the first time and planned their course of action, Claire had removed the glass covering and the light bulbs in the fixture above the dining room table and in the middle of Olivia's living room, replacing them with ordinary-looking lightbulbs that held a camera. Claire had fiddled with the bulbs and soon was able to transmit images and sound directly to her phone. With Denny's permission, Olivia had been given the task of monitoring the recording on Claire's phone.

"You should stay in your bedroom. If you feel the slightest bit weird, call 9-1-1 and tell them you have a domestic disturbance."

"Okay," Olivia said.

Although they expected his arrival, both Denny and Olivia jumped when David pounded on the door.

"Oh, my God. He's furious. I can tell by the knock." Denny fiddled with her wedding ring.

"Denny, whatever you do, don't sit down until David does. I don't want to give your husband the opportunity to stand over you," Claire said.

Denny nodded and gave Olivia a wan smile.

"It'll be okay," Olivia lied. She was quickly finding Claire's methods more than a little unorthodox.

Claire waited until Olivia was back in her bedroom until she opened the door. When she said, "You must be David Grayson," Olivia hit record. The camera worked like a dream.

"Where's my wife?" David demanded. "And who the hell are you?"

"I'm Denny's lawyer, Mr. Grayson. We're going to negotiate a fair divorce settlement, including child support for your unborn child today."

They were in the dining room now. Olivia watched as Claire wedged herself between David and Denny. "Sit down, Mr. Grayson."

"Don't tell me what to do," David said. "Denny, go pack. You're coming home."

"No, I'm not," Denny said. Her voice was strong and sure and full of conviction. "I'm tired of your moral-compass bullshit. You're a liar and cheat. I'm divorcing you, and if you don't play nice, I'll keep this baby from you."

244

"This is ridiculous, Denny. You're my wife. I want you with me. We'll work this out. Just come home." David wiped his eyes, as though he were crying, but Olivia didn't see any tears. "I love you, Den. I know I haven't been a good husband, but I've been working a lot for our baby. For us."

Amazed at how quickly David changed his tactic, Olivia muttered under her breath, "Don't fall for it, Den. Don't fall for it."

Denny nodded at Claire, who pushed an envelope towards David. "I wonder what your parents and their clients would say if those pictures were to make their way onto the Internet?"

David stuffed the pictures back in the envelope and pushed them back to the center of the table. "What do you want?"

"Child support, alimony for five years, so Denny can rebuild her business and start working. You'll get standard visitation, as long as you don't take the baby out of state without Denny's permission. You even think about not returning that child from visitation, these pictures go live and I report a kidnapping."

*My God, she's committing blackmail.* Olivia resisted the urge to call the deal off, not wanting her daughter to be part of such underhanded tactics.

David pushed away from the chair and moved towards Claire, his hands clenched into fists. Olivia pushed 9-1-1 and held her finger over the call button.

"Listen, you bitch, that's blackmail. You don't know who you're messing with."

Heart pounding, Olivia watched the situation play out.

Claire didn't back down. Olivia was surprised when Claire stepped close to David. "I'm messing with a manipulative socio-path who thinks the rules don't apply to him. I'm giving you an opportunity to act like a decent human being, to keep up pretenses for your family and your career." Claire sidestepped around David, took the paperwork and put it in an envelope. "But that's okay, David. You don't have to sign." She pulled a sheet of paper out of her purse. "Here's a summons. You've been served. I'll schedule an emergency hearing—"

"Okay, okay." David held up his hands. "I'll sign the paperwork." He turned towards Denny. "I'll do what you want. I'm asking you to keep those pictures to yourself."

Glad that Denny wouldn't have to suffer a long and drawn-out custody battle, Olivia breathed a sigh of relief. Being privy to blackmail was a small price to pay for her daughter's wellbeing.

While David read the marital settlement agreement, Denny sat still, her entire demeanor one of calm and poise. Olivia knew she was dying inside. David took his time and read every page. Finally he pushed the paper away and spoke to Claire. "I'll agree to this."

"Thank God," Olivia whispered as she let out a sigh of relief.

"Fine. I'm going to call my secretary. She's a notary and can be here in ten minutes," Claire said.

Olivia kept the camera running while Claire's secretary – who had been waiting at the coffee bar down the street – witnessed and notarized the signatures.

David was about to walk out the door when Denny called to him.

"Wait," Denny said.

"What?" David snapped at her.

"You owe me an apology. I've been faithful to you, been a good wife. Yet you always made me feel as though I was never enough."

David shook his head. "You won, Denny. Let it go. I'm not apologizing to anyone. I signed your paperwork, gave you what you wanted without a fight. Be glad for that." And with that, David walked out of the house and out of Denny's life.

Olivia joined them just as Claire shut and locked the door behind him. "That went well."

"Thanks, Claire," Denny said. "For the good lawyering and for the solid advice."

"I'm starving," Claire said. "How about a celebratory lunch? My treat."

"Sounds good," Denny said.

"Claire, you just blackmailed David," Olivia said.

"Not really. Based on what Denny told me, I feared he would become violent. I filmed our proceedings for our safety. I like to think of it as showing him our discovery." She winked at Olivia. "I won't mention the pictures again. I don't think I'll have to."

They made arrangements to meet and finalize the paperwork. When Denny excused herself, and Olivia and Claire were alone, Claire whispered, "I'll bet you $100 that David Grayson remarries within the year and immediately gets his new wife pregnant."

"Could be," Olivia said. *And with any luck, he won't want anything to do with Denny's child.*

# Chapter 37

Richard arrived on a warm spring day while Olivia was mulching her vegetable garden. He came around the side of the house, down the path. Olivia didn't notice him until his shadow, made large by a trick of light, loomed over her. She turned with her trowel in hand, ready to use it as a weapon.

"Richard?"

"I tried the front door, rang the bell. Guess you didn't hear me."

The past few months had taken their toll on him. He'd lost weight and his cheeks had a gaunt look to them.

"You could have called," Olivia said.

"I've been calling, as you well know," Richard said.

Olivia sighed.

"I heard you're going to volunteer for the Truth Project?" When Olivia didn't respond, Richard plowed forward, trying to fill the silence. "That's a step down, Liv. The money's not nearly as good, and you could find yourself in a dangerous situation. I know their mission is noble, trying to help the wrongly convicted. But you won't like it. Trust me. You should consider—"

Olivia held up her hand. "Don't you presume to tell me what I should or should not do. I'm not interested in your opinion. Are you going to sign the divorce papers?"

"We're going to have a grandchild. I came here to apologize."

Olivia exhaled and forced the tension out of her body. She tossed her trowel to the ground and took off her hat. "I don't want to fight you, Richard. All I'm asking is that you let me keep this house. Sign the papers. Move on. Find yourself a nice young wife who will stroke your ego and put up with your relentless bullshit."

When he held her eyes and met her gaze, Olivia saw the cold edge there. Why hadn't she seen that before? *Because I was blind with love and full of optimism.* Never again would Olivia make that mistake.

He nodded. "Okay. I'll sign."

"Good. Monday? We could meet at the bank and use their notary." She put her hat back on, ready for Richard to go so she could get back to work. But he didn't leave.

"I'm moving to DC. Going to work as a consultant. Denny will know how to reach me." He turned to go, but changed his mind at the last minute. "You know, Olivia, I never meant to hurt you. I always loved you and always put you first. I did make you happy, didn't I? You never even suspected there were others."

"Don't try to paint yourself as noble and considerate of my feelings, Richard. While you were screwing other women since the beginning of our marriage, you weren't thinking of me at all." She turned her back on him, finished with him, finished with their relationship. She sensed him walking away as she took off her gardening gloves and sunk her hands into the dark loamy soil, letting it ground her.

Hours later, she stood, arms aching, happy with her efforts in the garden. For the first time in her life, she had no grand plan, had no idea what her future held. Her life lay before her, a blank canvas ready for her to paint. She tipped her face up to the afternoon sun, knowing in her heart she was ready for whatever the future held. For now, she was content to just be.

# Acknowledgements

Many people have been generous with their time and resources as I wrote this book. Thanks to John Prentice, not only for his knowledge of the law, but for the help regarding the murder investigation. Kasey Corbit, attorney at law, double-checked my courtroom scenes, often taking away from her busy schedule to answer last-minute questions.

Kris Waldherr, Angela Baxter, Janet Robinson, Gloria Bagwell-Rowland, Kim Laird, and Peter Anderson beta read this book and gave me on-point constructive feedback. Big thanks to Abigail Fenton, my fabulous editor at HQ Digital. I had a vision for a novel featuring an older attorney on the brink of retirement. Abi pushed me to develop Olivia and the people in her life, all with an eye towards giving my readers a great story. She's a master at seeing my weak spots and pushing me to grow as an author. Also thanks to Helena Newton for her superior copyediting and all the team at HQ for their continued support. My husband, Doug, has supported me with his continual encouragement since 2006, when I decided I wanted to take myself seriously as a writer. Since then, I've published seven books, and have never looked back.

Finally, I want to thank my readers, whose kind words, reviews, and emails always make me smile.

#ReaderLove
Terry

# Acknowledgements

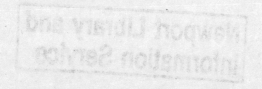

Dear Reader,

Thank you so much for reading *The Betrayal*, the first book in the Olivia Sinclair series. If you are so inclined, a review on Amazon, BookBub, and/or Goodreads would be very much appreciated.

I'm busily writing my next book, and I can't wait to share it with you. If you would like to be notified when I have a new release or when any of my books go on sale, you can sign up for my mailing list here. http://www.terrylynnthomas.com/

I enjoy connecting with you, so feel free to find me and introduce yourself on Twitter and Facebook. I do lots of promos and giveaways on social media and would love to hear from you!

Facebook: www.facebook.com/terrylynnthomasbooks/
Twitter: https://twitter.com/TLThomasBooks

Thank you again for taking the time to read my books.

Happy Reading,
Terry
#ReaderLove

Dear Reader,

Thank you so much for taking the time to read this book – we hope you enjoyed it! If you did, we'd be so appreciative if you left a review.

Here at HQ Digital we are dedicated to publishing fiction that will keep you turning the pages into the early hours. We publish a variety of genres, from heartwarming romance, to thrilling crime and sweeping historical fiction.

To find out more about our books, enter competitions and discover exclusive content, please join our community of readers by following us at:

*@HQDigitalUK*

*facebook.com/HQDigitalUK*

*Are you a budding writer?*
*We're also looking for authors to join the HQ Digital family!*
*Please submit your manuscript to:*

*HQDigital@harpercollins.co.uk.*

*Hope to hear from you soon!*

ONE PLACE. MANY STORIES

**If you enjoyed** *The Betrayal*, **then why not try another gripping thriller from HQ Digital?**

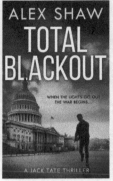